# Eclipse Of The Norns

Eyes of Midgard Book Three

**Lee Dawna**

LeeDawna Books, Inc.

This is a work of fiction. Names, characters, places, and incidents are either the product of the author's imagination or are used fictitiously. Any resemblance to actual persons, living or dead, events, or locales is entirely coincidental.

Copyright © 2026 Lee Dawna

All rights reserved. No part of this book may be reproduced or used in any manner without written permission of the copyright owner except for the use of quotations in a book review.

First edition

Cover design by Premade Ebook Cover Shop

https://www.premadeebookcovershop.com

ISBN 978-1-949192-34-6 (paperback)

ISBN 978-1-949192-33-9 (ebook)

Published by LeeDawna Books, Inc.

https://leedawnabooks.com

leedawnabooks@gmail.com

P.O. Box 824, Aurora NC 27806

~

This book is dedicated to those we've lost along the way. May we remember the roads they walked, the lives they lived, and the complexities of being human in a world full of impossibilities.

~

# Leah

I steady my breathing. Gelby can't hear the rapid beat of my heart through the crystal we're using to communicate, but there's no chance he'll miss the raggedness of the breath drawing in and out of my lungs. A satisfaction I'd rather die than give him. It's bad enough that the communication crystals we're using are visual, forcing me to see his face while he scrutinizes mine, watching for the impact his words have on me. Cruel words. Harsh ones. Words I never expected to hear anyone utter, especially someone I trusted enough to be intimate with. The Vasilis are known for their occasional dalliances just as much as they're known for not advertising their dating lives. None of their flings are allowed to stick around, and those jilted lovers are the only reason anyone ever hears about the appetites of the mighty Álfar. Gelby's appetite is one I can unfortunately confirm was rumored correctly.

I curl my hand into a fist, hating the barrage of memories. They're shameful. *I'm* shameful. As terrible at being a wolf as I was a daughter.

And unable to stop myself from making everything worse because there's a question I've been avoiding asking Gelby for over a month now and I can't keep myself from asking it today, even when I know I shouldn't. Even when asking is yet another betrayal. Of Collin. My family. The pack the Vasilis destroyed with their lies and accusations. The very people I hurt with my own lies and omissions, doing everything I could to deny and deflect. All to avoid the repercussions of my own heart. "What about Sean? Have the Vasilis heard anything about him yet?"

"Why?" Gelby's voice is cold, the bite of it frigid against the already icy temperature of Dökkbraek. A territory I never expected to find myself in. From the time of the vampires' first rising, the Ulfr have been their enemies—humans the divide between us. Vampir see humans as a food source. We see them as friends. Community. Lesser beings under our protection. But there are a lot of humans living in Dökkbraek. Safely. And even stranger than that, they're happy here, in this realm that exists beyond maps and knowledge.

I flex my fingers back open, focusing on the movement to keep myself from being wholly ungrateful to Keela. She's been a lifeline for Collin and me. Our only chance of survival. I'm grateful for the food and clothing, and even the shelter inside of her creepy castle. But I can never be grateful that the only crystals she claims to have are these. Gelby wasn't present when his father sent an army tearing through our pack lands, executing my family, but he's never rebuked the murders. He even defends Bishop's imprisonment of those too-few pack members allowed to live, and that fact grows more unsettling every time I'm forced to see the hardening resolve in Gelby's face. All thanks to Keela being able to provide us with everything we could ever need, except for a crystal devoid of this agonizing visual. "We made a deal, Gelby. You ask me a question. I ask you a question. And we both answer each other honestly. So, answer my question. Do you know where Sean is?"

Gelby's lip curls and I force myself to hold his stare. "After everything that Fae scum did, you're still concerned about his well-being? Why don't you ask me how *I'm* doing, Leah? I *dare* you."

I snatch the crystal from the table, severing the connection. The last thing I'm going to do is listen to Gelby Vasilis whine about me hurting his feelings. Yes, I took him up on his offer to have some consensual fun. That never meant I belonged to him, and I only ever went down that road with him because, at the time, I had nothing else to lose. Plus, Gelby is practically royalty. In Midgard anyway. "He's Vasilis, for fate's sake," I grumble, stuffing the crystal back into the velvet drawstring bag atop the sideboard.

"He's a supernatural male." Collin's deep voice cuts through the sitting room that adjoins the two bedrooms Keela assigned for us in Draugrkeep. I look up from the sideboard. Collin is different now. Abrasive. Rigid. His boyish ease gone—replaced with the hard lines and powerfully proud shoulders of an alpha. A mantel that fell upon him *that* day. The last one we spent in the territory reigned over by the Norns themselves. One minute Collin was fighting with Sean. The next, my brother was doubled over, the sudden influx of power painful in body and soul because for Collin to become alpha of the MacKenzie pack, our dad had to die. A reality that ripped us both in half.

I look down and away as my brother strolls deeper into the room, strength and confidence oozing from every pore in his body. They radiate from him the same way they used to fill the air around our dad. Collin stops beside me, his chin dipping even though he knows I won't meet his eyes. I haven't looked directly into them since that day, when he became alpha and our whole life devolved into the cesspool of pain that it is now. Because of me.

His hot breath is laden with annoyance. "Men of any kind can be possessive, but the more powerful they are, the worse their territorial nature becomes. Something my sister knows. But that didn't stop you from getting mixed up with the elf, did it?"

I keep my eyes low because even my wolf knows Collin's anger with me is justified. She was never on board with what I wanted to do in my flesh, but when I first said yes to Gelby, I had no idea he would want to turn our one-night stand into anything more than just one night of fun. Besides, I'm Ulfr. Even if I was willing to stick around until the powerful Álfar of the great Vasilis family was finished playing with me, Gelby and my relationship would have always had a looming expiration date. So, there's no real reason for him to be possessive. I'm not hashing that out with Collin, though. Not even my wolf buys that excuse, and Collin is my alpha now. One who has lost just as much as I have. More, even.

I swallow the lump in my throat and guide the topic away from my terrible decisions. "Gelby says Bishop will not yield." I give Collin the update he requested. The one that made me have to talk to and *see* Gelby again, because since becoming alpha of the MacKenzie pack, Collin has only spoken to Bishop once. That conversation was heated enough that I believed one of them would smite the other through the crystal somehow. Ever since, because of our *dalliance*, Gelby and I have been the bridge of communication. And each day, I wake up hoping that none of this is real. That I'll open my eyes and find that we're still in the land of the Norns. Because I'd rather live in that nightmare than this one.

I lift my eyes and focus on the bridge of Collin's nose. "Even though Bishop will not relent, Gelby assured me that our pack is being fed.

He also confirmed that Lance and the others have finally returned. The Vasilis picked them up yesterday."

A hint of a growl coats Collin's voice. "All of them? Lance, Ethan, Mark, and Nathan?"

My heart squeezes tightly over the pain I can feel through our bond. Collin would rather have any of those wolves with him right now, but he's stuck with me because the only wolves our pack has left are now in the bowels of the Vasilis prison. The rest are dead. Accused of treason and executed by Bishop. Including our parents, siblings, and all the pack elders. I slide my eyes back to the floor and exhale slowly. "Yes, all of them."

Collin stomps across the room and stands in front of our third-story window where we have a view of Dökkbraek's icy forest. The trees are beautiful, glimmering with the blood-red light of the aurora that stretches across the perpetually charcoal sky. Harlan, one of the Vampir who seems to be my shadow, whether at Keela's order or his own curiosity, told me this land is one of twilight because not all Vampir can walk in the sun, and that the shimmering red streaks in the sky are blood. A reminder of the oath his king made to Dökkbraek. A symbol to assure all Vampir that their king is eternal and will always look after them. Which contradicts the mourning ceremonies they've had for Abhartack this last month.

I don't know how the Vampir behaved before, but since we arrived in Dökkbraek and Keela broke the news of Abhartack's death to the horde, they've all been as crestfallen as Collin and me. We're united in our sorrow, vampire and wolf, and maybe that's why we're not acting as if we are the mortal enemies we've always been.

I watch Collin from the corner of my eye. With the confirmation I just gave him and the previous report of the dead and imprisoned that the Vasilis gave us, our entire pack is accounted for. Save for Sean, who Collin always thought of as his pack because in many ways, Collin was closer to Sean than his fellow wolves. And now, because of me, the last time my brother saw his best friend they were trading blows. I put my brother in a position to defend my honor and now we have no idea if Sean is dead or alive.

The last time any of us saw him, he was on his knees, bleeding from the hole Zara put in his heart when she ran him through with the sword Sean left behind in the rotunda. Then he was gone. Vanished. And we were on the floor beside that great well where the Norns looked down at us and out at Keela beyond a great shimmering wall where the vampire rampaged across the landscape. Only, the Vasilis and Monique were gone. Everyone was gone.

I lean against the sideboard and clasp my hands together. It doesn't matter that I still can't believe Liam MacKenzie is dead or that my father's death came at the hands of the Vasilis. He is, and it did. The Norns showed us Bishop's attack on our pack and then they left us with Keela. "There's more," I force myself to continue, wincing as a sorrowful, angry sound whines from my brother's throat. Lance and the others would most likely be Collin's chosen leaders, to replace those elders we lost, but now, even they are in captivity. "Gelby said the Völva coven has disappeared. He asked if we'd heard from Monique and I told him we hadn't."

Collin runs a hand up through his hair, eyes fixed on the forest beyond the window. "Did he believe you?"

I stare at the back of my brother's head. Though the Vampir are always watching us, Keela allows us to roam her castle and land freely. Most days, when we aren't in the dining hall or discussing the very few options we have, Collin is off letting his wolf run in the darkened shadows of that frosty forest. And when he's not doing that, he's with the human I smell on him more and more. I *dalliance* I don't begrudge him. We're hardly a pack so pack rules no longer apply. Collin is alpha. He can do whatever he wants. "I spoke the truth so Gelby should have believed every word. Keela is the one communicating with the witches, not us. And since she's made it clear that we don't speak for her, I answered only for us. If Gelby was using any kind of spell, my words should have shown truth, not deceit."

Collin's frustration is palpable. Mine too. But after my selfish failures, I don't even feel entitled to my rage. If I had only done what Collin asked and watched Sean from a distance instead of rushing in to mark him—as if that would make the Vasilis look the other way—then maybe Sean wouldn't have gotten so mixed up in the supernatural world. Even if he did, if I'd kept my distance, maybe Gelby would be an ally right now instead of our enemy.

Collin turns away from the window. "The witches are smart to use Keela as the loophole. Monique saw what happened. She knows that if the Norns hadn't intervened, Keela would have killed Gelby and Rohan."

A shiver runs down my spine. The day our father died is one I have many reasons never to forget. Keela becoming a demon incarnate is one of them. She was different the night before when she showed up with Abhartack to save us from the Skarthorn army. But she became death wrapped in human skin when Abhartack's head was severed from his body. "If the Norns hadn't intervened, Keela would have killed us all."

Collin's wolf rises, letting out a dissenting snarl. As a true alpha, he would never admit to such a thing without an official challenge, even though we both know we're only alive because Keela is allowing it. We don't entirely know *why* she's giving us sanctuary, but when the Norns left the three of us all alone, she seemed to snap out of her rage. The next thing I knew, Collin was vowing to kill Bishop and Keela was offering to bring us here. Since she's Vasilis, or *was* Vasilis, and the Álfar have declared our pack traitors, I thought it might be a trap. But Keela said we would have refuge here and Collin accepted the offer. If she's only harboring us to tick off the rest of the Vasilis, so be it. I don't care about their infighting. I only care about my brother and the MacKenzie pack members being held captive by the Álfar.

I glue my eyes to the cleft in Collin's chin. "Even with no evidence to prove their theory, the Vasilis believe the witches conspired with the Vampir, lifting the wards on the coven's compound so the Vampir could ambush the Vasilis. So yeah, the witches are smart to align themselves with Keela because with the vampire horde at her back, she's the only one of us who has a shot at standing against the Álfar. But the problem is, that's exactly what the Vasilis believe is happening. Gelby said they've received no confessions from any of our pack, but that Bishop still believes we weren't only working for the Fae because the Fae hired us to find a lost artifact. Bishop thinks we were working *with* the Fae. Just like he believes that the witches and the vampires were working *with* the Fae. All of us conspiring against him."

A coarse vibration echoes from Collin's chest. "The Vasilis can claim to believe the Ulfr, Völva, and Vampir are all in league with the Fae to overthrow Álfar rule in Midgard, but what they really want is war. Why else would Bishop deal himself this hand of self-fulfilling prophecy?"

I scrub my face. "I keep telling Gelby that the Fae only hired our pack to do what we do for every other kind—find things. And that we were just as blindsided by the vampire attack on the coven's land as the Vasilis were. Not to mention the fact that Dad and I fought with the Vasilis to expel the bloodsuckers that day. But Bishop has dug in his heels. He wants us to return to Midgard and face *questioning*."

"Tell him the queen of all bloodsuckers says no." Keela strolls into the room, creating no sound. She's like a mirage—there, but without having an impact on her surroundings. "If the Vasilis want to speak to you, they may come here. I'll greet them with the fairness they deserve."

Collin takes a step toward me, his eyes fixed on Keela. "You would directly defend us against the Vasilis? Even when turning us over to them would go a long way in elevating the status of the Vampir? You've been part of the Vasilis family for decades and that fact alone, regardless of whether or not you continue to have a relationship with the Vasilis, will bring status and reverence to the Vampir. Aligning, or *re*aligning, with the Vasilis will put you over the top."

Her lips curl, the ruby in the center of her jewel-studded choker pulsing, casting a bloody glow over her pale skin. Every time I see her, I'm convinced that her eyes are darker. More solid. It's as if what she became *that* day is all she is now. Then there's her hair. It's longer and lighter, which is oddly the thing that's the hardest for me to wrap my head around. Then again, I've never seen Keela Vasilis as anything other than a manipulative, bloodthirsty tramp, so what do I care if she's looking less like herself and more like a dead thing walking?

Her nostrils flare, head swinging my way and eyes narrowing as if she can read my unflattering thoughts. A low growl rolls through the room like the rumble of distant thunder. Keela smiles, dark splotches of shadow feathering underneath her skin. She pets one absently, fingers skimming along her hand as the shadow flutters underneath it. "Calm yourself, alpha. Unless you were indeed conspiring with the Fae, you have no reason to fear me. I've already proven to your sister that I can have her boy, Sean Winkle, if I choose. So that is no longer an issue between us." She turns her attention back to Collin. "And if I wanted your ungrateful sister's blood, there would be nothing you could do to keep me from having it. But it is not Ulfr blood that I want, and it is not a war that the Vasilis desire."

A thick, gravely sound crawls out of Collin's throat. "So, you mean to negotiate with them? Is that what this has been? Keep my sister and me alive to use as your bargaining chip?"

A dark laugh leeches out of her. One thick with the bite of hunger. "I have what the Vasilis want. What the Fae want. Even what the Völva want. And it is not *you*, Collin MacKenzie. Not entirely." Her eyes flick to mine before she turns away to pace slowly around the room. "They want power. And in far greater measure than even they know, power is exactly what I have."

Collin's attention cuts to mine and my wolf responds through our bond, letting him know I stand in solidarity with him and whatever choices he decides to make for us. Keela could easily kill us both, but if he chooses to fight, I'll go down fighting tooth and claw. I will do everything within my power to protect my alpha from this threat and every other. If he tells me to stand down, I'll submit. Because I would never allow a petty fight over a boy to get in the way of our survival. Sean made his choices, and I made mine. Now, Keela is the only ally we have so it doesn't really matter if I like her or not.

Collin's approving growl is low in my head. He turns and walks toward Keela, putting himself between her and me. "My father didn't send me on a mission to help the Fae overthrow the Vasilis, but if Bishop kills the Ulfr he just picked up because they were part of my search team, I *will* seek out the Fae and my sister and I *will* join them. Not because we seek power, but because we seek justice. I know your relationship with the Vasilis colors your judgment, but I cannot and *will* not let the atrocities committed against my family and my pack go unrevenged. There's innocent blood on Bishop's hands. I'll seek each and every alliance that can be forged to make him atone for that blood."

Keela turns back to us, dark eyes fixing on mine. "So will I. My king's life will be paid for in blood. Starting with that of Gelby Vasilis. Because, you see, I do have something *he* wants. And you, little wolf, are going to help me kill him."

## Collin

Crystalline mist sprays over my wolf's gray fur, our paws pounding against the frozen ground as we race through the underbrush, weaving between the tall, ancient trees of Dökkbraek's forest. The leaves here are etched with layers of heavy frost, reflecting the eerie aurora above us to set the woods ablaze with a blood-red shimmer. A gleaming cathedral of limbs and sorrow. A fitting reminder of the death clinging to my soul. Smothering me. My entire family slaughtered. Dad. Mom. All of my siblings. Every single one of them except Leah, the sister who's convinced herself that I hate her. Which I do. A little bit. But not the way she thinks or even deserves. I'm just angry, and I can't talk to her about it because every waking moment, I feel them. Our dwindling pack. Their sorrow is as great as mine and Leah's, and because I'm here and not in Midgard, I can't help them.

My wolf's anguished howl reaches through the forest, upward and outward, shaking the frost from the heavy leaves. My pack can feel that

I'm alive, a knowledge buried within a wolf that lets them know their alpha lives, but that's where my connection to the MacKenzie pack ends. I can't use the mind-speak between realms so there's no way for me to comfort or console them. I can't give them advice or offer them hope. I can't go to them. They're prisoners of the Álfar who now control our pack lands and if I go back to Midgard, Bishop will kill me. Compliments of the Fae. And if I'm being honest, compliments of the Vampir who are now giving me sanctuary. Yet here I am, safe while my pack suffers. A coward making a choice to shield his sister from the horrors to come because if I go to Midgard, so will Leah. No matter what she's done to make our situation all the worse, I can't bring myself to put her life at such obvious risk. Nor will I stand for Keela using Leah as bait.

I lower my head and thunder forward, powerful paws tearing into the frozen ground. Frost flecks my coat and steam rises from my hot, panting breaths. I want to find Keela so I can set her straight outside of Leah's hearing, but I can't. Keela's scent is masked somehow. I only know where she is when the vampire wants me to know. So, for now, I run. Like I always do. Trying to think. To forget. To force myself to feel something other than grief and rage. To feel the way I do in those rare, fleeting spurts of calm when Caroline is in my arms. *Human* Caroline. My guilty pleasure. A mistake. One I keep making. The same way Leah made a mistake with Sean. He always looked out for her as much as I did so I wasn't surprised to hear how hard he fought for her during their ordeal in the land of the Norns, but I was a little surprised to hear that she went out of her way to help him. With their history, I was even a little surprised that they made it out of there without her killing him. Smelling the scent of their sex on her was a complete shock. It still is. And it's one of the many things I wish I could forget.

*Fail in your quest, Collin MacKenzie, and casualty will have no guard. Bitterness will consume us all.*

I play the Seidr's words on a loop inside my head, using them to drown out my other thoughts. Because had I been in Midgard when my family was slaughtered, I would have felt more than the weight of their deaths. I would have heard their pleas. Their cries of fear. Once my father died and his alpha mantal passed to me, I would have heard the rage of my pack as the Vasilis slaughtered my mother and siblings, the pack elders, and any other wolves who dared to fight back.

If I'd been in Midgard, I would have been able to use the mind-speak to calm the pack. To organize them and give orders, even if those orders would have been to stand down. To survive. Once the mantal engulfed me, I would have been able to rise to the call of a true alpha, saving the bravest and most fierce members of our pack from slaughter and using them instead to help the others escape. But I was stuck in the realm of the Norns and without the might and will of their alpha, my pack fell. Those who weren't murdered were captured, and all I could do was scream as I felt the strength of the MacKenzie pack slip away.

To save my pack, I needed to succeed in the quest Dad charged me with. *Trusted* me with. So that I could be back with them when the Álfar struck. But I failed because all I ever did was complain about having to go on the quest to begin with. First, because Sean's dream of attending Merrymont was finally coming true and I wanted to stay there with him, being nothing but a stupid party kid. Then I complained that the mission was too vague for anyone to ever complete it. I whined about the quest being a waste of time and allowed my team to say the same things. None of us wanted to leave Midgard and because of my leadership, failure was the only option.

I even allowed the Seidr to saddle us with Zara, who not only refused to help my pack fight off the time serpents, but the very same dragon shifter who lied about the vultures. If Sean's magic hadn't been strong enough to cook the giant birds, Leah and I would be in a watery grave right next to him. Instead, we're in Dökkbraek, with no clue whether Sean is dead or alive. Because Zara somehow managed to find her way back to us—armed with a sword Leah swears was left behind when she and Sean swam away from the crucible the Norns had trapped them inside of. A blade Zara then ran through Sean's chest.

*But remember, young wolf, that one never knows what they think they know.*

I keep asking myself whether or not I believe Sean is dead or alive, but I'm not sure how I'm supposed to feel about either of those options. Sean was my best friend, but he disrespected my sister in the worst way. It doesn't really matter that Leah has been disrespecting Sean her whole life. What he did to her is something I can't ever forgive. And he's Fae, apparently, which makes any lingering feelings I have for my former best friend all the more threadbare. He's even the reason Leah and my dad were at the Völva compound the day the vampires attacked.

So instead of wasting time wondering if he's dead or alive, I need to figure out if the Fae were involved in helping the vampires gain access to the witch lands. Or was it the Völva who allowed the vampires to enter? If the attack happened because of the witches, was it because of negligence or intent? And who among them knew what kind of danger my family would be in once the plan spiraled out of control and left the Álfar just as suspicious of them as I am?

A mournful howl, as heartbroken as the echo of my wolf's own cry, reverberates through the forest. It's Keela, raw and unfiltered, pouring her emotions out to the trees the same way my wolf and I so often do. The sound leaves no doubt as to the depths of her despair. The emotion lingers here, embedded into bark and earth, seeping out into the air as a ghostly reminder of what we've lost. I turn toward the sound of her grief, only feeling a little guilty about interrupting her private moment. If she wanted to be alone, she should be out on the cliff overlooking the ravine that cuts behind the castle. That cliff edge is the only place she's forbade Leah and me from going. I'm not sure why but I don't care either. The same way I don't care to enter her private tower. She hasn't excluded that part of her castle from us, but I've ordered Leah to stay away from it anyway because it reeks of blood. Both Vampir and human. I'm disgusted by the human part but even Caroline defends Keela, and the quality of life the many humans in Dökkbraek enjoy. Humans who should be in Midgard. Not here in this cold and blood-soaked world.

Keela's sleek form comes into view. She's kneeling beside an ice-covered stream, her hand reaching down to rest on the glassy surface acting as a window to the freely flowing water beneath. My wolf shivers at the sight. After our encounter with the time serpents, we've sworn to stay away from bodies of water that are home to things other than ordinary fish, and those streaks of faint blue light glowing softly under Keela's palm are anything but ordinary.

I pad forward, frost crackling beneath my paws as my eyes track the way the gem at Keela's throat pulses. Its color matches the twisting ribbons of crimson rippling in the sky above us. Both the gem and the aurora bleed their bloody coloring over the ice-topped water, and it's about as creepy as I ever could have imagined a vampire world to be. If Sean was here, he would agree with me. Especially after getting a look at Draugrkeep—that great stone castle perched high on the edge of a massive void of howling wind.

"The needs of my Vampir are why Dökkbraek exists as it does," Keela speaks as I walk toward her. "This land belongs to us as much as we belong to it."

I stop where I'm at upon the moss-covered trail, my wolf tilting his head in question. Keela's dark eyes turn to meet mine, devoid of any trace of her sorrow. Nearly devoid of any trace of her former self. "You have questions about my land and I'm giving you answers, Collin MacKenzie. Many of my Vampir are old, but *all* of my Vampir can march in the night."

Even with her changing appearance, Keela is beautiful. Maybe even more so than she was before. But my wolf and I both know she's bad news, and I wish Dad would have let us bring Sean into our pack after his dad died, the way I wanted to, because then Sean's wolf would have done what our wolves do—keep us from falling into a vampire's trap. Especially this one's. Keela's rage is different than my own. Older. More purely evil each day. It's as if she doesn't need a reason for her anger, she only needs to exist. And now she's dragging my sister into the center of that rage. Plus, Gelby didn't intentionally murder Abhartack. Technically, Sean killed the vampire king—using a killing blow from Gelby that was meant for Sean. Still, when Keela gave us the communication crystals she made it clear that she would only speak to the Vasilis once amends were made for Abhartack's death. It's possible those amends also include Sean. She could have vampires out there hunting for him right now. A part of me says I should be okay with that. Another says that if Keela kills Sean, I'll kill her.

I shift back to my human form, grateful once again that Keela somehow managed to find spelled clothing for Leah and me. I cross my arms over the fabric of my plain black t-shirt. "Why are you telling me this, Keela? Because Gelby Vasilis lives in the sunlight and you think he doesn't know that you have vampires old enough to survive in it, too? You think you can stick Leah out in broad daylight and he won't expect her sudden appearance to be a trap?"

Her lips curl into a smile that would be pretty if it wasn't so sinister. "The Vampir are not simply predators, alpha. They are guardians upon the threshold. Abhartack, my king, was the first of his kind. And I am his queen. Day or night, I would take everyone's life to avenge his. Even yours."

I let my wolf rise to the surface. Enough for her to see our strength in my eyes. To hear it in my voice. She's been good to Leah and me and even the third-floor suite is nicer than I expected, but there's no doubt Keela has vampires watching and listening to our conversations at all times. Without the mind-speak, nothing Leah and I say would ever be news to Keela. The way anything Gelby tells us is never a surprise to her—whenever Keela finally decides to grace us with her presence.

Gelby is also the only person we're able to contact with the crystals. Leah found out they were spelled for only him when she tried to call Monique and the crystal she used exploded into a cloud of dust. It seems Keela believes she's the only one allowed to speak to the witches, and we only know she communicates with them because she's told us so, without passing along any tidbits of information they may have given her.

"The Álfar have taken over my pack's land and I'll seek justice for that, and for the MacKenzie lives that Bishop took. So I understand your need for revenge and Gelby's life for Abhartack's is fine by me. But Leah is *mine*. She doesn't do anything for or with you unless it's approved by me. Are we clear on this? The Ulfr are as sovereign as the Vampir. We are *not* your subjects, and you are *not* going to compel Leah to do anything that her alpha doesn't want her to do."

Keela turns her attention back to the stream, tracing a line of glowing light as it passes underneath the ice. "Just as you will not make promises to Caroline. She is *mine*. You will not change her, should she even ask to become such a foul creature as yourself."

A snarl bubbles up my throat. Shadows rush along her fingers, forming talons. She stabs them down through the ice, skewering that glowing light. It squeals and squirms...snuffing out, the water underneath the ice turning black as midnight under a new moon. "No one is sovereign, Collin MacKenzie. Not while the gods exist."

My hot breath forms a cloud of mist. "What are you saying, *Keela Vasilis*? You want to start a war with the gods? Because if whatever change is coming over you has you thinking you're a deity, then we've got bigger problems than your jealousy over Caroline's superior taste to worry about."

She retracts her talons from the ice, casting her gaze to a half-buried runestone on the far side of the stream. It's old, with ancient symbols carved into its surface. I've seen a lot of those on my runs through the forest. Some toppled over and others crumbling...all of them slowly being lost to time. "The gods were born of Chaos, the same as I was. But only one of us still chooses to serve that which birthed us. That's why the gods keep making plans based upon meeting me at Ragnarök. The *fools*." She disappears in a smoky mass of shadows, materializing in front of me, so close her chest skims mine. "While we wait for their next move, shall we play a game? I am hungry and you want a distraction. Let me give you the sovereignty you crave, Collin MacKenzie."

Her cold hand splays along my face, her eyes darker than they were seconds ago and the pull of her allure stronger than it's ever been. I can feel the danger of it humming underneath my skin. My wolf is still repulsed enough to resist her but since we've been here, I've tried more than once to combat that repulsion. To see if the ecstasy of her feeding from me would lessen the burden of my sorrows. I've never been able to get there, though. Because I have Caroline. The human who allows me to satiate the mostly manly and beastly parts of me. No strings. No questions. Hardly any words. Just pure physical release. I'm ashamed of myself every time, but for as long as I'm here and Caroline is a willing partner in our debauchery, I'm going to keep bathing in that shame.

I wrap my fist around Keela's forearm and tug her hand from my jaw. "My sister and I will pay you the life debt we owe you but we're not on the menu. Find some other way for us to repay you because we're more than happy to unite with you in revenge—you get Gelby and I get Bishop, but no MacKenzie will ever feed *or* kneel to you." I release her arm. "Bishop is going to try to attack Dökkbraek anyway, once he finds out there are humans here. Ones you and your vampires are *feeding* from."

She lifts her hand to my chest, stopping above my heart. "Bishop is a liar who brought those dear humans here, and I am Death. Bishop will die. Gelby will die. And the Vasilis will bend the knee to me, or I will kill *all* Álfar." The ends of her fingers dance with shadows, curling into those thick talons she used on the stream. "You have no need to seek out the Fae or anyone else. I will be your revenge. Even those Vampir who reside in nests outside of Dökkbraek will answer my call, as will all those creatures under my compulsion. Once I am finished honoring my king,

I will summon a great horde. They will fight at my side. As you will." Her talons rip into the fabric of my shirt. "Caroline will be no more of a toy to you than the one you abhor becoming. Turn her, and I will take everything you have left. Then I will skin your wolf and add his fur to my collection."

A beastly snarl rips out of me but Keela is already gone, nothing more than a blur of shadows fading into the dark underbelly of the forest. I drop to all fours, my shift complete before my front paws hit the ground. My wolf shakes out his mane, a rough, guttural noise vibrating up and through our jaws. There's no doubt that Bishop is going to regret ever releasing Keela from the Isle of Misery, and no doubt that my debt to her is bound to end in bloodshed. *Hers.* My wolf insists. I agree with him on that as much as I agree with his thoughts turning solely to Caroline. Our guilty pleasure. The woman whose toy *we* have become. He launches us forward, fluid and fast, chasing her scent. By now, his body knows the rhythm of this forest. The downed trees, low-hanging branches, and the dips and rises of the earth. I give him full control because in this form, we're pure instinct. Flesh, fur, and desire. In this form, life is easier. An alpha without a pack, given wholly to the whims of his reckless wolf.

## ~3~

Caroline lives on the far side of the human village, her cottage tucked away in a clearing all by itself. My wolf makes quick work of traversing the meandering path that cuts back and forth through the skeletal limbs of the ancient trees that keep her home hidden from view. The first night we came here, Caroline had been crying. We heard her sobs and let them draw us to her doorstep, where we curled up and kept a watchful eye on the forest, neither my wolf nor I in any shape to offer her comfort. She wasn't in any danger that we could sense, so we kept watch while she cried, empathizing with her tears. When she opened the door and found us there that next morning, my gasp was as shrill as hers. I wasn't prepared for the brightness of her amber eyes. Once I shifted into my human form, there weren't many words spoken between us. And we've kept it that way.

My wolf lets out a raw, emotion-filled rasp, his mind wandering to the satisfying feel of our first kiss with Caroline. Her lips felt like hope. Warm and tender, coaxing us to believe that one day, if we survive long enough, there can be something more than devastation in our lives. It's too much to hope for. The most we can believe is that we're a balm for Caroline the way she's the salve that soothes every aching part of us. I've never asked her what she was crying about or why she lets me into her bed. If she wants me to know, she'll tell me. The same way I would open up to her if there was ever anything I felt like sharing. Like how I was born to privilege within my pack and basked in a worry-free life. That I think the Norns knew exactly what was in store for me so they let my early years be bright and happy. They knew I would get to this place, where every carefree day is gone and there's no such thing as happiness.

Smoke curls from Caroline's chimney. Instead of being here pretending that I'm helping Caroline as much as she's helping me, I should be running for that deep ravine the way I sometimes feel Leah's wolf running toward it. I never have to stop her because unlike me, my sister is capable of stopping herself. My wolf pads softly over Caroline's porch, nudging her door and scratching at the bottom. She walks through the house, the floorboards squeaking under her feet. When she opens the door, her bright eyes once again take my breath away. She tucks a lock of dark hair behind her ear and steps aside. "Hi, Collin. I was hoping you would come tonight."

My wolf rubs against her legs as we cross the threshold, his big head nuzzling her hand. She runs her fingers through his fur and he purrs like the whipped cat both of us are. Caroline's touch is the medicine we need. I shift and scoop her into my arms, wasting no time getting my mouth connected to hers. She wraps her arms around my neck and I spring upright, shoving her away and turning back toward the forest. Leah's roar is distorted by distance and wind, but that sound is unmistakably hers. I drop back to all fours and race toward the sound. Toward Draugrkeep. *Leah! What's wrong?*

Her voice is fury and despair in my head. *The witch is here. She been lying to us. Sean is...Monique knows what happened to Sean.*

---

Draugrkeep is silent. Full of the kind of stillness that presses against your ribs and sends tremors racing down your spine. It's as if the castle itself is holding its breath, waiting the same way I am to hear what the red-headed witch has to say. According to Keela, the Völva have claimed not to know anything about Sean. But I've never trusted Keela and my wolf trusts her even less. *Where are you?* I ask my sister, trying to separate her scent from the sickly smells of the vampires.

*Dining hall,* she answers, the sharp blade of her irritation slicing through my head. Leah is looking for a fight but underneath that edge of anger is a tear of fresh pain. I can feel it throbbing its way through her, an emotion that's too raw for her to hide from her alpha. Sean disappeared on the collective worst day of our lives and since then, the absence of news about him has been both a blessing and a curse. He's been one less complication for us to deal with. He's been the source of the division between us.

I stomp down a wide flight of stairs and enter a long hallway, my shoulders as achingly stiff as the cold stone walls. Even indoors, where hearths blaze for the benefit of the humans who live here, the coldness of Dökkbraek clings to Draugrkeep. A cliché. A vampire castle that's dark, cold, and reeking of death. Wholly different from the warmth and freshness of Caroline and her cottage. The second I heard Leah, I abandoned that warmth, leaving Caroline standing alone with swollen lips and unmet needs. She deserves better. She deserves someone who has the ability to put her first in their life. That's not me and never will be. I don't even know if I'm mourning the loss of a friendship or the loss of a friend, and until I hear what Monique has to say about Sean, Caroline will remain at the bottom of my list of priorities.

I focus straight ahead, pushing through the doors that lead into the massive dining room. This space alone can hold hundreds of Vampir and it's only one room in this ancient castle. The size speaks to the strength of Keela's horde. I don't know how many are in her nest but between the smells and the few times I've witnessed them filling this dining hall, I'm both fearful and envious. Ulfr packs can be hundreds strong but it's rare. Once a pack begins to grow too large, nature takes over, gracing that pack with two clear and dominant alphas born to them in a single generation. It's a signal for the pack to split. The MacKenzie pack expected my generation to have two alphas but since no others were born to us, my dad prepared me for the possibility of it happening under my leadership. Now that most of my pack has been slaughtered, I won't have to worry about a split. I'll have to worry about rebuilding my pack. My lineage gives me strength but I'll need numbers, and I can't recruit them from here in Dökkbraek, though changing every last human in this land is tempting.

The dining hall is empty, save for the three females in the very back. Keela is perched on the arm of a chair, staring into a faraway corner while Leah crowds Monique against the sooty hearth of a fireplace just beyond where the queen's chair sits. *What's going on, Leah?* I check in with my sister before addressing Monique or even Keela.

Leah's eyes drill holes into the side of Monique's flushed face. *Monique saw Odin take Sean.*

"Odin?" I blurt. Monique's watery eyes meet mine and a deep, guttural growl rumbles from Leah's chest. A threat. My sister's primal instinct is to protect her alpha, even from danger that's only perceived. Monique has magic but the might of my wolf can strike faster than Monique can sling a spell. Especially at this close of a range. I reach them and place a hand on Leah's shoulder to calm her. "You saw Odin take Sean *when*, Monique?"

A tear tracks down her face. "The day...when you became alpha... Right after you collapsed, Sean was stabbed and Haldir was gone. It happened then. Before the Norns intervened to send us all away. Odin appeared, and he took Sean."

Leah's hand slams against the stone next to Monique's head. "The witch didn't tell us she saw Odin take Sean because she's a traitor, and she's only here now because she had a vision she doesn't understand and wants us to solve it for her. Isn't that right, traitor?"

Monique's terrified eyes flick to Keela and then back to me. I study the witch I used to consider a friend. Or, at least, not an enemy. "Is that true? You never told anyone about seeing Odin take Sean?"

"No," Monique defends. "I mean, yes. No..." She rubs at the back of her thigh. "Please, Collin. Leah's threatening to burn me alive but I swear I didn't betray the Ulfr. I'm trying my best to be helpful but until recently, I didn't have the power of prophecy. I'm new at this. A witch's powers are fully revealed when they turn sixteen so I'm too old to suddenly sprout new abilities, but here we are. And when I realized the rest of you hadn't seen Odin, or didn't *remember* seeing him, I freaked out. More than I already was *before* Odin showed up. As a...seer or whatever I'm turning into, I'd only just started to realize that, one way or another, all of my visions and prophecies had been about Sean. Then bam, Odin was there and everything clicked into place. But none of you knew that. None of you saw so I..."

"Kept it to yourself." Leah's jaws snap in front of Monique's face.

The witch turns away with a wince. "I told my coven. We decided to keep it secret until... We're trying to help you, Leah. I swear it."

I glance at Keela, who hasn't moved. Ulfr have good senses but Keela is known for being a lie detector. "Are you fine with Leah having roast witch for dinner? Or would you like to chime in with some helpful information? You're the one who's been keeping in touch with the Völva. Is Monique telling us the truth or not?"

Keela's eyes shift, taking me in. "The witch is speaking truth. I sense no deception."

I swallow down the building ire over her detached demeanor. Only an hour ago she was proclaiming she could annihilate the gods. I drag a hand down my face and turn back to Monique. "We've all been thrust into new situations lately. That's no reason to keep things from us. We're all being forced to travel roads paved from our nightmares and if we ever want to get on a better path, we have to work together, so tell us what you know and don't hold anything back or I'm going to let Leah have an early dinner."

I nod for Leah to step away from the witch. Keela should be running this interrogation since we're in her house, but I'll gladly take over if all she's going to do is sit there like a lump of coal.

Leah takes one single step away from Monique, her hand slowly peeling off the stone beside the witch's head. Monique doesn't waste time getting away from the fire. She shuffles to the side of the hearth and leans against the security of the wall, keeping stone at her back instead of flames. Her face is pinched and her eyes heavy with fear. She looks down, rubbing her hands over her long paisley skirt. "When Odin appeared that day, it was as if time slowed down. Some kind of glitch in the universe where I was standing in a void rather than...anywhere. When Sean and Odin disappeared, the noise of the world came rushing back to me. And..." She wipes her face. "I was grateful when the Norns intervened. The visions are one thing but the spirit-calling, when it possesses me and I start spouting words without actually being in control of saying them...it scares me. I've never heard of any Volva doing such a thing and then I...walked between worlds..." Her head shakes. "I was pulled there, into..." She looks up, tearful eyes on mine. "I don't know where I was. I don't know what's happening to me. It's terrifying. So, when the Norns sent me back to Midgard, I was grateful. I wanted everything to go away. To go back to normal. Then the Vólva had to run from the Álfar and I..."

"Continued to be a coward?" Leah shouts, chest heaving.

*You're not helping!* I yell back at her, making sure to blast through every other sound inside of her thick skull. She peels away from us, marching to stand on the opposite side of the table from where Keela is perched. Good. Monique is already afraid and she was terrified back then. Scared and unsure. Just like the rest of us. I move to the table and pull out a chair for her, motioning for Monique to sit. "We understand. Just tell us what else you know and maybe what you've been going through will spark something that makes sense to all of us."

Monique gingerly moves toward the table, highly favoring her right leg. I glance at Leah. *Did you do that to her?*

Leah pulls out a chair and plops down. *I wish.*

My gaze cuts to Keela, the queen whose fixated focus is back on the dark, empty corner. Leah's sigh is audible in my head. *Keela didn't do it either. Monique said it was Jofir, because the traitorous witch went to the Vasilis first but unlike us, they didn't buy anything she was selling. They were going to lock her up. Jofir intervened. Instead of taking Monique to the prison, Jofir pretended that Monique bested her in a fight and let the witch escape. At least, that's Monique's story.*

I look between Keela and Monique. Surely Keela would tell us if Monique was lying. She can't want a Vasilis spy in her castle. Then again, none of the kinds have ever really intermingled like this before and Keela isn't exactly Keela anymore. She could also be lying to us about her loyalty to the Vasilis. Leah and I might already be inside of a Bishop-approved prison.

I sit down next to Monique. The closer the better when it comes to sensing any sort of change in her body that would indicate a lie. "Go ahead. We're listening."

Monique fingers the ends of her red braid. "Since I've been back with my coven, I've been feeling more like myself. But two days ago, I had a vision that felt more like a…convergence of energies. It's hard to explain."

Leah huffs out a breath. "Just tell us about it the same way you told the Vasilis. You know, the Álfar who told me just this morning that they haven't seen a single Völva. That you're all in hiding and they think we have something to do with your spectacular evasion." She leans her chair back and kicks her feet up onto the table's edge. "Or maybe that's only Gelby telling me that because you've concocted this whole story with the Vasilis. You are a proven liar now, and it's suddenly much less odd that the Völva have been able to stay well outside the grasp of the Álfar."

A thin smile spreads over Keela's blood-red lips. She likes the infighting, especially when it's Leah who is riled up. Before I can yell at my sister to knock it off, Monique slams her palms flat against the table. "Call me what you want, Leah, but I didn't ask to be put in the middle of any of this. The same as Sean didn't ask for what's happening to him. If he's even still alive. Which Gelby hopes he isn't, by the way. And not because of the threat Sean poses to the Vasilis. Gelby has gone mad with—"

"That's enough." My alpha's snarl bleeds into my words. Leah's guilt is so thick it coats the back of my throat and worse than that, it's drawing that smile on Keela's lips even wider. "You're not in a position to rebuke anyone, Monique. Just tell us about your vision."

She looks up at me. Even though her eyes are full of tears and her lips are trembling, she's filled with the defiance that all witches have. An instinct that's wired into her even though she's outnumbered and outmatched. "In my vision, Sean was sitting on the top of a balance beam scale. Like the ones depicted in the human courts of Midgard—the scales of justice. There were chains wrapped around him. Ones made of thread. They were draped over him like a spider web, completely engulfing him." She focuses on the space above my shoulder, as if she's seeing the vision all over again. "There was fire...coming from Sean. But it wasn't the dragon fire we all saw him wield. It was different. Still powerful. I could feel it on my skin and every time it burned a section of chain to ash, more grew back to take its place. Only, in those moments before it grew back, it wasn't Sean I saw underneath. It was...claws...scales...faces...fur...always something different. Never Sean."

She lowers her gaze and none of us speak. Not until Leah drags her feet off the table and sits up straight, her fury subsiding. Replaced with worry. Panic. "Sean is Fae, not Dreki. We all saw him use the faelight like any other Fae would. And we all saw him wield the dragon fire like no other Dreki ever has. He also heals faster than any other supernatural we've ever seen, and Beatrice said that Sean was a Fae *and* a dragon from an old lineage. But that's not possible. So, what if your vision is telling us that Sean is some long-lost supernatural kind? A Fae who can shift? Has that ever been recorded before?"

Monique swallows. "In the vision, I could feel Sean's magic. It's Fae. And old. The *ancient* kind of old." Her eyes tick to Keela and back. "But Fae is only one of the magical signatures Sean has. There were others. *Many* others."

I slide my elbows onto my knees. "What are you saying right now? That Sean is some kind of hybrid? Has that ever happened before?"

Monique looks pointedly at Keela. "Yes."

Keela's attention snaps to Monique and the witch shudders, her face going pale. Keela hasn't been outright violent since we arrived here. She hasn't been anything like the whirlwind of destruction she was in the land of the Norns. But Caroline mentioned some Vampir have gone missing, and a few humans too. She also told me that patrols of vampires are roaming all of Yggdrasil's worlds, dragging back what she's been told are violent criminals who serve as food for the new queen with a notoriously insatiable appetite. Caroline says it's because Keela doesn't want to feed on her own, weakening her horde at a time when the Vasilis are on a rampage. But maybe that's not what's happening here at all.

"Keela's differences are obvious, even to her," I point out, hoping to end any line on conversation that's going to drag us into the pit of exactly who and *what* Keela is. She's never fit the narrative of the other vampires, but we've all just accepted the lie that she is one. Even the Vampir have accepted her and made her their queen. "Just focus on what your vision revealed about Sean. He's Fae, and what else? A dragon?"

Dread flickers over Monique's face. "I don't know. Beatrice once thought he was Dreki but I didn't feel a dragon's presence in the vision. It was hard to really tell what I actually did feel, though, so I don't know. It was all jumbled, like he's..." She studies her hands. "The power I felt swimming within that vision means Sean is more than a hybrid. I think he was purposefully created. By Odin. A weapon created for a very specific reason."

The air quakes, as if the castle finally let out its held breath. All of our eyes dart to Keela. The queen is looking back at us, her head tilted in that predatory way it so often does. "Created by the meddling, many-faced god who thinks Yggdrasil will favor him in Ragnarök."

A drop of fear mixes with the worry plunging into my gut. Between Keela saying the gods are preparing to meet her at Ragnarök and Monique believing Odin created Sean as a weapon... "Are we living the end of days? Is that what we're saying?" I look from the hard lines of Keela's face to Monique. She's sitting perfectly still, tears glistening as they cascade down her cheeks. I lean over and clasp her hand in mine. "Is that what you're telling us? That Odin...created Sean as a weapon because Ragnarök is upon us?"

Monique doesn't answer. I tighten my grip on her hand. Until the Vasilis took Sean to the Völva compound, he was human. Up to that point, every magical test my dad had ever ordered proved him to be nothing more. The Vasilis and all Álfar will fight with Odin. It was expected that the witches would too. Not the Vampir. And probably not the solidly gray-area Ulfr—whose strongest pack has now been eliminated, their alpha driven into the arms of the vampires. "Is Sean with the Vasilis? Is that where Odin took him? To get him ready for whatever kind of weapon he's supposed to be?"

Monique chews on her lip. "I don't think so. Jofir says no—"

"As if anyone can trust an Álfar!" Leah bursts from her chair. "Or a witch. All of you are promising to help when all you've really done is used Sean to burn down your coven house while conspiring with the Fae to kill any Álfar who got in the way of the vampires getting their queen! Which started a war with the Vasilis and got our entire family killed!"

Leah isn't wrong and the witches do need to answer for their role in provoking the Vasilis. Ambushing the Álfar was seen as an act of war, and no one in their right mind could have thought the Odin-blessed army of elves would see the attack on the Völva compound any other way. Especially when the sole purpose does seem to have been to retrieve Keela from the Vasilis. Unless it was meant to spark exactly what it has. Division. A drawing of the battle lines. Our shifter abilities come from Loki so it's always been rumored that we would fight on his side. A side considered dark. Less than noble. A side filled with fiends and freaks like the Vampir. That's part of why Ulfr have worked so hard to have our own communities where we simulate with humanity and follow their laws while abiding by our own strict rules. It's a way of separating ourselves from the ideological stain of where we came from. To maintain our own codes of loyalty and honor. To give all to ourselves and our pack. But in the end, if the old stories are true, then Loki's child, Fenrir, is the ultimate alpha, and that means he can simply call to us and Ulfr everywhere will be powerless to refuse the summon. We'll be unable to do anything other than follow the great wolf into battle.

I shake off the shuddering thought, my wolf bristling at the idea of anyone ordering us around. For now, I'm still the most powerful alpha known in Ulfr society and until that changes, all wolves, including Leah, will give me their total and complete submission. *Stop.* I order Leah. *Control yourself or leave.*

She clamps her jaw shut so hard her teeth clack. I gnash my own teeth together. Despite how powerful and scrappy Leah is, she has always known that the alpha mantle would come to me, not her. A wolf's power is known at birth and when an alpha dies, the mantle of all the previous alphas in that lineage passes to the next most powerful wolf. The only way to circumvent that is in a fight-to-the-death battle. Alpha versus challenger. If the challenger wins, they receive the full weight of the dead alpha's mantle. That's why older alphas have to be careful. Especially those from mantles that aren't as powerful as the MacKenzie line.

I let go of Monique's hand. "You're not sure where Sean is. Let's leave it at that. What other information do you have?"

She dips her head, sliding a hand to the satchel tied around her waist. A tear falls against the canvas fabric as she digs through it, removing a small scroll. It's dingy and old, the brittle paper crackling as she works to untie the wide golden ribbon from around it. "Beatrice has been helping me interpret the visions. The new one and the ones I had before. Neither of us knows why I'm suddenly turning into an oracle but Beatrice thinks all of our sudden life changes are related. And she has a theory regarding the visions."

Leah snorts, derisive and cold. Monique's fingers tremble while I try harder than ever not to broadcast my feelings. Keela is watching us. Studying and dissecting every movement and every scent. I don't need her filled in on the depths of the tensions between Leah and me, or between us and the witch. We might all end up fighting for the same team but we're not on the same side. I gesture to the scroll. "What is that?"

Monique inhales deeply, as if trying to gain the courage to tell us. "One of my prophecies spoke about bonds that honor fate and rites that were lost to time. It referenced the need for balance, and the voice that came over me said *many hearts. One face.* I immediately thought of Odin because before that prophecy, there was one that referenced eyes, or *an* eye. It said *eyes once seeking wisdom now buried in ancient mire, hidden in the place where shadows are drawn.*"

Keela rises from her perch, movements fluid and silent. Like that of a shadow. Monique's hands shake even more as she smooths the thin, fragile parchment over the table. "The Völva have mostly grimoires in our collections, but a Seidr visited our coven long ago, before I was ever born. She gave this scroll to the coven, as a bonus to what the Seidr had already paid us for some spells. No one really cared, it seems. It's just an old prophecy and even the Seidr claimed not to know what it meant. The coven basically discarded it. Filed it away and forgot about it. Then when Beatrice was barely twenty, she was visited by a Seidr who reminded her that the coven had more than grimoires in their collections. Once Beatrice grew into her position as our head, she had access to all of the collections and started searching through them, looking for anything that might not be catalogued. She found this and has been trying to figure out what it means ever since."

Leah leans forward to get a better look. "What language is that?"

"An old one," Keela answers, her words hitting more like a threat than a statement.

Monique's face flushes, eyes staying rooted down onto the parchment. Dread settles over me, weighing down my bones. Now, more than ever, I believe the Ulfr have been used as pawns. It's hard to come to any other conclusion when the Seidr is coming up again. I don't know how many of them are out there but those fate-cursed fortune tellers are directly linked to what's been happening. "What does it say, Monique?"

Her voice is soft and shaking as she begins to read, her finger trailing underneath the unfamiliar letters. "Knowledge old and silent read, secrets locked in shadows told. Bound and woven, endless night, a balance tipped, the sundered to hold. Blood and bone, a prison lost, souls of many, an omen cast. Beyond the threads, a lifetime spread, touched by death, in godless sight. Sacrificed, one for another, forged anew, a flame to devour. Guarded well, a choice to make, glory or ruin, will or wrath. Stir the relic, birth the old, one face to hold what fate foretold." She pauses, finger trailing down the page to where the last line is scrawled in a different handwriting. "Balance back where it all began. Beware the fulcrum—it does not choose freely. It remembers."

All of our eyes flutter toward the gem in Keela's choker. It pulses into a bright flare of bloody red. The vampire places her hand over it, offering no explanation. I turn my attention back to the scroll, unease unfurling inside of me like a sail on a great ship. "What does Beatrice think that means? And who wrote the extra part?"

Monique lifts her head, staring straight into my eyes. "I did. Because Beatrice was right about Sean being an omen. He's a message spread across lifetimes, with the power to draw us together or rip us apart." She looks at each of us, lingering on Keela, then on Leah. "I think Odin intended for Sean to unite us but things aren't working out how he planned. And that means there will be consequences. For all of us." She slides the discolored parchment off the table. "Ancient things are awakening. All of you know it's true. Just look at what's happening to Keela."

A warning snarl ripples over Keela's blood-red lips. Monique blinks, chin lifting as her sad, weary eyes take the ever-changing vampire in. "Be angry with me all you want, but that doesn't change what's happening. Sean is the fulcrum. That's why I saw him atop the scales." She waves the scroll in the air, looking at all of us. "He's *this* prophecy wrapped in flesh, forged by Odin as a means to tip the balance at Ragnarök. But something is wrong. The Vasilis are losing allies and upsetting the peace the supernatural world has come to know under their rule. That's why Odin took Sean. And it's why Collin is right. Unless we all start working together, we're not going to have a world left to go back to. Sean isn't *in* prison. He *is* the prison. And ever since he showed up at Merrymont, our lives have been hell. As the fulcrum, it seems he's made his decision. Wrath. And that decision is *not* tipping the scales in our favor. So, either we figure out a way to get the Vasilis to trust us again or we prepare for war. Time is running out. We all have a decision to make. A side to choose."

## ~4~

## Sean

"Again," I breathe out in frustration, wiping the bloody spit from the side of my face. I've spent so many years working on my physique that my physical strength is a given. Which means absolutely nothing when the point of these training sessions is for me to rely on my magic. Ever so slowly, I'm unlocking those magical threads inside of me, coaxing them forward and testing each strand to see what it does. The Fae magic is the most dominant and it's the one I need in a fight. But it's the magic I have the least control over.

Ilda raises her perfectly sculpted brow at me. She's one of those visions you have to see to believe. Tall, blonde, and a body that makes her skintight battlesuit her best weapon. But she prefers to attack with the sword that's never far from her grip. It dangles loosely at her side, more like an extension of her arm than a weapon. One she's not going to use on me again because she thinks I've had enough abuse for one day. Her mistake.

She turns away, the length of her ponytail flowing down her back like a waterfall of spun gold. She struts toward the training room door and I peel myself off the concrete floor of the only indoor room I'm allowed to train in. My flame-throwing abilities haven't been the same since Zara shoved that longsword through my chest, but according to Natalie, that's because the soul of the dragon shifter that was trapped inside of me was injured. Or killed. Something Odin is ticked off about. He spent centuries binding souls together until he created a monstrous mix that was going to be his ace in the hole when it came to the Armageddon battle all of these people call Ragnarök. But Odin forgot something important when he Frankensteined souls and shoved them inside of a human baby. He could suppress the medley of supernatural power with fire runes and old spells, but those runes and spells didn't ward against my human spirit. It's rebellious by nature, and I grew up in a world where there's this little thing called free will. "I said, *again*."

Ilda's shoulders tense at my tone, her feet coming to an abrupt stop. She's too proud to let me get away with disrespecting her. Which I do as often as I possibly can because beautiful women bring nothing but misery. Odin paid the MacKenzie pack to look after me, which brought Leah into my life—the girl who destroyed my childhood. Then Odin intentionally bumped into me the first day I stepped foot onto Merrymont's campus, putting himself in my path so he could fray the edges of the spells he placed upon me. That began the process of my awakening and led me to Keela—the vampire I *still* love, even though I've never had a reason to. I love her even when I can hardly think of anyone other than Leah. It's Leah's face I keep seeing. The look she had when I told her I wanted us to be together, and the pain in her eyes at the end, after I betrayed her. After I brought her more misery than she ever gave to me.

"Are you scared, Ilda?" I use my self-disgust and hatred for all things Odin to taunt the Norse warrior. "Worried about pushing a half-trained Fae to his limit because even on my very worst days, I'm still more powerful than you?"

She slowly turns back toward me, her piercing blue eyes as deep and wrathful as the northern seas. Ilda is a top general of the Einherjar—Odin's army of harvested souls. Keela once vowed that she would meet her friend Aether in these hallowed halls where the Einherjar train, but I've looked and asked, and Aether isn't here. Neither are my parents.

I roll my neck and order twin balls of fire and faelight to my palms. I might not be able to flame up like I used to but I still have fire. What these people call elemental instead of dragon. So long as it gives me a shot at burning every strand of hair off Ilda's head, I don't care what kind it is. I juggle the orbs, voice echoing through the bunker-style room. "Here, kitty kitty..."

She lifts her blade. It's etched with ancient runes. Ones that remind me of the blade Zara ran through my chest. The one Leah and I found, back when I should have been enjoying the two of us being alone in a watery world. Stuck or not, we had food, shelter, and before I crushed Leah's spirit, she'd been laughing. Happy. I'd never seen her like that before. So relaxed and at ease. It caught me off guard. Just as much as the realization that my old feelings for her were alive and well.

Ilda advances. She won't kill me because that would make her precious Odin mad, but I heal really fast so she never has a problem pummeling me until I'm bleeding from every pore on my body. By that point, my brain is too scrambled to care about the fact that my entire life has been a lie. That I'm not even *me*. I'm a whole bunch of old, dead, reincarnated somebodies. One of them a Fae who just happened to have the power to command fire. I launch a flaming ball at Ilda and follow it up with a line drive of faelight. She flips and ducks, bending in a dizzying display of slashes and strikes. She moves like a dancer, graceful and quick, her feet barely touching the floor as she leaps out of the way of two more fireballs and splits down low to evade the third.

"Why are you here?" She scowls, ticked off that I almost managed to get an orb past her magic-repelling sword.

"Because Odin won't let me leave," I answer, attacking her again and putting everything I have into the magical assault. The Einherjar worship the ground Odin walks on. Literally. But from what I've learned about their god this far, I'll never be inclined to jump on his supposedly righteous bandwagon. Odin can kiss both my cheeks. And not the ones on my face.

I throw a disc of faelight that breaks apart in midair, using the spectacle to shove some orbs of fire toward Ilda's too-pretty face. "Why am I in this room? Because when I finally take you out, I'll know I can defend myself in the real world."

She pirouettes away from my attack as easily as I knew she would. She's not even breathing hard. Meanwhile, I'm sweating buckets. Not from the physical but from the effort of trying to control my magic. To make it go where, when, and how I want. But I've been through this before. The training room is chipped and charred because of the sessions we've had these past few weeks. Ilda always wins. But each time, I get better. Stronger. Smarter.

I circle her, keeping my eyes on her feet instead of the sword humming with the wisdom of centuries of battles. "I'm in this room because I would rather die than fight a war for Odin."

She tracks my movements. When Ilda attacks, it's pure physical strength, her body as honed as her blade. When I attack, she absorbs the blows with an unyielding flurry of grit, striking out with lightning-fast slashes. Ever calculating. Always advancing. Keeping me one ill-thought-out move away from feeling the dance of her blade against my throat. "To deny Odin is to deny yourself. He is the father of us all. If you insist upon disrespecting him, then I expect that you will get your wish." Her eyes gleam. "Your death will be swift."

I grin at her, because she hates it. "I can live with that."

I launch another assault of faelight and use a burst of my newfound supernatural speed to dart toward the far wall instead of directly at her, unleashing a volley of fire as I go. She ducks and rolls, and advances on me. One of my fiery orbs slams into her shoulder and she lets out a sharp hiss of air. I silently congratulate myself on the rare hit and run up the wall, using my own strength to defy gravity for the solid heartbeat I need. Ilda hesitates and I twist my hips, pushing off the wall, shooting a full sheet of faelight slicing down. A little to the right so she'll have to move left. Which she does. I extend my leg, slamming my heel into the side of her head. She staggers, stunned by the blow, and drops to a knee. I hit her with another punch of faelight. Her head snaps back but her leg sweeps out, removing my feet from the ground. I lash out with another ball of fire but it's a wild sling, accomplishing nothing but another scorching streak across the ceiling. My back slams into the concrete floor and Ilda is on top of me, her sword at my throat. A triumphant smirk spreads across her lips. "You're here because you fight with too much emotion, and that's why I'm not afraid of you. Too much ego, and absolutely no rhythm."

"Don't forget honor. He has little of it." I cringe at the sound of Riggs' voice. He's another one of the Einherjar's top warriors and from what I can tell, he and Ilda are a couple. One of those *no public displays of affection* types, because they're too serious for all of that. Too busy being perfect war specimens for Odin.

Ilda whips her blade away from my throat and launches herself off of me, showcasing her strength and agility by landing five feet away with the lightness of a falling leaf. "I was just getting ready to start the honor portion of our lesson. Want to help me teach him?"

Riggs snatches the massive battle-axe from his broad back and swings it in a crushing arc. I prop myself up on my elbows and glare at him. Like Ilda, he's tall and imposing. The two of them together exude the kind of raw power that commands respect. I refuse to give either of them an ounce of it. Especially Riggs. I'd rather pluck out his overly bright green eyes. "Well? What are you waiting for?" I get to my feet. "Is this better? More *honorable* for you if you don't attack a man while he's down?"

Riggs tilts his blade, showing off the gleam of the deadly sharp edge. I draw faelight to my hands. Like a warrior with a thousand battles under his belt, Riggs calmly moves around the perimeter of the training room. I follow him. The last time we fought, he nearly sliced my arm in two. That's when I realized how important my healing abilities are. To Odin. He created me to be practically indestructible so I could conquer for him. Destroy. Do his bidding without anyone being able to stand against me. But I don't work for Odin, and Riggs gets a sick pleasure out of knowing he can do quite a lot of damage to my body. So do I, actually. There's pleasure in those brief moments of mind-numbing pain. "You're looking a little sluggish, Riggs. How old are you again?" I expand the ball of faelight in front of me. "I bet you wish that when you died, Odin would have done something special with your soul. Like give it to me, so he'd care more about what happens to you."

His lip curls but I don't react. I wait. Watching his every movement. The twitch of his eye, the position of his feet, how his grip tightens on the axe. His cheeks sharpen, his snarl moving into a full-blown smile. I turn but I'm too late to correct my mistake. The hilt of Ilda's sword slams into my temple. I drop to my knees. Riggs chuckles, sliding the reinforced iron of his ax back into its sheath, the leather grip smooth and silent as it settles into place between his shoulder blades. "Your defiance is a lot like your self-loathing. It will earn you two things. Pity, and eternal death. If you want to survive, learn to control your emotions. Learn discipline." He turns to Ilda. "Let's go. Bjork is waiting for us, and we have enough discipline to know how to answer the call of our betters."

The two of them sweep out of the room and Natalie sweeps in behind them, laughing. "I came to see how your bright and sunny disposition was affecting your magic training. I'm glad to see it's going so well."

I sink back on my heels. "Glad my pain amuses you."

She crosses the room and offers me a hand. "You can beat Riggs and Ilda both, probably even at the same time, but you choose anger over discipline, and believe me, it pains me to say that because I'd rather not agree with Riggs on anything."

I wave off her offered hand and climb onto my aching feet all by myself. She shrugs, brushing the ends of her dark, curly hair away from her freckled face. "I'm not here to argue with you about how Ilda and Riggs are right and you're wrong. I found something you need to see. It's about your soul bonds."

Natalie is one of the shorter people here but though she's on the mousy, book-smart side of things, she's just as deadly with a blade as Ilda. I follow her out of the training hall and across the open courtyard. Valhǫll is a series of long, corridor-style multi-floored buildings, all connected through a grassy central atrium where a statue of a man rises up in the center. He looks like he's been hobbled together from a bunch of other statues. An arm from a marble work, a knee from rough stone, a bronze shoulder, a gold hand... Some of the pieces are strong and new while others are worn and even wrinkled. It's supposed to represent the many faces of Odin. One day, I'd like to have enough power to knock it down.

"Don't even think about firing on that statue again," Natalie scolds. "I barely got the scorch marks off from your last attack."

I shrug. "Where are we going?"

She points toward the hall that's three over on the left. "The bókahús. I've been sifting through the dusty tomes in the back and found some interesting...tales."

I'd be intrigued if she hadn't found a lot of interesting tales. They've all amounted to absolutely nothing when it comes to figuring out what kind of souls are inside of me and what I can do about them. She's adamant that she won't help me circumvent Odin or his wishes and insists that I should train with his army so I can lead them the way he wants. But she's too curious and fascinated by me not to do research into the very things that seem like they could help me do the exact opposite of what Odin wants. For that, I'm grateful. Even if all it's been so far is a dead end.

I lift my eyes to the skyline, taking one last glimpse of the view before we enter the library. Or the bókahús, as Natalie calls it. Valhǫll reminds me of Montana. It sprawls across a prairie and there are rugged mountains off in the distance. Those mountains look down on lush valleys and green forests. Above their treeless crests, the big sky is wide open, giving us warm days and cold nights. Only, there are no stars in this world's night sky. Every time I climb atop one of the branches of the hall and watch the sky go from the dark edges of dusk to the crisp pinks of dawn, it's the lack of stars overhead that proves to me that I'm not in Midgard. My Earth. The human realm where life was anything but easy, and yet still so much better than it is now.

I open the library door for Natalie, confused as to whether or not I'm even alive anymore. I'm as flesh covered as anyone else here, but they all died. Their souls were retrieved and brought here, to this immortal realm where they were given solid form again. Natalie said that's not what happened to me. That I'm not like anyone else in Valhǫll because Zara didn't kill me.

Natalie walks ahead of me. "You're making that face again. Is it brooding or pouting? I keep forgetting which unhelpful mood you prefer."

I bite back the scathing retort that's balancing on the tip of my tongue. Natalie is the only person here who I trust, and mostly because she's the only one who looks at me as if I'm a person instead of a weapon. A weapon I never would have believed myself to be if the Norns themselves hadn't shown me Odin's manipulation. How he played the long game, retrieving souls and holding them inside a series of powerful stones until he captured all the magic and force he wanted. Then he used his own magic and what he manipulated out of others to cast soul bonding spells, branding me with runes and layering his own magic over everyone else's so none of them would ever be able to sense their magical signatures on me. At least, that's what the Norns showed me. But I trust them about as much as I trust Odin. They could have manipulated those visions, so all I can really rely on is the fact that the Vasilis claimed not to be able to detect the source of my magic, and the look of shock on Beatrice's face the day I nearly burned her alive. Beatrice, the witch I knew as Bonnie. "If this newest interesting find of yours explains how I can *un*suppress all of these souls inside of me, I'll drop the attitude and stand up straight and tall, just like your boy Riggs."

Natalie rolls her eyes at me, sarcasm so thick I can cut it with a chainsaw. "No wonder your friends love you. How could they not, with all your charismatic charm?"

My fingers twitch into fists. "Which friends are those? The Vasilis? Yeah, they started out acting like they wanted to be friends but then those Midgard-ruling elves tortured me and got Leah and me stuck in the land of the Norns. But maybe you're talking about my shapeshifting best friend who lied to me our entire lives."

She cocks a brow. "I was referring to me. I consider you a friend, and I think you're particularly hilarious."

She turns away from me, cheerily greeting a group of warriors passing by us in the hall. Within the ranks of the vast Einherjar army, everyone holds a job that keeps Valhǫll running. But it doesn't matter if they're emptying trash, landscaping, offering medical care, scrubbing pots and pans, or tending to the many different varieties of animals housed in the valleys—everyone here is a warrior first and the doer of their job second.

Except for me. Because I'm not a simple one-dead-soul reincarnation like they are. I'm Odin's *special* creature. A mutt full of the remnants of ancient souls that should have died a long time ago. And that's why I'm nowhere close to being finished brooding over the fact that Odin is a thief. He took what didn't belong to him and now that he's imprisoned me here, I've started having memories that aren't mine. There are faces in my dreams that I don't recognize, and things I suddenly know that I never knew before. Which brings me back to the question of death. If my souls were bound into one, and Zara killed one of the pieces of the whole, doesn't that make all of me dead? Dead the way the Einherjar are. Or am I still alive the way I was before I came to Valhǫll, but with one less soul? At least one of the souls inside of me, two if I count my original human soul, isn't immortal. Natalie says some of the others are probably only longer living beings too. Not considered immortals by any supernatural standard. That means there's a good chance they've outlived their life expectancies. Will they die now that they've been awakened? Since they're tied to my human soul, will I die too? *Dead* dead?

Natalie grabs my arm and pulls me through a door in the back of the hall. "Come on, pouty face. If Ilda didn't break you this time, maybe I can still manage to cheer you up."

I tug my arm free as we walk through the passage. "Maybe I should go provoke Ilda into beheading me. Then you can have fun writing down all of the interesting ways I'm either still miraculously alive or finally dead."

Natalie groans, pushing open another door and springing down a set of spiral stairs. I follow her, because I've told Natalie everything. Confided in her. All in hopes of getting her to help me, which is exactly what she's trying to do. If there's a way to get out of being used by

Odin, I want to know. Even if it means that I have to die a permanent, un-reincarnatable death.

The stairs lead to a large room outfitted with tall countertops overhung with flexible lights that are bent over stacks of books. "Welcome to my office!" Natalie beams, undeterred by my sour company. "Well, the place I spend most of my time anyway. Being a scribe means not only recording current history, but making sure the older records are kept in good order. Some of them are ancient, and in languages I haven't yet learned to read. But some of them..." She heads for the longest counter. It's piled with books and littered with parchment. "Odin gives us wisdom to do our jobs so even though a lot of the oldest tomes are thought to be full of lore, I started to wonder if that's only because those languages have been lost to time. So instead of trying to actually decipher them, a scribe only perused them, picking up a few things here and there before writing them off as fairy tales."

I move to the counter and look down at all the strange lettering. "So, you decided to read the languages you don't know, and found out you *do* know them?"

She shakes her head. "It doesn't work quite like that. Odin gives us the advanced ability to learn, but we still have to put in the effort. I haven't had the time, so I pulled what I could read, even if only a little bit." She smooths her hand over the polished leather of a bound book with three interlocking triangles etched into the spine. "This book talks about the World Tree. It tells how the tree is rooted in the center of the cosmos, with the trunk rising into the clear sky where its crown gives life to the land of the gods."

She opens the book and flips to a page covered with the raised image of a tree. It lifts from the bottom of the page and stretches out beyond the edges. I run my finger over the trunk. It feels like bark. "This is the World Tree?"

Natalie nods, tracing the outline of the tree's canopy with the tip of her finger before sliding down the page, all the way to where the trunk disappears into a mass of roots. "Here is where the land of the Norns is rumored to be. Where they tend to their mystical well. The waters are sacred and not allowed to be touched without permission from the Norns."

I snatch my hand away from the book. "I didn't touch them."

She laughs. "Maybe you should have, because they're said to hold the secrets of life. Of *existence*. That's how the Norns do what they do. They drink the water. Bathe in it. And use their gifts to decipher the old magic held within those waters. Some say this magic is a piece of Chaos itself. That it whispers to the Norns, driving them to weave their destinies. And some of those destinies are so certain that the Norns carve them into the bark of Yggdrasil itself."

I study the raised image. "What does the Norns defacing a tree have to do with me? I want answers about me, not a lesson in Norse mythology."

Natalie sighs. "Fate is a delicate balance of past, present, and future. Ever-changing. Unpredictable. And yet, it's orchestrated. It *has* to be, because the cosmos demands balance."

I fold my arms over my chest. "You mean the Norns demand it."

Natalie smiles. "The sisters are bound to the rules of the cosmos. They manipulate fate for the purpose of balance. Each sister is respected for what they do, each of them charged with contributing their own unique perspective as they guide their threads into the tapestry of life."

I let out a sharp snort. "The Norns play games with people's lives and come up with stupid challenges to make us *prove* ourselves so they can judge us, based on rules they make up. I've been on the receiving end of that judgment, and I watched lives get destroyed because of it. So even if the rest of you want to worship the Norns the way you do Odin, I won't. Like Odin, the Norns are free to weave themselves right out of my life."

Natalie reaches for a parchment on the counter behind her. "Most of us don't abhor the Norns the way you do, but we don't worship them. We revere them. As you should. Because their influence over any life is profound, but it's especially far-reaching when it comes to those with more challenging destinies. Like yours."

I look down at my hands. Faelight rises from my skin—tiny threads of glowing magic intertwining with flame. "If Odin left me alone, my life wouldn't be complicated at all. The Norns should be making *him* go through tests to prove himself. Not me. And not Collin or Leah."

Natalie looks up at me, a deep crease between her brows. "I suppose you've earned the right to be testy, but try not to be utterly disrespectful. Unless you really do want Ilda to behead you."

I take a deep breath, massaging the temple Ilda landed her perfect blow on. Odin is rarely ever here. He pops in from time to time, decreeing things or decrying me, and then his army of stooges goes about training and working, while fitting any of his new demands into their schedules, waiting for that glorious day when their precious Odin decides to need them. When I asked what would happen if everyone decided to lounge around and not do any of the things Odin asked, they all just looked at me as if I'd sprouted three heads. Since then, my idea for a Valhǫll-wide vacation has been met with the kind of scorn that leaves a bruise. Which is fine, because it takes me all of thirty seconds to heal these days. Still, Natalie is trying to help me and if she can figure out exactly how I was created, that could lend itself to uncreating me. Then maybe someone will let me leave this place instead of always saying it's impossible to leave without Odin's permission. I don't want to be here, separated from the girl whose heart I broke. Or from the one I sometimes feel like I'd rather rip out my own heart than be without. "I'm sorry, Natalie. I'll try to stop insulting your gods and your *revered* ones...in your presence."

She flips the parchment over. There in the center is the faintest sketch of a sword. *Zara's* sword. "Good. Because I know why you were stabbed. And I know what happened to the dragon. It's gone, Sean. Released. Which is exactly what you've been wanting to know because if one of them can be released, maybe all of them can."

## ~5~

"The Norns shape lives. Even those of the gods." Natalie pulls another book across the counter. This one milky white with pale red lines forming the silhouette of a flame. "You're not the only one who insists upon being angry about your destiny, Sean. Every god has circumvented the Norns. Or tried to. It's a common thing to want to change one's fate. To make it better, even if not for ourselves, but others. The same way you made different choices once the Norns showed you the reality of what you are." She reaches past me, sliding a stack of three books over to the odd white one. "Those different choices are why the sisters themselves have long been angry with the gods, claiming the gods manipulate their power the way you claim Odin has manipulated you. But many of the gods believe the senselessness of fate is what will bring on the final destruction of the cosmos. They essentially put more stock in their own solutions than trusting the Norns to keep everything balanced."

A tense breath slips past my teeth. "Because balance doesn't always favor the gods, so the greedy, power-hungry Odins out there change every single thing about other people's lives and set them on twisted paths for no other reason than the wants of the self-serving god."

Natalie groans, flipping open the top book on the stack. Its edges are black and pages full of what I can only assume are supposed to be words or letters. She drums her fingers against one of the pages. "This book breaks down how each sister of fate has specific dominion over an aspect of time. Urd deals with the past, and Skuld governs the future, while Verdandi is the embodiment of the present. Together, they're tasked with upholding the sacred laws of the cosmos. Which means they're supposed to be impartial." She gestures toward me. "They're not supposed to directly engage, the way they did with you. On the rare occasion they give someone an audience, their message is always cryptic and poetic." Her eyes gleam. "Like that of a Seidr."

I study the lines of unreadable text. Collin told me about the Seidr he had a run-in with, and I told Natalie everything, agreeing to be completely upfront with her. I don't think she was prepared for the brutality of my honesty. *I* wasn't even prepared for it. I'd hidden my feelings for Leah so deep inside my vault of things I didn't want to feel that they broke the last remaining tether to who I was when those feelings leaked out and spilled down my heart like an oil slick. One that makes my hunger for Keela more confusing. I was getting used to the idea of Keela being my soulmate, then Leah tipped everything upside down and now wanting Keela feels too complicated to be right. My choice is Leah. At least, the part of me that I think is really me chooses Leah. But that doesn't stop other parts of me from wanting Keela. "You think the Norns broke their rules for me? And the Seidr did too?"

Natalie bites her lip, looking around to make sure no one else is in the room with us. "Yes. On the Norns, anyway. So, this morning, I asked myself why they would do such a thing. And that's when I found this." She removes the black-edged book and opens the next one. It looks almost identical to the first except for a stamp of a raven's wing in the dead center of the cover. Natalie opens it and begins rifling through the pages. "Every move the Norns make is significant, but what they did with you was outright pivotal. Which made me think about the ancient runes. Ones said to have been placed in the realms so long ago that time itself has forgotten about them. They're supposed to hold ancient secrets. Prophecies written by the first seers to ever live."

I point to the book. "And now they're written in this book?"

Natalie lowers her voice to barely an audible whisper. "No. But Urd is the embodiment of memory so she wouldn't have forgotten about them the way everyone else did. And Urd's literal job is to constantly contemplate the accumulated wisdom of the past. Which means that Urd, more than her sisters, understands the importance of their actions. And Urd would have also remembered that Odin *sacrificed* himself in order to read those ancient runes."

My brow knits. "Is that how he learned to do what he did to me?"

Natalie shrugs, pointing to the page she's finally settled on. "This is the song of the cosmos. I'm still working on deciphering all of it but it speaks of bones, woven and mixed. Sacrifices and secrets. Guarded wells and godless sight. And...an anger that threatens both glory and ruin."

The blood drains from my face. "That's what the Norns said about me. That my anger threatens glory and ruin."

Natlie nods excitedly, going back to the book with the three interlocking triangles. "I've spent so much time going through book after book, reading old historical recordings and prophecies, connecting pieces of every story that has anything to do with Ragnarök and how it might relate to your inevitable role, that I nearly missed the real lead." Her nimble fingers open the book and flip to the image of the tree. "There's another well." She runs her fingers across the page. "Somewhere around here. It belongs to Mimir and is called Mímisbrunnr. It's said that Mimir drinks from the well daily and that the water gives him immense knowledge." She flips to the back of the book. "Odin, already wise, sought to gain even more knowledge by asking Mimir to let Odin drink of the well. This story details how Mimir granted Odin's request, but only after Odin made a great sacrifice. To gain the wisdom of the well's ancient waters, Odin sacrificed his *eye* to Mimir's well—and gained untold knowledge." She looks up at me. "This book records exactly how Odin became known as the one-eyed god."

A weight presses against my chest, a burden heavier than the others I carry coming into focus. "What does this have to do with Zara?"

Natalie's eyes widen, as if she's surprised I haven't already connected her widespread dots. "There's a poem that talks about humility and the path of sacrifice. Of how a pure heart is better than the cleansing fire of regret. Toward the end, it mentions Odin's token given in sacrifice." She reaches behind her and snatches another piece of parchment to add to our growing pile. "Here. This is another poem talking about the same thing." She runs her fingers beneath words written in symbols I can't read. "The seeker of wisdom, armed with a symbol of thine own face, shining like the stars above. Tears poured out, what fate now sees, left in the well on crystal bed." She runs her fingers around the sketch of what looks to be a bed of crystal and then goes back to the book with the tree. "This book claims that Odin's sacrificed eye was turned into a powerful, unretrievable artifact by the sacred waters of Mimir's well. It was encrusted in the same crystal that grows along the bottom of the well.

But later, in this book"—she moves to the stack beside the white book and tugs the bottom book free—"it's written that one whose sacrifice was greater than Odin's could retrieve the Eye."

"Aether?" I ask, throat dry. "Aether gave up something important to retrieve the eye?"

Natalie leans close, still keeping her voice low as if she's afraid someone will overhear what she's telling me. "It's hard to tell who sacrificed what. All we know is the amulet is real and Aether ended up with it. Then he put it inside of you, which he was probably only able to do because the Eye recognized itself in you. You know, because of the amount of magic Odin had to use just to keep you glued together in this charming little form." She straightens, grinning. "Urd knew the Eye was in play the second it was retrieved, because the cosmos knew. Because the cosmos flows through Mimir's well just like it flows through that of the Norns. It's what connects everything. And it's why it's so hard for the gods to circumvent the will of the Norns. But the gods *have* managed to get their way, like when they attempted to create a brand new fate weaver and gave birth to the Seidr. And with Odin successfully creating you. But the instant something happens, the Norns *know*."

I scan the books and parchment scattered in front of us. "They know, and start working to fix what the gods broke?"

Natalie claps, and then hushes herself, eyes scanning the room again. "The Norns aren't demanding balance for the sake of being tyrants. They demand it because the cosmos needs it. *Has* to have it. If they don't do their job, there will be consequences. For all of us. I think that's why Aether ended up with the Eye, and how it came to be inside of you." She holds up the picture of Zara's sword. "Just because someone pulls a fast one and gets something past the Norns, doesn't mean the Norns are then helpless to correct the imbalance. When something happens, Verdandi knows about it immediately because it's part of the present. Urd knows about it seconds later because it's part of the past. And Skuld is able to see every possible future ramification. And they've had ages to plan out exactly what needed to be done to counterbalance Odin capturing souls. Over two decades now to counterbalance how he put those souls inside of you."

I lean against the counter. "They sent Zara to assassinate me?"

Natalie swallows. "Well, first, I think they stuck you in that rotunda with Leah MacKenzie hoping she would use this sword on you."

I nearly choke on my tongue. "The Norns wanted Leah to kill me and because she failed, they sent Zara to finish the job? Why didn't they just kill me themselves?"

Natalie places the parchment beside the white book and finally opens it, turning to a page that's marked with a thin silver chain. The letters and words on the page are printed by hand in tiny neat rows. "The Norns are as stuck as you are. Their job isn't to impose upon anyone's free will, all they can do is try to give them purpose, and I guess Leah decided her purpose wasn't to stab you. The same can't be said for Zara." Natalie moves the silver chain aside. "This book is a history of the Dreki and while I can't read most of it, once I found the parchment with the image of the exact same sword you described as the one Zara used on you, I knew I had to try. The sword is called Firebrand, and it's a true rarity. A weapon forged by the ancient Dreki kings and imbued with what this text calls the eternal flame."

"What is that?" I ask.

Natalie shakes her head. "I haven't found an explanation for it yet. All I know is the sword is somehow tied to the essence of the kings themselves and used as a way to prove the purity of a bloodline, to make sure all of the Dreki rulers hail from those original kings. This part here says that a young dragon in line for the throne wouldn't be able to maintain the transference of power they would get if their elder were to perish before the younger dragon's fifty-first turn. Meaning years." She runs her finger down the page. "This part says Firebrand was imbued with some sort of magic that would hold the soul of the deceased dragon until the too-young heir reached maturity. At which point the heir would spill their blood upon Firebrand's blade and receive the power from their dead relative. The power that is rightfully theirs."

I think about how the sword felt in my grip and what Leah told me about the Dreki. How they puff themselves up on pride and honor, and yet can't get along with each other long enough to even mate. "The sword holds dragon souls, but only those of the kings?"

Natalie studies the next page in the book. "That's what it seems like. Which means the dragon soul inside of you must have been one of them. Or one of their heirs, I suppose. The kings all disappeared a very long time ago, thought to be dead or having never existed at all. It seems now that they did exist and their bloodlines ran dry because their sword disappeared, making it impossible for any Dreki king to ever rise again."

I think back to Monique's words right before the Vasilis forced me into the land of the Norns. "Beatrice, the head witch I told you about, said I had the fire of some old dragon bloodline."

Natalie smiles. "You also have the flame of a very ancient Fae. And it makes sense that a dragon like Zara, who you said lived with a Seidr, would recognize the sword as a very important Dreki relic. You even said she called you a thief. I think she knew the soul of one of her Dreki kings was hijacked and that she could use the sword to free it. To absorb it.

Because you might have had the soul of a dragon, but you didn't have its blood. Which is what the Norns wanted all along. To stop you from having as much power as you did."

I rake both of my hands through my hair. "I guess two ancient flames is too much for any one person to have, but did Zara take Haldir because he's the bloodline of the kings, or is Zara the bloodline and she took Haldir because she needed him for some other reason?"

Natalie heaves a sigh. "I didn't consider Zara being the heir but you're right, she could be. If that's the case, she wanted Haldir either for her mate to help rebuild their numbers or for her security detail because female dragons are usually smaller than males and don't have as much power. But we don't have time to worry about what she may or may not be doing to Haldir because I found something else this morning and I think it might explain how your souls are interacting with the Eye, because Odin never intended for you to have that Eye. The Norns did, so it must be a negative for Odin that you have it."

I scratch the spot on my chest where Aether punched it inside of me. "The Vasilis never found an amulet so I'm assuming I absorbed it the way Firebrand absorbs dragon souls?"

Natalie motions for me to follow her to another counter that's piled and littered with books. "From what you told me, the dragon inside of you was dominant, either overriding your Fae magic or just faster at gaining control of itself after the awakening. Now your Fae is dominant but you're a broken creation. You're not wielding magic the way you should be able to. Some things are slowly coming to you and Ilda's last report to Odin said your instincts and enhanced senses are getting better, but the results have largely been disappointing."

I shuffle through the books. "Agreed. So next time you speak to Odin, tell him to send me back to where I came from."

Natalie flips open the largest and thickest book on the table. "Don't be sore over me simply stating the truth. Odin is dripping with disappointment. You're soaked in anger. And the Norns interacted with you in an extreme way." Natalie stops on a page only a tenth of the way through the great tome. "Odin went to great lengths binding your souls together but neither he *nor* you can access the power of the souls the way he thought would be possible. I think we can safely assume the Norns are behind foiling Odin's well-laid plan to have you be his great warrior. You losing the dragon soul is one thing, but what better way to interrupt your ability to access the others whose combined wills would demand that you obey Odin, than to fight Odin with his own power?"

"The Eye," I mutter, perusing the page. A few of the symbols actually seem to form words I can read.

Natalie smooths her hands over the page. "The stories mentioning the Eye turning into a relic never explain what power the Eye possesses, but one can assume that it's probably imbued with some of Odin's own power. *And* it was turned into an artifact by the water in Mimir's well. Water whose power is supposed to come from the cosmos itself. And the cosmos was created from the very same Chaos that created Odin."

I scratch my jaw. "And that means what? That I'm more powerful than Odin now?"

She winces. "No, I'm not saying that. I'm only saying that it's not a stretch to assume the Eye possesses power that came straight from the Primordial Void. The place where Chaos itself lives. Chaos being what created the cosmos—Yggdrasil, the great tree whose existence the Norns do their best to balance." She taps the page. "This book tells of how it was there, inside the void, that Odin and his two brothers were born. But they weren't the only ones. They were simply the ones who drew first blood." She swallows. "They did it for the greater good. Slew other creatures from within the void to create Midgard, a place they immediately set upon protecting. Especially after they used what they found there to create mankind. Odin's brothers helped form and shape humankind from logs, but it was Odin who breathed the breath of life into them. That's why his focus has always been on humans and Midgard. He's trying to save that which he created." She motions around. "Valhǫll isn't just a vanity project so Odin can have an army. It's a place he created and gave his own power to so that human souls could come here and live as the supernaturals and gods do. For eternity."

I snort. "Yeah, unless they get killed in his stupid battle and have to die for a second time."

She frowns. "You're missing the importance of what I'm telling you, Sean. Odin's duty is to the gods and to Midgard. The Norns have a duty that keeps them planted between the void and the cosmos. It's creator versus creation, even when it comes to you and your battle with Odin. But he *is* a creator, and so *is* Chaos. And because you absorbed the Eye, that dual power to create is inside of you. Which is why..." She hesitates.

I put my hand on top of hers. "It's okay, just tell me. I can handle whatever it is."

She looks around. "The Eye was put inside of you right after Odin began to lift your suppression spells to allow those individual souls inside of you to emerge, each of them capable of rising to the surface to use their power for whatever and whenever you needed. But you're not operating that way and you're suddenly seeing and knowing things you didn't before because the Eye is creating something new inside of you.

I think it's fusing your souls together, making them one in a way Odin never expected. Never wanted." She swallows, removing her hand from underneath mine and jamming her finger into the page of the big book. "Chaos is creating a new kind. You. And there's no telling what parts of you it's going to keep and which ones it's going to delete."

"A disruption the Norns were counting on." The air ripples, Odin's voice booming through the room. My spine stiffens and Natalie jumps, turning away from the table to stand with her head bowed, giving Odin the deference I refuse to give. "A disruption bolstered by the petulant mind of the Eye's host." His voice shakes the floor underneath me, a bolt of gold light spiraling upward, twisting and fading away like spent starlight. In its wake stands Odin, his cold eyes locked on mine. "Thank you, Natalie. I knew you would figure out what was wrong with my creation."

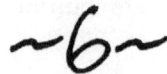

# ~6~

Natalie's head shakes, the set of her jaw disagreeing with the lie her head is trying to tell me. She befriended me for Odin's sake. Getting me to trust her so I would open up and tell her all of the things Odin wanted to know. "You spied on me. For him."

A tear slips down her cheek. I look away, squaring my shoulders to Odin. "Weapons and pawns. Pieces on your board. That's all any of us are to you. Objects for you to use."

He walks toward me. "Everyone has a purpose. Natalie's was to keep an eye on you, help you figure out whatever it was you thought you needed to know. Yours was to bring down the other side in Ragnarök. That's why I crafted you, after all. Over the course of many centuries, and with the greatest of care."

I narrow my eyes on him. "I'm no fan of the Norns but if they say Ragnarök is a winless battle, then it probably is."

Odin shifts forms, becoming a cloaked figure in a wide-brimmed hat. "It is not the whims of gods and men that usher Ragnarök, and I will not let it be the whims of fate that decide how it will end. The sisters try to find balance where none exists. They feed on Chaos, where nothing and everything exist together. And they do this while placating to the supplications of the cosmos."

I fold my arms over my chest. "It doesn't matter how many words you toss around because even if they convinced me that fighting for you would save the world, I wouldn't do it. I'll watch everything burn into nothing and pat Chaos on the back before I so much as a lift a finger to help the *god* who thinks he has the right to manipulate and prey on emotions. To destroy lives. All to give himself a pointless advantage."

Odin shifts into another form. Wearing another one of his many faces. This one rugged, strong, and worn. A warrior. "I fight for an existence that benefits all kinds. I fight to keep us all from going back to the existence my brothers and I fought to escape."

My temper flares. I lower my arms, allowing my fire to dance up from my fingertips, clawing and crackling over my wrists and all the way up to my shoulders. Natalie sucks in a sharp breath of air but Odin only watches the flames as they rise. I take a step in his direction. "You cared so much about your weapon that you hired a pack of wolves to watch over me, and then you didn't bother to help my parents. You let them die, and you didn't save their souls, because you didn't care about them any more than you care about anyone else who doesn't serve a purpose that's beneficial to you. So go ahead and keep hiding behind your many faces while pretending you're something to worship because I see what you truly are, and I will *never* serve you. All I'm going to do is fight to go back to the existence I came from."

Odin stands there, a mask of polished patience. "So you've said, and you are free to choose. Though, even without the great dragon and the setbacks the Norns have caused, you are still capable of shattering the very threads of the foretold battle."

I add a dizzying mix of faelight to the flames covering my arms. "The only thing I want to shatter is you."

Natalie bolts to the other side of the room and Odin chuckles, morphing into the old man he first appeared to me as. "That's too bad, my boy. If you refuse what the Third decreed you for, then I will have to create another who will accept the honor." His eyes drop to my chest. "And I will be taking back what belongs to me. The Norns should have known better than to direct its fate to you."

I open my mouth to tell him again where he can shove himself but runes shimmer in the air all around me and my body goes stiff. Rigid. Utterly still, like that monstrosity of a statue in the courtyard. Sound sucks away. Air. Scent. Leaving me in a vacuum where sight is my only sense. Slowly, a sound like the drip of water fills the silent void. It isn't until I taste the tang of copper in the back of my throat that I realize it isn't water. It's blood. Mine.

Sound comes rushing back. Natalie is screaming from behind a wall of wind, the vortex stealing the tears from her eyes as terror seizes every feature on her face. Every freckle. But it's my own terror that transforms my shredded throat into a wreckage of gurgled shouts. Snakes of Odin's magic burrow into me, ripping me apart from the inside, his voice ringing out like the distant toll of a bell as he watches holes gape open all over what was once my body. "I made you to unmake the boundaries of kinds. To win wars. Unite kingdoms." His face shifts between its many versions as he speaks. "I created you to conquer. It's a pity you chose anger over glory. A wolf over your ability to mate with the Dearg Dua."

My jaw falls open. Not because I want it to. My flesh is melting, tendons and bone dripping away. Odin is killing me. I can feel the life draining from my cells. He's killing me. *Dead* dead.

## Zara

Wind howls through the barren landscape where I first set eyes upon Collin MacKenzie, the swift-moving air sweeping away the heavy layer of sulfur. I wish it wasn't. I'd rather have that pungent scent filling my nose, overpowering the smell of Haldir. The heavy yoke of his body weighs me down, tugging and pulling against my center of gravity, causing me to stumble through the volcanic field. I adjust him over my shoulder, grateful to have gotten this far. Thankful even to the traitorous witch who bound my dragon. The guilt of her actions forced her to send potions of strength to the Seidr and it is only through those potions that I have been able to fulfill my mission. Still, I am tired. This journey has been long. Made worse by the witch's trickery. No matter her attempts at amends, I will not forgive her.

I stumble again, heaving Haldir's dead weight higher onto my shoulder. His elbows bang into my back, hitting against Firebrand's enchanted leather sheath where it rests along my sweaty spine. The Seidr was right in all of her predictions. Even now, the shift in the wind signals that change has come. A reckoning. A chance to right long-forgotten wrongs. Even if doing so means committing new trespasses against the kings and their heirs. But what I do, I do for all Dreki.

I move around the base of the volcano, closing in on the hidden door to the Seidr's lair—where she was free to see into the future and weave new paths. Where she was free to train and guide me. I whisper the words the Seidr gave me, knowing they'll work to open the door, and knowing there will be no time to mourn the loss of what I will find inside. Already, a spot of moss grows along the threshold.

I push the door open and carry Haldir inside, paying attention to every detail of the home around me, the way the Seidr always told me to, admonishing me to remember that there is a purpose to all things large or small, and that those purposes will reveal themselves. In time. Already, I see a sack by the small table in the back of the room. One not ordinarily there. And I see what I have been dreading since the moment I ran Haldir through with Firebrand. The Seidr, lying cold and stiff in front of an equally cold fireplace.

I heave Haldir from my shoulder, dropping him into my arms and settling him on the knotted rug beside the Seidr, allowing the tears to come because they will not hinder me. Will not deter me from what must happen next. I cross Haldir's magnificent arms over his broad chest, cupping his hands over his heart. His face is one it would have been good to know. "Sleep well, my prince. May the souls of our ancestors rise up to meet yours." I wipe the crust of blood from the corner of his mouth and bow my head, asking for the ancient dead to heed my call. To welcome him among them. Had it not been for Firebrand, I could not have subdued Haldir long enough to force the poison down his throat. Had it not been for the Norns disliking Odin even more than they dislike me, I would not have been given the chance to claim Firebrand for my kingdom.

With the agony of a thousand cuts, I move away from Haldir and crouch down next to the Seidr. She is a mother to me, but she would not be honored by mournful words. I unsheathe Firebrand. "I found it." I show her the blade, still wet with the blood of the heir, as she said it would be. A tear tracks down my face. "I'll finish it now. For both of us." I touch her cheek, blinking away my clouded vision. "Damned or divine, may the soul the gods created find mercy wherever it goes."

I rise from the floor and store Firebrand back in its sheath, moving to the only object out of place in the room. I lift the sack, crossing its strap over my body in the opposite direction of how Firebrand's sheath crosses me. There's no need for me to inspect the contents. I already know this small sack contains everything I will need to finish my quest. The Seidr sees all options and has never failed to meet my needs, even when obtaining my needs has caused her to deal with beings she otherwise would not have. Even when my needs put her at great risk. When they hastened her end. For all of this, she has prepared me.

I end my flow of tears, shutting them off and storing my emotions away. A warrior, as I am, cannot have such feelings of sorrow. Of regret. A Dreki tasked with what I must do cannot feel at all. My kingdom before all else. Even the life of my mother.

I lift my head, fire burning inside my empty heart, and cross the threshold, stepping back out of the Seidr's now cold home. The door closes behind me and I open the sack, removing a jar of golden cream brought to the Seidr by a powerful Surtr who came all the way from his land of giants to gain an audience with she whose origins began the blending of kinds. I open the jar and dig my fingers into the silky cream, slathering it heavily along the edges of the door, whispering old words as I go. Just as the Seidr prepared me to do.

My fingers slide across the bottom of the door and back to the top, where I began. I remove my hand and the cream on my fingers disappears but that on the door glows bright red, sizzling and cracking. The glow fades, leaving nothing but solid stone in its place. I recap the jar, the Seidr's lair now a volcanic tomb. One where the bodies inside will remain undisturbed.

I drop the empty jar into the sack and take out a solid green stone. One whose weight feels too heavy in my palm. What I do next will not only change the course of fate for what remains of the Dreki, but for what remains of all the worlds of Yggdrasil. I place the stone at my feet and break it under my heel.

### Sean

My body is cold. Numb. My mind suspended somewhere between the dreams of life and the torment of death. It's dark here, edges of cutting stone sprawled beneath me while an expanse of memories lay scattered above me like grains of warm sand, inviting me to walk among them. Some are mine. Others are ashes of a past that doesn't belong to me. Not to the human I was. They belong to those odd and foreign souls Odin took from their still-living bodies, capturing them for himself while leaving their flesh to rot. Their bones to be lost to their families and their kinds for all eternity. Rulers and those of great power among the supernatural kinds were robbed of their souls while they slept. Targeted by a vengeful god all so their powers would not pass on or die off, according to the natural order of each kind. Odin stole them while they lived so he could build himself a warrior. And now, Odin understands he chose the wrong human to convert.

I rest my consciousness atop that place where my human heart beats underneath my ribs. Odin has been trying to do to me what he did to the others. Harvest my soul. So he can take back what he endowed it with. So he can try again to create his perfect warrior, using the very same souls he's already collected. But the Eye works against him, binding his magic to me and drawing the magic from those souls away from them and into me, turning my human soul into something else. Something more. The Eye leaves the others weak and bare, so even if Odin does collect them from me, they will not be powerful the way they once were. They'll be nothing more than dark, whispering pits.

I allow my consciousness to move closer to the souls. It's getting harder to separate them from one another. The Eye sucks on the very threads of their beings and every time Odin dissects me, they blur together even more. But they are separate from my soul now. No longer attached. The Eye undid what Odin was so proud of accomplishing. Not to save any of the souls, though. Not even to save mine. The Eye thrums and coils through my veins, hiding in plain sight as it takes those elements it deems worthy to enhance its new creation, folding them into my soul, mixing and weaving, mending and darning. Patching my soul the same way the collective healing abilities it has cleaved from the others patches my body, healing what Odin has destroyed.

The others call out to me, voices that are not my own shouting to me from my deepest, most intimate parts. They know the great dragon is gone. They recognize his absence and some of them want that for themselves, to be gone from inside me so their souls can take their final flight. Others want to stay, to become one with what the Eye is creating.

And yet some plead for sovereignty within me. Those like Erik, who are weak without the power contained within my body. Erik is the reason I feel unnatural things for Keela. Her allure is why some of the others love her too. Despite the Eye's dismantling of their souls, they're still full of wants and desires, and those wants and desires impact my own.

I reach for Erik's memories. They're of Keela with blonde hair. Human. Smiling. Crying. The two of them lived lifetimes ago. Her stealing his heart and then coming back from the dead as...something else, to rip the beating heart from his chest. Unlike all of the others, Erik is the only soul Odin retrieved after death. He bargained with Hel to obtain Erik, and even though Erik's last memories of Keela are bitter, he loves her. And like Odin, he's angry that I didn't do more to become her mate. That I let Abhartack get to her first.

"Sean," a soft voice spills over my shoulder. I startle. This voice is from outside. Somewhere beyond my body. "Sean," the voice speaks again. Hushed. Frayed. "Sean, wake up. Please, wake up."

I will my consciousness to move toward the voice. To see the back of my own closed eyelids. "Who are you?" My voice is hoarse. Too rough against the inside of my ears.

"It's me. Natalie." Her tone is urgent. "Can you open your eyes? You need to be able to see."

Her words strike an odd chord. In this vessel made of memories, my eyes *are* open. I *am* seeing. I could stay here, reliving the lives of my souls instead of my own. Stay here healing. Preparing. Waiting for the next time Odin comes to rip away flesh and bone, searching for the very thing that's inside the blood he spills across the floor as if it's nothing at all.

I focus on the backs of my physical eyelids, rolling one of them up like a window shade. The light from Natalie's lantern sends the heavy shade crashing back down. But she's real. She's there. Kneeling beside me on the hard dark stone. I test my voice again. "Odin sent you to play nurse?"

"No," she answers, hands moving to my arms and sliding behind my back. I let out a sharp hiss as she tugs me upward. "Sorry," she whispers, "but we have to hurry. Odin finally left but he won't be gone long and no one is supposed to be in here so if I'm caught..."

I blink open my eyes, squinting and wrapping an arm around my middle, hunching forward over my legs and doing my best to hold myself upright. "Odin left already? He's only been ripping me apart for three days, I thought he'd be psychotic enough to keep it going for at least three more."

She touches the patches of new pink skin covering my throat, hands trembling and tears falling. "I'm so sorry. I didn't know he would—"

"Stop." I bat her hand away. "I don't need your pity. I don't need anything from you."

She hiccups a sob. "You do, Sean. Because you haven't yet given up what Odin wants so he'll back to...to do this to you all over again."

I try to shift my weight forward. To stand. "I'd rather spend my life being this close to death than give Odin anything, so let him come back." I slouch against the stone, my legs not yet on board with functioning. "Let his magic chew through me. I don't care."

"But I do," she whispers. "The Eye is acting as a shield, somehow protecting you from the worst of what Odin wants to do to you, but it doesn't matter if the Eye is infused throughout your body or not. If Odin can't eradicate it and harvest your souls, he'll find someone who can. He'll collect magic users and artifacts until he's able to reap what he wants. And you will suffer, Sean. More and more each day."

I wrap my hands around one knee and bend it, hoisting my leg into an angle until my foot is flat against the stone floor. My bare foot, my clothing long gone. "Good, because if I'm suffering, that means Odin is too. Every time my lips grow back, I'll smile about that."

Natalie pulls a dark gray shirt from her crossbody bag, fitting it over my head. "The Norns must have foreseen your anger and rebellion as one possible outcome, and that's why they intervened to ensure you would get the Eye. They knew you would be tenacious enough to stand against Odin, if you had the ability to. So, they gave you the Eye and hoped you would do what you're doing now instead of joining him in his cause. Who am I to interfere with their will?"

The soft cotton of the shirt pools around my hips, my arms fitting easily into the loose sleeves. "I thought the Norns wanted balance. Not for Odin's side to lose in Ragnarök."

Natalie retrieves a matching gray pair of sweatpants from her bag and starts them over my foot. "They wrote the cataclysm into Yggdrasil's bark so it will come, and they will not allow Odin to stack the deck for when it does. To seek to change fate on the level at which Odin has done…it's unacceptable to the Norns."

I meet her eyes, my own hands taking over to finish working the sweatpants up my legs. "And it's now suddenly unacceptable to you?"

Her face holds only sorrow. "The way you're being treated is unacceptable to me, so I want you to listen to what I have to say because Odin is not the only one who knew you would end up at Merrymont where Keela and her brothers could be found. Skuld knew too." Natalie removes a slip of paper from her pocket. "Keela is the key. She either helps the gods win or she ensures they lose. That's the only logical conclusion because Odin himself led you to her, and if the most powerful vampire in the history of the cosmos is in love with you, then she will fight on Odin's side so long as you do. Being the queen, *all* Vampir will fight for Odin. Or..."

"They'll fight against Odin because I fight against him," I finish for Natalie, shimmying the pants up and over my hips.

She casts her eyes down to the paper. "Or they'll fight for whichever side Keela wants them to, which could be the one that opposes you if you don't choose her." Natalie looks up at me from underneath her lashes. "Fate seems to have rested a lot on the shoulders of your dating life. The high-born Fae, Aether, was connected to Keela. He got his hands on the Eye and gave it to you at *her* house, where you were then immediately set upon by the Vasilis. Instead of getting close to Keela, Aether's actions raised their alarm bells. Bells that took you directly to the Norns, who put you through a trial that separated you from your feelings for Keela. Enough to derail you from Odin's mission to see you undergoing the vampire mating ritual that Abhartack was ultimately able to complete in your absence. All of that led to problems for Odin, but Abhartack is dead now." Natalie stands, her hand beginning to move in zigzagged patterns with harsh lines and sharp corners. "Skuld knew what would happen to you when Odin started to uncoil his magic. The sisters used their combined wisdom to chart a new course for you. They're giving you a choice, just like you wanted. So, take it, and choose wisely because your choices affect us all."

A shimmering light begins to swirl around me. I scoot away from it. The light follows me. I swat at it. "What is that? What are you doing?"

Natalie shakes her head. "I'm sorry. I didn't know what Odin would do and now I don't know where else to send you. No place is safe for you, but your friend Collin was hired by the Fae to look for their lost artifact. Aether *had* a powerful artifact. So, I believe what the Fae had Collin looking for was the Eye. Since the Fae had it, and you have Fae powers, I'm hoping they can help you. If so, then my sacrifice will be worth it."

I bang my fists against the wall of light, the increasing velocity beginning to blur Natalie's face. "Wait! What do you mean by sacrifice? Natalie, wait!"

She steps away from me, picking up her lantern. "Whatever comes next, Sean Winkle, may it be you who gets to shape it. For the betterment of us all."

My body grows hot, everything around me spinning faster and faster. I try to yell but the words die in my throat. I try to use magic but it won't form. This vortex of light sucks me deeper inside, my body morphing, my atoms being pulled apart. I try to fight it. To tell Natalie that I'm not worth sacrificing herself for. When Odin returns, he'll kill her for sending me away. I throw my head back to scream but my body breaks apart. Molecule by molecule, I become one with the light.

## ~7~

The vortex spits me out onto a patio of moss-drenched stone. I fall hard on my hands and knees, a slash of crisp air cutting through my still-reforming lungs. The shimmering winds die down and blink out of existence with a snap. I cough, gasping while my cells realign themselves into the solid, defeated being that I am. Whatever spell Natalie used to send me here, it's infinitely worse than the portals the Vasilis like to shove me through.

Fresh air crowds my airwaves. Presses against my skin. A cruel and unmistakable curse for how stark this contrast is to where I was, and how Natalie risked her eternal life to remove me from Odin's chamber of torture. I push up off my aching arms and sit back on my haunches, looking down at my skinned hands. The blood left on them as they heal. The blood that will be on them if Natalie dies because of me. She betrayed my trust but if she doesn't survive whatever Odin does to her for letting me go, I'll add her death to my list of grievances against the many-faced god. And against myself.

I flatten my palms on my thighs, drag in a lungful of the painfully clean air, and squint at the too-bright landscape around me. It's lush with blooming trees and flowers, fruits and low-growing vines. The vegetation spreads in every direction, flowers and foliage crisscrossing to make impossible patterns. But it's the ivy growing along the ground, against the edges of the moss-covered stone, that sticks out to me the most. It glows with a shifting luminesce of colors, fading from soft pink to warm yellow. Pale green to dusty orange... All along the ground and throughout the understory, the ivy glows, casting its gentle spray of shifting color.

I inch forward, my knees stinging as I stay low, cautious of even the ivy. This land might be a giant flower garden but even the bushes those flowers grow on can't be trusted. For all I know, this land of the Fae might be infested with cannibals masquerading as roses.

In front of me, there's a pool of still water, its edge shaped from the stone I'm gingerly making my way across. Nearby vines and flowers hang over those edges, dipping themselves beneath the crystal-clear surface. As I approach, the water hums. My chest answers it with an ancient aching moan. It's Eldemar, the Fae whose power I'm slowly absorbing, the Eye making it my own. He's rising to the surface, whispering his name and begging to have himself dipped into the cool waters of his homeland. A place he never believed he'd ever see again.

My skin beads with sweat and fire sparks at my fingertips, the need to touch the water becoming overwhelming. I get closer and lean forward, dragging my burning fingers over the smooth surface. The water is achingly cold. Exquisitely perfect. I lean farther into it, letting my arm sink up to my elbow. Three arrows split the air where my head just was, lodging themselves into a tree on the other side of the pool, sending flower petals cascading down into the water. Slowly, I lift my arm from the water and show my hand to whoever is behind me. "I'm not here to hurt anyone."

"We don't care," a voice as sharp as Ilda's blade calls out. "Stand, trespasser."

I pull my legs forward, keeping my movements slow and steady as I tuck them under me and raise myself away from the pool's edge, unfurling my still-healing body to its full height.

Hands at my sides and fingers spread, I turn to face the voice. Three Fae males stand shoulder to shoulder, each holding a gleaming silver bow nocked and ready with their next arrow. The men are dressed in matching silver outfits that glimmer with golden embroidery, thick bands of gold and silver wrapped around their cuffs and the necks of their high-collared uniforms. The one on the left is taller than the other two and has an antler-shaped tattoo in the center of his forehead. The one on the right has rows and rows of braids dangling down around his shoulders, and the one in the middle has a nose and chin that are as pointy sharp as his voice. "Who are you?"

I keep my palms on full display. "I'm the guy you just tried to kill. Which isn't very nice. You could have said hello first."

Pointy face releases his arrow. It slams into the stone at my feet, vibrating there for only a second before it disappears. I raise a brow at him, noting the arrow nocked back in his bow. "Neat trick, but you missed again."

The other two release their arrows, each tip skimming the top of my shoulders, slicing through the thin fabric of my shirt and scoring the skin enough that blood begins to bead and soak into the fabric. The Fae in the center moves forward. "How did you get into the queen's personal garden?"

Satisfaction beats through me. If this is where Natalie had to send me, then at least she put me right at the top, where I'll know if the Fae are friends or foes sooner rather than later. Which is good, because I'm ticked off and looking for a fight. If I can't take out Odin, another enemy will do. I call a ball of faelight to one of my palms. "I'm a Fae, like you, and your queen is going to want to talk to me."

Antler forehead rushes forward, a glow of his own faelight encasing his nocked arrow. "Drop your magic!"

I take a deep breath and call fire to my other palm. "I'd rather not. So, let's play a new game. You take me to your leader, and get me some food, and I won't cook and eat you."

---

Back when I was just a human, I would go out of my way to be respectful. Collin was the arrogant one. I'm starting to think arrogance comes with being supernatural. That would explain my inability to be nice to the guards who are forming a semicircle around me, one behind and two beside, just a step back from my shoulders and arched three armlengths away. They've never dropped their bows, keeping those arrows pointed directly at my head. I lift my hand to my mouth and pretend to cough, letting sparks fly from the closed fist covering my lips. Braids stumbles, his back brushing against the gleaming leaves of the garden lining the trail they're marching me down. Pointy face barks at him in irritation and I don't bother to hide my smile. I'm assuming these are the queen's guards because of their shiny outfits and where they claim to have found me, and even Eldemar finds it funny that they're spooked by me. Ever since I showed them the fire, their hands have been shaking and their feet unsteady.

Light is beginning to fade from the sky and as it does, the petals and leaves all around us shimmer as if they've been dusted with starlight. Tucked among them are creamy-white statues of Fae and other beasts, all cut and detailed with a precision that makes the hair on the back of my neck stand on end. Unlike the statue of Odin, these are so realistic that I wonder if they once lived and breathed.

The path opens up, the canopy rising higher above us with each step. The moss fades away, leaving nothing but impeccable white stone beneath it. We step onto the widening patio, the size of it growing ever larger as it spreads toward the castle straight ahead. One that looks as if it was ripped right out of the pages of a fairy tale. A castle where the most beautiful and kindhearted princesses in all the land would live. The dimming sun reflects off its crystal walls, the height of them so tall they disappear into the heavens, joining the sunlight to cast a shining dome over all the princess's land. The castle is surrounded by heavily flowered garden walls, the length of it disappearing right into those perfumed walls. "Wait here," pointy face orders, shuffling past me and rushing toward the castle.

The two remaining guards spread out even farther, taking a position a few steps in front of me now, as if they can stop me from getting to the castle if I decide to make a run for it. They're not the only ones watching me, though. The same statues I spotted on the way here are scattered all over the castle's patio, tucked away into sections of bushes and flowers as if they're each tending to their own personal garden. Or hiding in it. Watching. All of their eyes on me.

There are also tall urns of cascading flowers dotted across the patio, some of them forming a sort of walkway, the color-shifting ivy spilling over their sides and across the stone to form a colorful carpet all the way to the towering crystal doors that are sliding open as if on a breeze, parting for a woman whose hair is the color of my flames. She's draped in jewels, her ornate white gown one some heroine in an old English movie would wear. A movie like the ones my mom used to watch.

She approaches smooth and fast, every element of her appearance crafted to show just how important she is. How *royal*. The most understated thing about her is the chandelier of a crystal crown sitting atop her mass of flaming hair. My two guards fall to their knees, the pointy-faced one at the queen's side calling a length of faelight to his hand and jabbing it in my direction. "Kneel before the queen."

I flick my eyes to the other Fae standing with the queen. He's on her right, and he's tall. Taller than the rest of them. And he's assessing me the same way I'm assessing him. I tilt my head, keeping my eyes on the man whose clothing tells me he's on similar royal footing as the queen. "I think I'll pass on bowing to anyone. I'm having a really crappy year and ten minutes from now we might be trying to kill each other, so…"

The man beside the queen moves his hand and vines dart out of the urns, running across the stone like rabid snakes. They wrap around my ankles and leap up to seize hold of my wrists. I call on my fire before they can pull me to the ground. The man's eyes grow wide as his precious magic trick goes up in smoke.

The guards surround me but the queen holds up her hand. "That will be enough, Vigmund. Take Toreyn and Fodrik to the kitchens. Tell the cook to prepare a special meal for our guest."

I press a hand to my stomach, hoping all the bits of my digestive system are healed. "Thanks, I appreciate the hospitality." I glare at the man who must be the king. "At least someone around here has manners."

His nostrils flare but the queen pays no mind to either of us. She walks forward, examining the ashen remains of the vines, suspicion flooding her features as she looks up at me. "My guard tells me you claim to be Fae." She walks in a slow circle around me. "You aren't unimpressive in your physical form, and I can feel the power of my people within you, but you're hardly exquisite. And *all* of my people are remarkably, unattainably exquisite."

She stops in front of me, her closeness making every nerve ending in my body tingle. Not with desire, but delight. Anticipation. "Well, that should clear up that I'm not *yours*. I just happen to have your magic."

Her eyes flick to my hands. "Show me again. Prove to me that what you possess is the Waking Fire."

The king moves to stand beside her, his face a solid block of ice as he stares directly into my eyes. I stretch my arms out to the side, lifting my palms skyward. First I call on the faelight, letting it swell in the middle of my hand. Then I call the fire, allowing flames to dance along my fingers and curl upward like a wave, crashing backward to cover the ball of faelight in a burning glaze. A little trick I've been working on. To show Leah. One that takes a lot of energy and focus to hold even for these few seconds. I drop the magic and lower my arms. Now isn't the time to be wasting my resources, and if I do ever get to see Leah again, she may not want to see my face, let alone my magic tricks. I take a breath. "I don't know what Waking Fire is. I've been told this is elemental so if that's what you're talking about, then yeah, I have it."

Her suspicion only thickens. "No Fae has possessed such fire in centuries. The Waking Fire was lost to us long ago."

I shrug. "You should probably talk to Odin about that. He's been trying to kill me for days, by the way, so no offense when I say this, but if Odin couldn't kill me, I doubt you and your people can get the job done. So where is this food you were talking about? I'm starving."

She lifts a hand to her delicately long throat. "Odin?"

I crack my knuckles. "Yeah, I have a few things he wants. One of them is something I've heard you Fae are looking for. So, let's cut to the chase because I just learned supernatural beings existed and since then, I've lost my best friend, the love of my life—or two of them, and I've been tortured by the Vasilis, the Norns, and Odin." I glare at the silent king. "I won't be bowing, scraping, or begging. You either want to take me in and help me, or you want to give killing me your best shot. Make your choice and let's do this because I can't remember the last time I had food." I look back at the queen. "I've been too busy trying to remember all of the lying, manipulating supernaturals who deserve the kind of punishment they've been doling out. Are you like them? Or was my friend Natalie right when she put her faith in you being smarter than all the others?"

I wake to trickles of sunlight filtering through clear glass windows, the bed beneath me softer than a cloud must be. Last night, after eating every single morsel of food the queen's cook put in front of me, I was brought to this room by Braids—also known as Toreyn. I don't remember much after that, save for the Fae food souring on my stomach. I threw it all back up. Then I crawled to this bed and had the best night of sleep I've had since this whole supernatural nightmare began.

I roll over and stare up at the gold-trimmed ceiling above the bed. This room looks expensive but I doubt there's a bad room in Queen Sóleyva's crystal palace, and I'm sure she has a dungeon just as cheery as Bishop's or Odin's. She was friendly enough last night but that could all change today.

I sit up. Being here is drawing Eldemar closer to the surface. With the Eye syphoning his power, I'm not sure if his conflicting emotions are because there's something about Queen Sóleyva that both appeals and repulses him, or if he's weak and realizing that in time, the Eye will take from him everything that makes him Fae. If that happens, will he cease to be supernatural? Will I become immortal?

I lean forward and scrub my hands over my face. Sóleyva is leery of me and I don't blame her. *I'm* leery of me. But she spent last night asking me questions while I stuffed my face, her silent king watching in disgust as I shoved things in my mouth two at a time and didn't bother waiting until I swallowed to answer his queen. Sóleyva was inquisitive while he was cold and mute. Despite his silent vigil, I answered her questions honestly, even when my answer was to tell her that I wasn't going to answer her question. That response annoyed the king but he never spoke a single word. Either because he didn't want to or he can't. He didn't even react when I told them I had the Eye. I didn't tell them I *am* the Eye, only that I had the amulet and its location was for me alone to know. Or to at least keep concealed until they convinced me I could trust them. The queen was put off by that answer but then she laughed, offering me more of the marshallow-like substance she called divinity. It's as good as the name suggests. And my overindulgence is probably responsible for my stomach's revolt. That, or Queen Sóleyva decided to test my immunity to poison.

Dueling blooms of peace and unease circulate through me. I get out of bed and move to the bay window overlooking what Toreyn called the Seelie court's south garden. My sense of smell is getting stronger. There are scents wafting up from the garden and others filtering in from outside my room. I can't pick out what they are or pinpoint the culprit, but at least I can tell which direction they're coming from. That seems like a helpful skill to have. But heightened senses don't mean I'll ever have privacy. I was there when Keela used magic to see through a solid wall. Magic she said Gelby taught her to use. Magic that's probably used by the Fae too. Queen Sóleyva probably had someone watching me last night, to see if the poison worked or to see what I would say or do when left alone in this room. So far, my actions have been to vomit, sleep, and stare.

"Good, you're awake." The queen's voice sweeps across the room behind me, as if she's out to prove my thoughts about this appearance of privacy are true. On near-silent feet, she comes to stand beside me in the soft glow of her land's dawn. "Stunning, isn't it?" Her hand waves out to the view beyond the window, where leaves shimmer as if they're etched from the same crystal as her palace, each curve of them too perfect. Every glittering flower too colorful. And the eyes of those eerie statues...they're still watching me.

I smooth a hand over my bare shoulder, where all that remains of her guard's attack is a day-old smear of blood. "It's hard to believe any other place could be as stunning as this one."

Sóleyva smiles so brightly her reflection shines in the window glass. She's as stunning as any flower in the garden, and I wonder if it's her light that's responsible for what shines down from the sunless sky. "We are in the heart of the ancient land the first Fae settled. They are the ones who poured their magic into this terra, elevating it to the pinnacle of beauty you see around us today." She points beyond the garden walls, where yet more gardens grow. Wilder and thicker than what surrounds the palace. "Out there, where earth and sky meet, you can still hear the supplications of my ancestors...*our* ancestors, their magic a whisper that carries all the way to the mountains in the west."

My magic stirs in response to her words, as if it hears the call of the ancestors and wants to join them. "Is that where the Unseelie court is?

There are two factions of Fae, right? You Seelie get along with the Vasilis and the Unseelie don't?"

She steps between me and the window, causing me to take a step backward. Her hand lifts, palm hovering over my shoulder without touching me. My skin itches and I look down. The blood is gone. I rub the clean spot, just to be sure it isn't only an illusion. "How did you do that?"

She lowers her hand. "You were greeted like someone found trespassing on my sacred soil. In a place where I often bathe, no less. So, you are lucky my guards did not treat you as foul as the Unseelie would have." She studies my face. My normal, round, human ears. "You do not look Fae, but I can feel that the Fae magic inside of you is strong." She sighs, brows dipping in disappointment as she looks me over once more.

I crack my neck side to side. I kept the extent of the hodge-podge of souls inside of me a secret. It's enough for her to know that I'm the only one who can tell her where Odin's Eye is, and that I have a Fae soul inside of me. What she doesn't need to know is that Odin stole it from one of her people and stuffed it into my human body. "Strong Fae magic, but I'm not one of you and never will be."

The queen's eyes smolder with passion. The covetous kind. The kind that says she likes power. "Your existence breaks all the laws of our nature but we Seelie are not so easily spooked. My assessment has proven you to be worthy of being counted among us, so it is a good thing indeed that my guards are not as vile as the Unseelie. It is good that your friend sent you to *my* court and not theirs."

She steps to the side, snapping her fingers. I turn to follow her. Two Fae rush into the room, their arms laden with bowls of fruits and platters of interesting-looking breads. And a dessert dish full of divinity. They place the items on a long, low table that's surrounded by plush seats and pillows—a strange sort of sitting area on the side of the room farthest from the bathroom, which ensured I didn't make it over there last night.

The queen loops her arm through mine and leads me toward the table, the skirts of the gown she's wearing swooshing around her ankles. Though not as elaborate as what she wore yesterday, this gown still holds all the markings of her status. It's made of layers of thin fuchsia-colored material that drapes over her body, the waist cinched with a wide silver belt pelted with what I'm certain isn't anything close to the cubic zirconia stones my mom used to wear. Without the crown on Sóleyva's head and her hair cascading down her back and over her shoulders, she looks much less regal than yesterday, but every bit the royal that she is. "Please, sit and enjoy breaking your fast. You have seen much in your short history as a supernatural, but not nearly enough. The king and I are most eager to help you figure out what strange mix of curses have befallen you, but first you must eat. Nourishment is important to the Fae, and you will soon get to know all of the wonders of our food."

She lets go of my arm and I sit at the table, lifting the glass of pink liquid to my lips, imagining the *wonders* she's talking about are poisons. But if all they do is make me throw the divinity back up, it's worth it. I feel like I could eat a dragon the size of Haldir right now. "Your king doesn't seem thrilled to help me with anything, and I thought the Seelie and Unseelie were working together now?"

She flicks her fingers as if washing away the very premise of my words. "King Riktr is only protective, which you cannot begrudge him. And we have never been friends with the Unseelie, but never fully enemies either. You know, maybe even more so than I do, that the lines between who can be trusted and who cannot are never solid."

I look beyond her to the land that's just as beautiful today as it was yesterday. She's right—who can tell the difference between friend and enemy anymore? "At least your cages are gilded and full of food."

Her laughter is like rain on a spring day. Refreshing. Rejuvenating. "If generosity stifles you, then by all means, consider me your captor. Otherwise, feel free to come and go as you please. Explore our land. On your own, if you wish." She nods to the door on the far end of the room. "You'll find your personal bathing chamber stocked with everything you'll need to make yourself presentable in my court. Clothing is in the wardrobe."

A jolt of dizzying thoughts ricochets through me. "You're serious? I can just walk out of here? Alone? And go wherever I want?"

She folds her hands in front of her. "You have been through quite an ordeal, Sean. I mean to help you. You are, after all, one of my own. A *loyal* member of my court, I hope. As much a willing ally to me as I willingly am to you."

Her words hang in the air like a layer of broken glass, daring me to inhale. To deny her. I take a slow, small breath. "My whole life, it turns out that everyone else has gotten to choose what I do. Choices they made based on what they wanted from me. On what they could get because of me. And I've been told that I'm just supposed to take it because an arrogant god decided to take away my free will. He laid waste to everything I might ever want in this life because all that matters to Odin is how the rest of us can serve him. Is that what you want, too? For me to be *loyal* to you so you can get whatever it is you want from me, and to heck with whatever it is that I want?"

Her delicately curved brows rise. "You didn't choose what you are, but you bear the weight of it all the same. And now that you are beginning to understand what you are, it is time for you to stop seeing yourself as this pitiful thing. Stand with me and I will show you how to burn fate itself. How to manipulate it for the best outcome. For *us*, and even for the cosmos. Because we may not be able to stop Ragnarök, but we *can* put off that dire end. Shape the worlds of Yggdrasil for the good of us all." Her lips tick up into a beautiful smile. "Fae first, of course."

My skin crawls. I told her almost everything that Natalie told me about why Odin created me, and I even filled Queen Sóleyva in on how Zara took the dragon soul when she stabbed me. I didn't give her any more detail than that, and I only gave her that much because I worried she could sense a lie and I needed to give her something to entice her to help me. Or to at least not attack me. "I'm helpless to do anything about my own situation and yet everyone thinks I can change the fate of the entire cosmos."

She leans forward and sweeps her hand across my brow, smoothing my messy hair aside. "Odin meant for you to unmake the fate of the world. I mean for you to *re*make it. To follow in the footsteps of our ancestors and make a better world. For all kinds, and for the Fae. Both Seelie *and* Unseelie." Her palm slides down to cup my cheek. "Many centuries ago, the Waking Flame was lost to my family. It has now returned. In the veins of a boy who has been wrecked. Physically. Emotionally. A boy who has barely begun to live." Her face is serene, every bit the fiery queen I saw yesterday, but now, so much more than that. A lifeline. Her magic a calming presence as it caresses me.

My heart begins to beat with a rhythm that is not my own. I melt into her touch. Her palm glows, glittering where it makes contact with my skin. "Heal, Sean. Some of your wounds may never go away but they can heal into scars you can be proud of. As my own emotional scars have."

She moves closer, pressing a chaste kiss to my lips. "Welcome home, Sean. I will help you, and quickly—before you burn yourself alive using powers you do not understand."

She withdraws her magic and sweeps away from me. I instantly miss the soothing effect of her magic. She stops at the door, glancing back at me with a calculating gleam in her ruddy eyes. "By the way, where is the Eye, dear?"

My anger rises. Joining her court might be a good idea but right now, all I want is to just *be*. "I forgot to tell you something last night."

"Oh?" She grins.

I narrow my gaze on her. "The Norns say I have an anger problem, and I've already been burned a few times by people using kindness to manipulate me, so keep your magic hands off of me or we're going to play a game of touch that neither of us is going to like the ending of."

She laughs. A hearty, contagious sound that brings a smile to my lips, despite how mad I'm getting. She places a hand over her heart. "My dear Sean, you are amusing. But, you see, it turns out that you are very powerful, and you are *mine*. The Waking Fire belongs to my family, and I take care of what is mine. In whatever ways I deem appropriate. You may not like all of them, but you don't have to. I am your queen, and that is enough." She winks and opens the door. "Do clean up. I don't allow swine in my court."

---

Toreyn opens a door along the side of the palace and waves me out into the courtyard ahead of him, pointing toward a maze of trailheads that angle off to cut through the gardens in different directions. "The queen takes her evening meal at dusk. Be back in time to make yourself presentable before joining her table." He turns on his heel and goes back inside, slamming the door behind him. Toreyn was waiting for me when I came out of my room, dressed in the least offensive outfit I could find—a dark green tunic and matching pants that make me feel like I'm getting ready for my shift at the local hospital. Maybe he's nippy this morning because he doesn't like the clothes either. Or maybe he's mad that he's been put on escort duty. But at least all he had to do was escort me through the palace.

I'm still shocked that Toreyn didn't argue when I told him I'd being going on a walk alone and I won't be sticking around to see if he or the queen changes their minds. I pick the closest trail and start walking, winding myself away from the palace. If Queen Sóleyva really lets me do this by myself, it will be the first time since I stepped foot onto Merrymont's campus that I'm being allowed to make my own choices. There are no ravens urging me to go down one path or the other. No compulsions or strange pulls. Only me. Walking on my own.

My senses are growing stronger and I don't hear anyone following me, but that doesn't mean much when it comes to magic. I reach a cross section in the trail and choose to turn left, slowing my hurried pace and willing myself to relax. To enjoy this moment even if it's only an illusion of freedom. To be grateful for the interesting plant life and that fact that I kept down all the food I gorged on this morning. Including the divinity.

Feet steady and unhurried, I turn down another path, this one on the right, and wander along it. Up ahead, a twisted tree trunk juts out from the edge of the forest, the twining vines hanging from its branches brushing so low over the ground that if I wasn't paranoid that someone, or some*thing*, was going to jump out at me any second, I wouldn't have noticed the hidden path cutting off the main trail. I carefully pull the vines aside and duck through the mass of leaves and heavily perfumed flowers. The moss-covered trail gives way to packed dirt, and it's hard to tell what I'm walking toward because this path is narrow and overgrown, everything green and flowering and hanging down in my face. I take this as a sign that this trail isn't commonly used. That's a small win. If the queen is only letting me have a head start before sending Toreyn or one of the other guards after me, my detour down this less traveled path might slow down their progress in finding me.

I scan a shrub littered with iridescent flowers whose bright colors shine like neon signs. It's distracting enough to make me miss the briar bush beside it. The hem of my tunic snags on a red-tipped thorn and I tug the lightweight material free. I may not like the style but the clothing is softer than any other cloth I've ever felt, and if I saw a t-shirt in this color, I'd probably buy it. For that matter, if the Fae are going to treat me with basic rights and dignity, why not buy what their queen is selling? My life will never go back to what it was pre-Merrymont. I can't even return to the realm where Merrymont exists. The Vasilis control Midgard and now that I know what I am, I'm more certain than ever that their end goal will always be to kill me. Going back to Midgard puts me directly in their line of fire so why not stay where I'm being offered an ally? The queen's end goal might be to only keep me alive until she gets the Eye, but since I am the Eye, she can't ever kill me. Not unless she can do what Odin himself couldn't.

I pluck one of the neon flowers from the bush. Joining the Fae means giving up on ever seeing Leah again. Ever seeing Collin again. The siblings might be fine with that but me being fine with continuing on without them is about as likely as me getting used to wearing this Fae clothing. I need to figure out how to talk to them and asking Queen Sóleyva to help me with that will prove to her where my true loyalty lies. The MacKenzie family. Them first, not the Fae.

I crush the flower in my fist and head farther down the trail, less enthralled with the brightly colored flowers and silver-leafed vines now that I've started thinking about Leah again. What I did to her and how I'll probably never see her again. Never see my home again. My parents' graves... A lump forms in my throat. My mom would have loved this place. She planted flowers all over the yard of the house I grew up in and when we vacationed, Dad always made sure to add a botanical garden to our list of stops. For her. Everything always for the woman he loved.

I shove the crumpled neon flower into my pocket and lift a hand-sized bloom that looks as if it's carved from the sky. It smells like Mom's roses. My mom who always liked Leah. My mom who always believed that I would end up at Merrymont. She said it was where I belonged. That she could feel it in her bones. Maybe her mother's intuition told her that Merrymont would lead me to what my heart really wanted. Leah. Always Leah.

I drop the bloom, leaving the sky-blue flower behind. Maybe mom always knew Merrymont would lead me here, to this land where I'm being offered acceptance. I walk deeper into it, the sky growing brighter with every step. I run my fingers over the shimmering foliage as I pass, fire coiling tightly in my chest. This mesmerizing place brings up too many memories for me to ever be happy here. I want to go home. I don't want to remake the world or fight fate. I just want to go home.

"Come on," a low voice growls from somewhere ahead. "Where are you?"

My magic presses against my skin. I know that voice, and the shock of hearing it in this garden crashes through me like a puck in a pinball machine. I crouch low and make my way through the foliage. I haven't mastered stealth the way other supernaturals have but I'm getting better. I use my newfound skills to move as quietly and quickly as possible toward the voice that's burned into my memory.

Light splits the canopy, casting bright rays into the clearing beyond the end of trail. In the center of the clearing are three black stones that form a triangle. Each stone is eight feet tall and four feet wide, and through the light-infused gaps between the stones, I see Zara. The traitor who left Leah, Collin, and me for dead.

Anger collides with the heat of my fire and the power of my faelight. With a show of supernatural agility, I explode from the garden edge and into the triangle, launching off the side of a black stone and twisting in midair. My heel connects with Zara's jawbone. She sprawls across the cobblestone bottom of the triangle. I hit her with a blast of faelight. She shakes off the impact and jumps to her feet, eyes blazing. "*You.*"

I launch another volley of faelight. "Yeah, it's me, Zara. Surprise! I didn't die."

She dives through one of the gaps between the obsidian stones, taking cover behind it. "I took what didn't belong to you. Whether you lived or died was not my choice to make."

Fire flickers to life in my palms. "Do you say that to all the boys you stab? How's Haldir, by the way?"

Half of her face slides into view, her one eye watching me. "Why are you following me?"

I ready my flames for the next attack. "Since you left me for dead, I've been a little busy. Finding you hasn't really crossed my mind but now that you're here, killing you is front and center." I shudder at the memory of the vultures. The way they dove toward us. Toward Leah. "Come out and face me like the coward you are, Zara. The last time I killed someone it was an accident. I want to know what it feels like to do it on purpose."

She slips back into her hiding spot. "If you aren't here because you're following me, why are you here? Have you joined the Fae? Or are you here with the witch?"

My fire flickers. "What witch?"

Zara's body fills the gap between the stones, Firebrand held tightly in her grip. "If you aren't here to protect the high witch of the Völva coven, then you will step aside and tell no one of my presence here. Leave me to conduct my business and the next time we meet, I will continue not to kill you…Eye of Odin."

I throw the fiery orbs. Zara ducks back behind her stone and the fire dissolves at the edge of the clearing, as if it knew my intent wasn't to set the whole Seelie court ablaze. "Why are you calling me that?"

Zara jumps from the stone she's behind to duck behind the next one. "Once I found the rotunda and saw the runes, you finally made sense. Though, it's curious that *you* are who Aether chose to give the Eye to. I expected him to find a great warrior to bestow such a gift upon."

Her words quake through me like ripples over that clear, still water surrounding the rotunda. The fire dancing in my upturned palms flickers out, the orbs of faelight hovering over my head exploding like shooting stars. "You could read those runes?"

Zara stalks from behind the stone, eyes narrowed on my fading magic. "That, and the Seidr gave me missions. Tasks to complete. I completed them. One being to give Aether a soulstone and to warn him about a dangerous allegiance between his father and the Seelie queen. One that hinged on the power they believed the Eye of Odin would bestow upon them."

I absently run a hand over my chest and Zara gives me a knowing smirk. "When I met Aether, he did not yet have the amulet or even believe that the Fae possessed it. Then I met *you* and found out about your encounter with Aether. Even without the runes, your fate was not hard to figure out."

I study the hilt of the sword. The rubies encrusted on the bottom. The ones Leah said represented the legendary dragon kings. "So, you figured out what I was and what? Decided to take back your ancestor and kill another dragon in the process? Did you get rid of Haldir because he wasn't useful to you? Or is *he* who should be holding that sword right now?"

Her eyes narrow. "If it did not suit the Norns for me to have Firebrand, they would not have led me to it. The moment I heard you and Leah describing the sword you found, I knew the time serpents brought me to the Norns so I could intercept it." She tilts her sword, allowing it to catch the light. "In accepting Firebrand, I understood what I must do."

I allow flames to break over the lengths of my arms, still amazed at how it knows not to burn my clothing. As if it operates on my will alone. "How *noble* of you, great and wise dragon. No wonder there are so few of you. You're all selfish and greedy, just like the gods and everyone else I've met in this messed up *cosmos*."

Her head cocks, eyes studying the flames as they form rolling loops that travel up and down my arms. "Dreki are not nearly extinct because of our own greed, but because of the cruelty and greed of other kinds. Of *gods*," she spits the word, stowing the blade in the sheath strapped across her back. "I did what I had to do for all Dreki and I would make the same choice again today. No single life is more valuable than the dying embers of my kind."

"So he's dead," I spit back at her. "Did the Norns know what you were going to do to Haldir? Do they know what you plan to do to Beatrice? That's who you're talking about, right? The witch who isn't here because the last I heard, it's going to be a long while before she recovers from *me* almost killing her."

Zara's jaw twitches. "The witch is here. I'll take her life to settle my own grievance against her, but Beatrice's presence today is only a happy coincidence. My final task for the Seidr happens to be here." She nods to the stone behind me. "When I gave Aether the soulstone, I told him to place it here. If he did, his soul still lives, and that's the last place I have to look so stand aside and let me get on with my task."

I look to the upright stone behind me and then back at her, stammering, "W-what?"

Chin held high, Zara stomps past me, dropping to her knees in front of the black stone and reaching around the edge to where the cobblestone butts against the obsidian. I follow dumbly behind her. "You're serious? Aether is...alive?"

She pulls a dark cloth sack from underneath the stone's edge. "Figuratively speaking. He wasn't arrogant enough not to heed my warning so this little gem now holds the essence of his soul. His magic, anyway. To my knowledge, he cannot be reincarnated. The witch's magic isn't that strong. But if I had to guess, this is why she's here. It was her magic that created the stone and if she is able to retrieve it, she may want to use it as leverage to get what she wants from the Fae queen."

Zara opens the pouch and dumps a perfectly cut gemstone into her palm. Its color shifts like the ground ivy, from deep blue to vibrant purple. "We were *both* chosen by those who control destinies so it does not matter what you think of Dreki. You held the soul of a dragon king, but not his blood, so you could never claim his throne." She stuffs the gem back into the pouch. "I do not fight for glory or riches. I fight for the honor of my ancestors. I fight for the restoration of my homeland. Many sacrifices have been made along the way and I did not cower from them. Nor will I. I remain as unyielding as the Norns. The question is, what do *you* stand for, pawn of Odin? Do you stand against him by aligning with the Fae? Or are you here to bring the Fae to their knees before him?" She gets to her feet and extends the amulet to me. "I don't know why Aether chose you to receive the Eye or how it came to exist inside you. All I know is the Seidr asked for Aether to place this soulstone here and then she tasked me with retrieving it upon her death." Zara's eyes bore into mine. "Consider this my debt to her paid. You are, after all, the soul thief. Who better to tend to a soulstone than the thief himself?"

I step away from her. "I don't want it. I already have Fae magic and whole bunch of souls."

Zara advances, yanking my palm up and smashing the soulstone's pouch into it. "Maybe so, but where I am going, I have no use of Fae magic. Just remember that there has never been true peace among the realms. Each kind favors their own, and you are *alone* in what you are. You either fight for survival or you die. This stone will help you negotiate with the Fae. Take it, and trust no one. Especially the witches."

I close my fist around the pouch. "Especially *you*. You could have told me all of this before but instead, you *stabbed* me. Lucky for me, I'm pretty hard to kill. Odin made sure of that."

Her eyes flick to the edges of the garden behind me. "Even gods can be killed. Someone just has to figure out how." She plucks an orange stone from the pouch at her hip and tosses it behind her. A portal sizzles to life. "I have removed one soul and rewarded you with another. Use Aether's gift wisely, Sean Winkle."

She steps into the portal and I rush forward, contemplating hitching a ride to wherever she's going. I've given enough to Odin. The Norns. The Vasilis... I won't be used by anyone ever again. God, fate, or Fae. "Wait, Zara. I..."

The edges of her body begin to fade, the portal closing around her. She smiles. "When you see the witch, tell her that if she is not dead by the seventh moon of the king's rise, I will be back. And I will witness her last breath."

The portal snaps shut and I instantly regret not going with her. Not killing her. Not deciding fast enough which of those things I should do. I press a hand to where she stabbed me. A crude, sour laugh bleats from behind me. Before I can turn around, roots skitter across the cobblestone and wrap around my ankles, dragging me from the obsidian triangle and out into the clearing surrounding it.

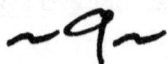

King Riktr's roots squeal and hiss like living things, scurrying away as I blast them with flames. I jump to my feet and they retreat into the earth, their wailing fading away as they tunnel back to where they came from. I shove the dark pouch into the deep pocket of my pants, dropping it next to the crumpled neon flower. If Aether is what the king is after, he should have sent his roots after the stone, not me. "That's twice now that you've shown me your neat little trick. Now it's time for me to show you mine."

King Riktr stalks from the thick foliage, spreading his arms out to the sides. He bends them at the elbows, wrinkling the delicate filigree of his long-sleeved tunic as every living thing around us—every shrub, tree, and blade of grass bends toward him. He closes his fists and they all turn to look at me, flowers swiveling like heads on limbs. *Growling* at me. "You barge into my realm, defile our sacred site not only with your presence upon the stone but with that of a vile reptile, and now you dare to threaten me. But you forget who this land *belongs* to."

I cross my arms over my chest. "First of all, I didn't barge in, I was sent here. Secondly, I didn't invite that vile reptile, I found her here. And thirdly, exactly what kind of sacred things do you do here in your stone triangle? Or should I ask the queen? I'm new to all of this supernatural stuff but let me see if I've got this right... The queen is in charge of the Seelie court and the Unseelie court is ruled by a king. A king that isn't you. You're just a title with no real power. Almost as if you're not really a king at all, just a mute figure who stands and sits beside the queen like an obedient dog."

He's fast, closing the distance between us to only a few feet in less time than it takes me to blink. "Your *rarity* is why the queen hasn't killed you. She likes to *collect* rare things."

A cold shiver ripples down my spine. "The statues? They were alive once, weren't they? The queen turns people into stone. Like Medusa."

His eyes burn with hatred. Envy. "Who is this Medusa? You didn't tell us about her."

I unfold my arms and take a deep breath. "She's nobody. Just a bedtime story like the ones Bishop weaves into his magic and delivers around Midgard on Christmas Eve to keep humans in the dark about what's really going on all around them. That's probably the reason I have this boiling rage growing inside of me every second of every day. A lifetime of lies and magic. And now a king who doesn't know when to stop pressing his luck."

King Riktr thrusts his finger into my face, teeth grinding. "We don't have much time so you listen to what I have to say, *child*. The queen's true mate was murdered centuries ago. Since then, she has collected...things. I won her heart only because of the rarity and strength of *my* magic. There is no loyalty on her part. Only mine." His jaw clenches. "I am loyal to my queen and she deserves *me* at her side. Not you."

His words hit like a blow to the solar plexus. "You think the queen—"

"I don't think, I know," he seethes. "Because I know her. The Unseelie king was killed by the Vampir, and his heir was killed before that. For treason. Therefore, until the Unseelie can determine who is next in line, there is a void in their hierarchy. The balance of power is shifting and if the queen believes you will help her take it all, to rule over both kingdoms, then she will be rid of me and take you as her king. But you are not loyal to her. You are no more Fae than you are anything else." His face pinches, as if smelling a foul stench on me. "Your valor is stolen. At best, you are to be our greatest weapon. But you will *never* be our king. Do you understand me?"

I lean into his face. "I don't want your spot and I'm not interested in your queen. If you don't want me to change my mind about sitting on your throne, leave me alone. I was thrown into this game that all of you are playing and I'm tired of being forced to do things I don't want to do, so the next time you get this deep into your feelings, remember which one of us has the Waking Fire before you go and pull another stunt with your little plants, or I'll set your whole freaking world on fire. Do you understand me, *king*?"

He straightens. "I do, *soul thief*."

He flicks his hand and roots burst back out of the ground, shooting tendrils that wrap around my hands and bind my wrists together in front of me. Seven guards armed with bows and spears filter into the clearing from the garden path. The king's voice lowers. "Do not make this worse for yourself. Leave those on. Because the queen knows you've visited this site and she is not pleased."

The Seelie throne room makes the rest of the palace look like a hovel. I stand just inside the golden arched doors, decorated generals from the Fae army dressed in their military best standing at attention beside and behind me, guarding my way out. Compliments of the king. He spoke only to his cadre of personal guards as they led me back to the palace but his words were meant for me. Warnings. Explanations. He commented on their uniforms, detailing the subtle differences that distinguish his personal guards from those of the queen's. To anyone on the outside, the king was simply at ease with his royal guards, talking about things that would interest them. But I understood his game. He was giving me information about their military rankings, and I'm not dumb enough to think he was doing so for free. He wants me to avoid the queen's guards, and he wants something more from me than only my pretend servitude. I've left his handcuffs on and the Fae lining the sides of the long room in front of me all have to be basking in their king's ability to subdue me. But to the queen, Riktr is signaling much more.

The king stomps up the aisle toward the back of the room, his steps haughty and attention straight ahead, ignoring those Fae lined up along the edges of his path as they bow and scrape. Behind them are sheer walls of clear crystal that showcase the glittering, sparkling landscape around the palace. Even the stone terraces glow moon white and the silk draping over the columned openings shimmer with vines of iridescent blooms. And here inside, it's no less sparkly. Every surface is made of crystal, a prism of colors breathing out from it as if the crystal itself is alive. And if the room and all its surrounding glory aren't enough, the Fae themselves are dressed in shimmering, glowing fabrics. Some of the women's gowns are ornate while others are soft and light. The men are mostly dressed as I am, in a matching tunic and pants, but their colors are anything but plain and the few who stand out among all the others must be wearing so much jewelry because they're thirsty for the queen's attention. Or maybe the king's. Either way, it's the eyes of the men that spark with the most suspicion as they turn to look at me. The women are mostly curious, and maybe a little afraid.

I catch the eye of a tall blonde with a fuchsia gown cut down to her belly button where flecks of gold paint radiate out like rays of the sun. She blinks. Looks away. Steps back in the row and begins whispering into the ear of another woman whose eyes dart away as quickly as mine find hers. A man in a long gray robe etched with brightly colored runes straightens to his full height and whispers into the ear of the woman next to him. Her eyes are on me and when I meet her stare, she inclines her head. I break eye contact, my gaze immediately slamming into that of the queen. Tonight, her gown is as sheer as the crystal throne she sits upon, the folds and layers spread around her to spill over the crystal and down onto the carved thick wood of the dais her throne rises out of. Soft waves of light, like moonlight cast upon water, move over the trailing fabric, as if she's an ethereal being sitting on top of a shimmering mountain of pillows. And because no fairy godmother is complete without a crown, hers is crafted from the thinnest and purest crystal, inlaid with silver, gold, and opals. It rises high into the cathedral ceilings of the room, so much taller than the chandelier that sat on her head the first time I saw her. But it's this pale display of color set against the contrast of her flaming red hair that makes her breathtaking.

I don't realize I'm bowing until I see the smudge of dirt on the top of the thin-soled shoes that were left in the wardrobe for me to wear. I jerk upright, getting ahold of myself. A flicker of amusement ghosts across the queen's face. I feel my own flush. The queen turns her attention to the smaller throne perched beside hers, where the king is now sitting, his own crystal crown atop his head. Only his is much, much smaller than the queen's. "Remove your shackles. I'm sure Sean meant no disrespect today. After all, I did not forbid him from traveling anywhere he wished." Her attention moves back to me. "It is curious, though, how you keep finding yourself in my sacred and private places when our kingdom is so large."

Murmurs rise from the gathered Fae and I start to burn the handcuffs away but they disappear, disintegrating into dust until not even the tiniest speck is left. I don't bother thanking the king. Instead, I wonder if the crown that appeared on his head the second he sat down would disappear like his cuffs if I went up there and threw him off his throne. His eyes narrow, burning with a rage to match what he's seeing in mine. He inclines his head in acknowledgement of our mutual hatred for one another and I do the same. The queen laughs. "Well now, it seems a walk in the gardens has put you more in touch with your Fae side, my dear Sean. Sometimes we need only to connect with nature to restore ourselves."

Her voice is a rustling purr of inuendo. She expects the king and me to be odds. To fight for her. Maybe that's what the Fae do—constantly vie for position. Higher status. I flex my hands and pull my eyes away from the king. "You're right, I've always loved being in nature and the fresh air did me a lot of good. I think it was my old, ancient, super powerful Fae who probably led me to your sacred place. But he doesn't remember exactly what we do there. Can you remind me? Is that where we murder traitors?"

A chorus of sharp inhalations rises from the dozens of Fae lining the walkway between me and the dais. The queen stands, a crackle of energy wafting out of her, humming through the throne room. Everyone falls silent. "Leave us," she commands. "I have business to conduct with my newest subject."

Murmurs ripple through the room, joined by the scuffle of soft-soled shoes and the rustle of clothing. I feel the weight of the king's glare boring into me. I clench my fists and open them, working the blood through my hands in an exaggerated way to make sure he remembers that I *allowed* him to parade me in here wearing cuffs. Tension builds between us. A string being pulled taut. The last of the spectator Fae exit the throne room and the queen nods to a lithe Fae in a dark gray tunic and matching pants who stands just off to the side of the dais. "Bring her."

My pulse jumps and tiny sparks of flame burst from my fingertips. Steel grinds against steel as the sword-wielding guards around me draw their weapons. The queen laughs softly. In a *he will learn* kind of way. "There's no need for your fire. Put it away." She motions to the side of the room where the Fae in the dark gray disappeared through a hidden door in the wall. "We've had yet another unexpected guest and she would like to speak with you." Her eyes home in on mine. "And if you would stop expecting me to use violence against you, then I won't have to. Our games can be fun. For both of us."

I work to douse my flames and satisfaction joins the queen's now calm demeanor. She retakes her throne and I clench my jaw, returning the king's scathing glare. He was at the clearing long enough to hear Zara call me a soul thief and if he heard that, then he also heard her use Aether's name and talk about the soulstone. But I've been with him since that time and he hasn't mentioned any of this to the queen. And I watched Zara portal away. If they don't have her, the only other important *she* would be Leah. Or Keela, but I don't think even this army of Fae could subdue Keela. Not the way she was after I killed Abhartack.

"I can be a powerful asset..." I begin to plead a case. For Leah. The hidden door opens and the lithe Fae slips back out, followed by a hunched figure whose gnarled hand clutches tightly to a staff etched deeply with runes. Beatrice. The witch I nearly roasted alive. I move toward her. The queen's royal guards shove me back. "Beatrice..." I call over their shoulders, guilt and shame washing over me at the sight of her. She looks decades older than she did when she first placed her hands in mine.

The witch shuffles her way across the room to stand at the base of the dais. She bows her head. The queen's face is still a mask of calm but her magic pricks over my skin, needle-sharp this time instead of soothing. "I didn't realize you were such good friends with our guest."

"I...she..." Words fail me as Beatrice's near-broken form turns toward me.

"It's good to see you again. Alive." Her raspy voice still holds hints of power but she's nothing like the strong witch with the gleaming eyes and confident air that I met at the coven house.

The queen waves a hand and her guards move aside. I approach Beatrice. Carefully. The memory of how scared Monique was when I saw her after I set fire to the coven house bleeding into my slurry of current thoughts. I stop a couple of feet away from the old witch. "I can say the same thing to you. It's good to see you alive. I'm so sorry about what I did to you, and to the other witches."

Beatrice leans more of her weight onto the cane. "We know you did not intend to hurt us so I hope you feel the sincerity in *my* apology when I tell you that I am sorry for my role in what happened that day. Sorry for my coven, and sorry for the pain those actions have caused you ever since. Had I recognized the handiwork of a god upon you, I would not have tried to break the magic with such force."

The queen rises from her throne and descends the dais steps, coming down to where we're standing. "Yes, if only any of us had known Odin was betraying the most powerful kinds by stealing the souls of our ancestors to create the powerful Sean Winkle, I wager a great many things would have gone differently."

Beatrice observes the queen, hand tightening on her cane. "The gods keep their plans more closely guarded than most, but at long last, it appears all is being revealed."

I look between the women and glance at the still-seated king. "Why? Why are so many secret moves being revealed now? Are we really that close to a world-ending war?"

The queen's voice is edged in steel. "Ragnarök is the gods' favorite leash. It keeps us divided. Questioning. The threat of war a constant blight on our doorsteps. But, like you, we wish only to be free. To live by the merit of our own choices. Yet your very existence ushers war to every kind. Your anger and betrayals fueling the flames of that war. So, it is curious that you continue to make enemies of those who would accept you."

I shove my hands up through my hair and run them down the back of my tense neck. "I'm not trying to make enemies of anyone and I sure as heck never intended to start a war. I *exist* because of Odin, not because I decided to rampage through anyone's world."

The queen raises a brow at the witch. "There you have it. He doesn't want to go on a rampage. Nor do I. Your quest for allies must continue elsewhere. The Fae will only defend the Fae."

Beatrice leans forward, her cane creaking under the pressure of her weight. "And what happens when there is no one left and the Vasilis come for you? The Fae *caused* the last war, according to the history the Vasilis tell. A history where they record how that war brought the death of Bishop's wife, the mother of his two sons. The Vasilis may have entered into a long-lasting treaty with you but we both know they will *never* make true peace with the Fae. They will come for you, with Odin's blessing upon them, and who will help you in this fool's dream of victory then?"

The king finally rises from his throne. "The Vasilis are not the only ones who lost loved ones in that war. The queen's own mate was ripped from her and slaughtered by those Odin *blesses*. They are not saints and Bishop is no god. You yourself exposed his selling of humans, ushering them to their slaughter like cattle all so he can line his own pockets and keep his threadbare treaties in place."

"Wait...what?" His words slam into me like a gut punch. "Odin *sells* humans? For what?"

"Food, mostly," the queen answers with a shrug. "We don't eat them so we weren't privy to Bishop's back-room deals until the Völva gave us the little tidbit." She eyes Beatrice. "Information you received during your dealings with the Vampir, correct?"

Beatrice straightens as best she can, trying to square her shoulders as she addresses the queen. "My dealings with the Vampir came on the heels of *your* dealings with the Vampir. The Völva have only ever lobbied for peace, and it was not only our own actions that brought the full weight of the Vasilis upon our heads."

The queen's tinkling laugh echoes through the room. Her hand rests against her chest. "Are you accusing the Fae of bringing brimstone down upon you? Fae, which now includes Sean Winkle, Odin's very own special creation. A creation he may be cross with, but one he would not see destroyed by any hand but his own nonetheless."

The meager traces of fight leave Beatrice's body and I step to her side, clutching her elbow in an effort to keep her standing upright. "I doubt Odin would care who killed me, so long as he got back what he wants. But what's going on?" I lift Beatrice's chin. "Did the Vasilis do something to you? I thought you guys were friends?"

The corners of her worn mouth turn down. "The Vasilis have attacked their allies in Midgard. Most of my coven escaped Bishop's wrath, but…"

A pit opens inside me. "But what, Beatrice? Tell me."

Her gnarled hand comes to rest on my forearm. "Rohan and Gelby have rejoined their father in Midgard. They flanked him during his assault on my coven, but they were not with him when the Vasilis descended upon the MacKenzie pack."

"Descended upon the MacKenzie pack…" I roll the words over in my mouth, a deep sorrow engulfing my rage.

Beatrice's fingers tighten on my arm. "What Ulfr Bishop left alive, he imprisoned. Save for two, who through fate's hand were not present when the attack occurred."

I let go of her and sit down on the dais steps. Up until now, I didn't know if anyone made it out from the land of the Norns. I didn't know if they were alive or dead. I spent my time with the Einherjar believing that Leah and Collin were safe and back at home with their family. That

Keela was safe and returning to the normalcy of what her life seemed to be before me or Abhartack came into it. I spent my time imagining that they had all moved on and forgotten about me. "Collin? Leah?" Their names are heavy on my tongue.

Beatrice nods, voice thick with sorrow. "The only two wolves of the MacKenzie pack left alive and free are your friends. The rest of their family—father, mother, siblings—they were all killed by the Vasilis."

I lean forward and put my head between my knees, sucking air into my protesting lungs. "Bishop killed…Liam MacKenzie? His…" I can't say the name of his wife. His kids. Collin and Leah's younger siblings. "Why? Why would Biship do that?" Faelight seeps from my pores, growing bright and thick as it spreads out of me, coated in a sheen of Waking Fire. The guards pull their queen away and the king retreats to the back of his burning dais. Beatrice lumbers backward and I watch the scrape of her cane against the floor, my lava flow getting ever closer. A catastrophe unfolding before me, but I'm helpless to stop it. Bishop killed the Ulfr. Because of me.

# ~10~

## Collin

My wolf is restless. I set him free, the bite of cold in Dökkbraek's forest as welcome as my unwanted thoughts. I'm tired of being here. Sick of puzzling through Monique's twisted words. Even if half of what she says makes sense, I don't know what I'm supposed to do about it. Keela is showing her face less and less and Harlan tells Leah that his queen's behavior is normal. That she's going through stages of grief. Which sounds blasphemous coming from a filthy vampire.

I give my wolf the reins because I know exactly where he'll take me. Caroline's skin will make me forget the troubles of my pack and how helpless I am to do anything about it. How helpless I am to do anything about Sean or Bishop. I can't even help my sister. The one who has never once asked me about my infatuation with Caroline even though I know Leah can smell the human on me. I'm haunted by the guilt of allowing this craving for Caroline to continue and I can't hide the shame of my actions from Leah. As Ulfr, and especially now that I'm an alpha, I have an obligation to my pack. One that includes finding a strong mate to produce strong wolves with. Binding my emotions to a human is wrong. For me, the human, and my future mate. Most of all, it's wrong for my pack.

My wolf bounds onto Caroline's porch and I shift back to my human form, rapping my knuckles against the worn wood of her door before the anticipation of her sweet release is overshadowed by the weight of my duty. "It's open!" Caroline calls from inside.

I twist the knob, a little put off that she isn't coming to let me in herself. She's never *not* opened her door for me. "Hey, it's me," I announce as I enter.

"I know," she calls back. "I recognized the knock."

A frown drags down the corners of my lips. I move through the living room, heading for the kitchen where her scent is strongest. Caroline is sitting at a small round table positioned between a window and the back door of her house. She barely looks up at me so I pull out a chair and sit next to her, scanning the open notebook in front of her. Forasmuch as she's become my temporary solace, we've never done this before. Sit together at her table. Sit next to each other without the sole purpose of basking in one another.

Caroline uses her lavender pen to carefully form the letters of each name she's listing in her notebook, and all I can think is that her dark hair smells like jasmine, not lavender. I clear my throat, nervous now, feeling like I've never talked to a girl before. "What are you working on?"

Her head shakes. "I don't know. At least I hope I don't."

I read the first ten names. I don't recognize any of them. "Who are they?"

She chews her lip, looking up at me with an uncertainty that breaks my heart a little. She's not sure if she should trust me. I straighten in my seat. "If they need help, tell me. I'll do everything I can to help them. I don't have much pull around here but I'm still an alpha."

Her lips move, as if they want to smile but don't have the energy to. "Thanks, but... Remember how I told you some people have gone missing? Vampir and humans both?" I nod and she sighs, placing the pen along the top of her notebook. "Well, none of them have returned, save for a few of the Vampir, and they only come back to recruit more people. It wasn't much at first, but now it seems as if we're losing at least five people a day." She slides the notebook in my direction. "I started with the most recent and I'm going back to try to remember everyone else, but Dökkbraek is larger than it looks and the Vampir come and go from other realms so..."

I scan her list. Seventy names already. "Do you think the Vampir would take the humans on their food-finding missions?"

She shakes her head. "Humans would only slow the Vampir down and get in their way. I...whenever anyone asks those who *should* know what's going on, those Vampir say the humans are helping them patrol our borders. But there aren't any threats along our borders. Abhartack has wards in place. No one gets in or out without his permission..." Her voice trails off, as if she's only now remembering that Abhartack isn't alive anymore.

A knot of dread forms in my stomach. "Things are changing. If Keela is sending forces to secure the borders then seventy isn't so large a number."

Caroline swipes the notebook back to her and picks up the pen. "No one has ever entered Dökkbraek uninvited. *Ever*. Rumors claim the safeguards were put into place by a powerful coven of witches who are loyal to Abhartack. They created wards that no one can get through. That no magic can break."

It's possible the death of her king destroyed the wards and the comfort of security that Caroline has always lived with, but it's the fact that witches are involved that's making my wolf rise. Caroline's mouth falls open as he looks at her through my eyes, turning them into the dark reflective orbs of a canine instead of a man. "The Völva. They were sworn to Abhartack?"

She closes her jaw and bites down on her lip. "I...no. I don't think so. I've hardly heard them talked about and never in connection with Abhartack's coven. The two have always been separate. But then again, one coven has always been considered a rumor while the Völva are verifiably real."

"And Abhartack is dead now." I chastise my wolf as much as myself for the pain those words cause Caroline. Abhartack was beloved by her, and by everyone else in Dökkbraek, human and Vampir alike. The first time I heard a human lamenting about how much they missed seeing their king stroll through their bustling streets, talking about him like he was an ordinary man, I thought I was losing my mind. Hallucinating. "If there was a coven working with Abhartack, they could be *not* working for the new queen. There could be enemies gathering on the borders." And that would explain Keela's constant absences.

Caroline shakes her head. "Abhartack *chose* Keela. Even before he brought her here, he told us she would be our queen. And everyone loves her...we're happy she's our queen. And half the humans on the list are too old or too out of shape for any kind of combat. The Vampir wouldn't take them out on patrol, and especially not farther out than the Vampir themselves ever go."

I lean close to Caroline's ear, aware that the vampires have hearing that's even better than my own. "I've known Keela for a very long time. She has an appetite unlike any other vampire."

Caroline shoves me away but I wrap my arms around her and hold her against my heart, voice low in her ear as she struggles against the bands of iron I've wrapped around her. "I'm not trying to hurt you, but you need to listen to me. Keela feeds much more often than all the Vampir you've grown up around, and she possesses powers of persuasion none of the others can remotely compete with. Other worlds won't like the vampires raiding their lands for her so Abhartack might have treated you with respect and encouraged this gross cohabitation, but maybe his choice of queen was only a smart choice if he lived. A mate to keep her from slaughtering all of you."

"Stop it!" Caroline screams, chest heaving. I let go of her and she jumps to her feet, sending her chair crashing backward into the floor. "Our kinds have lived peacefully for generations. As equals. If you think that's gross...that my *mother* was gross, then you can get out of my house and never come back."

I jam my finger into the list of names. "Your mother was human. So was your father. I've seen the picture of them on your nightstand. Your *step*mother was a vampire but that doesn't change anything. If you think it does and that I'm wrong about what might be happening here, then please inform me of your stroke of genius because ten minutes ago, you didn't even have a guess. At least I'm coming up with a very real, very possible scenario. War is coming. So maybe your queen is killing two birds with one stone. Feeding her bloodlust and turning humans into vampires to build her army."

Caroline takes a saucer off the kitchen counter and holds it like she's going to throw it at me. "If so, then I hope she takes me. I'm trained to fight and I will feed my queen just as gladly as I'll fight for her because she is right to call for blood in retribution. It's *justice*. Fair. Blood for blood. Gelby Vasilis killed Abhartack so she's going to kill him. I support her decision and will do *anything* to help her."

My wolf howls for me to stand down but I can't. Not when I should be doing exactly what Caroline wants. Leaving and never coming back. "When Keela takes you up on your offer, remember that I told you her motives are darker and more dangerous than you want to believe."

I get out of my chair and stalk for the front door. Caroline follows me. "Keela is dangerous but that's the point. I'm not afraid of her. She's going to save us. *All* of us. Are you going to help her? Or keep pretending that you don't want to kill every last member of the Vasilis family the same way she does?"

I fling the door open and stomp out of her house. "I'm an alpha. I save myself, and it sounds like you and the other humans here better start figuring out how you're going to do the same."

---

## Leah

I walk the edge of the cliff behind Draugrkeep, pace brisk. Keela forbade us to come here but I need space away from the others. Distance from everyone. Including Collin. As my alpha, he can find me if he wants to. So can Keela and the other Vampir because I can't mask my scent. The most I can do is keep my emotions on lockdown, the way I learned to keep them from being broadcast back when I first realized I had feelings for Sean. If Dad found out, he would have sent me away. To make sure I didn't risk ruining our family line. If the pack found out I even had a crush on a human, it would have been ruin enough. Political suicide when it came to finding a match or a mate. That's the whole reason I never asked anyone for advice, even theoretically. I was as alone then as I am now. Save for Harlan—my shadow. He's never far from wherever I am but he rarely comes close enough to bother me. Though, if I feel like talking, all I have to do is look in his direction. He'll be here in the blink of an eye.

I stop where the forest curves closest to the chasm, stepping out onto the ledge with Dökkbraek stretching out behind me, the uncrossable ravine in front of me, and the crimson sky above me. The aurora is darker now than it was when we first arrived. The wind whipping from the chasm colder. Harsher. A bitterness in the hiss of it against the castle walls that makes me want to leave this place that's so different from home. But this is all we have left. A shadow-draped forest thick with frost and silence, and the constant threat of death. I close my eyes, focusing only on the howl of the wind. Monique's vision changed a lot of things. Some of them more important than others. My hand moves over the pocket holding the velvet pouch heavy with the communication crystals. I'd be lying if I said I didn't bring them with me because I hoped to use them to contact Sean. I'm ashamed to admit how willing I am to waste another one, should it explode like the last time I tried to contact someone other than Gelby. It's pathetic. But my fear that Sean is actually dead, like all the others, is growing.

I take out one of the crystals and sit cross-legged on the edge of the ravine, running my hand over the gem while holding a single face in my thoughts. A haze of white light begins to billow through the crystal. When it clears, Gelby's face appears. "It's too dark there, Leah. I can't see you. Why don't you open a portal and come to me? I'm sure your pack would like to see their little princess."

A tear slides down my cheek. "If I come to you, will you exchange me for all of them? Let them go to live free, with Collin, and keep me locked up in their place? In my brother's place?"

Gelby leans so close to his crystal that I can only see his eyes. "Why don't you come here and find out?"

"Why don't you go speak to Bishop about him selling humans to the Vampir?" I clap back at him. "I'll work on getting a portal open while you work on finding out why your traitorous father betrayed all of us."

Gelby snorts. "Are you so determined to pretend you are friends with the Vampir your kind has hated for all eternity that you let your people suffer while you make up lies in defense of your sworn enemies?"

I bring my own crystal to my face so he can see the shine of my wolf's eyes in the dim light of this world. "We are not you. Ulfr don't pretend to be friends and then stab everyone in the back. Sean didn't even know about you, and you still treated him the same way you've treated every other kind. Bring him into your fold and then do everything you can to hurt him until he bows down to you."

Gelby's eyes flare bright blue, vines of magic sizzling out of them and down over the hard bone of his cheeks. "I did everything I could to help him until he revealed himself as Fae. And guess where he is now? He's with *them*, the scum who murdered my mother and slaughtered thousands of innocent lives. So do not speak to me of right and wrong when you still go out of your way defend *them*."

"You are not the only one who has lost a mother." The words rip out of me, old wounds mixing with new. "Sean watched his mother die in a war all her own. He stood by her side while she battled cancer and he couldn't do anything to help her. None of us could. And there was no one for him to fight and no place for him to seek justice." Tears streak down my face. "Now *both* of my parents are gone. My brothers and sisters. But unlike Sean, who all of you play with like his life means nothing more to you than his mother's did, my brother and I *can* fight. We will seek justice for our pack. For all of the innocent lives slaughtered by the one *you* call father."

"Good." Gelby lets his magic grow brighter. Thicker. "Because if you come here, Leah, I will kill you. Slowly."

A gasp cuts through the ferocity of the wind and I shove the crystal back into my pocket, cutting off the connection with Gelby. Monique winds her way from the forest to my side, her steps steady, her voice anything but. "He...Gelby...he didn't mean that. He..."

I climb to my feet and dust off my legs. Not so long ago, I thought of Monique as a friend. After what happened with Sean at her coven house, she aligned with the Ulfr in our resolve to get him out from under the thumb of the Vasilis. Now I know that she's no better than the Vasilis. Full of lies and omissions. Self-serving before everything else. "Gelby meant every word, but you already know that since you've been hanging out with him lately."

Monique draws herself closer to the cliff edge, her clumsy foot knocking a loose rock over the lip of the chasm. She stares down into it, the wind rushing into her face and her red braid flying wildly behind her. "Gelby is taking in too much power. Since the Norns...he's been channeling more magic, casting more spells, and marking himself with powerful runes. The magic is warping his mind. And...he's mad with jealousy." She glances at me. "I half believe the Vasilis are only holding the Ulfr because he thinks that's how he gets to keep talking to you."

A twig snaps in the forest and I look that way, toward where I know Harlan is most likely perched up high in a tree. Watching. Listening. Probably spying so he can report my conversation to Keela. "The Vasilis only care about the Vasilis. The same way you only care about your coven."

Monique turns toward me. "That's not true, Leah. I care about you. About all of us. And Gelby's words just now...that's not the Álfar I know. The Gelby I know would never say that to someone he cares about, and I know he cares about you."

My hot breath clouds in front of me. "I'm done with this conversation. So take notes from the vampire who's out there watching us right now because they're always watching, but unlike you, they know when I want to be left alone."

Monique tugs her braid over her shoulder and smooths the loosening strands. "I'm not leaving you alone because the Norns are always watching too. And other destiny seers."

"Like you?" I scoff. "Maybe you should thank Sean for your newfound abilities. He might have triggered them when he threw you into that wall. I wonder what new power you would find if I threw you off this cliff?"

She tosses her braid back over her shoulder and pulls a circular bundle of sticks from her pocket, holding it against the folds of her skirt and out of view of anyone in the forest. "The Seidr is dead. The one Collin went to see."

I shrug, not bothering to attempt taming the wild whip of my hair in the wind. "So?"

Monique moves closer. "Collin's Seidr is the same one who told Beatrice about the scroll. The same one who gave Zara her quest. The same one who then directed the path of Collin's quest. And the very same one who *speaks* through me."

I blink at Monique. "You know the Seidr is dead because she possessed you?"

Monique's eyes shine with a layer of tears. "Not possessed exactly. The Seidr's spirit is able to channel through me because...I'm...her blood. Many generations removed."

I take a step away from the witch. "You're saying you're a hybrid. Like Keela and Sean?"

She looks down, scanning the ground at her feet. "I don't think so but none of my coven know for sure. They didn't even know the Seidr had a son who impregnated one of my ancestors. It seems she bred with purpose and even with only a small trace of her bloodline inside of me, she's able to connect with it and use me as her conduit. A bridge between the spirit land and those of the living."

I shake my head. "Why did you lie to us? You said you didn't know how your power was possible."

Monique sniffs, eyes coming back up to meet mine. "I didn't lie. I don't *know* how any of this is possible. Small things are being revealed to me, like a vision of the Seidr's son and the ancestor he mated with. I was able to go back and trace her through our records. None of her children or grandchildren...none of her line up until me have had this power. That's why I followed you today. So I could tell you first because I'm on your side, Leah, and I'm trying my best but I'm way out of my league here. I know it isn't fair, but try to put yourself in my shoes. How would you know a vision about Sean tied into an old prophecy unless you already knew about the prophecy? How would you know the symbolism in a vision was talking about Sean unless you had experienced something similar before?"

I study the red rims of her eyes. She's been crying and I'm finding it hard to care. Since our father died, Collin has transformed into a hardened alpha, one made from sharp, unrelenting stone. Maybe I've undergone a similar transformation because my desire to hurt Monique is raw. Unrelenting. Even though I know I *shouldn't* want to hurt her. I blow out an exasperated breath and run my fingers through my hair as it whips and splays in the wind. "Zara cut down both Sean and Haldir. Do you know why? Was it some sort of Dreki infighting?"

Monique studies the air, as if the wind holds some kind of answer. I shake my head. "Never mind. It's just that…the sword Zara used was the one Sean and I found in the rotunda. It had markings about dragons but I didn't consider that it was important for Sean until after we arrived in Dökkbraek and I replayed everything that happened."

Monique's eyes refocus on me. "If Zara retrieved the sword, it must be important to the Dreki, but I don't know why."

My chest tightens with the weight of my next words. "Can you find him? With a location spell?"

Monique slides the roots back into her pocket. "If you have something of Sean's, I can try. But…" She meets my eyes. "He may not be the same Sean you remember. The way Keela is not the same Keela we've always known."

"Is that the astute secret? You're using your clever spells to hide from my forest?" Keela's cold voice makes my skin crawl. I swing around to see the shape of her emerging from the dark confines of the forest. A creature who moves more like a spirit than flesh and blood. Her gaze settles on Monique. "What else are you hiding, blood witch?"

Monique's eyes go distant again, as if there are things I can't see all around us, speaking to her. My wolf shudders. "The problem with secrets is that they're more likely to break us apart than unite us," I answer for Monique. "And that's what we're supposed to be doing, right? Uniting? So the question is yours to answer, *blood* queen. What do *you* know that you're not sharing with the rest of us?"

Keela's eyes cut to the edge of the chasm. "What I know, little wolf, is that you have nothing of Sean's. Not even his heart."

A snarl rips out of me and I gnash my teeth, my wolf rising. Keela chuckles and Monique's head whips back, a horrifying scream launching out of her throat. I grab her before she falls over the cliff, pulling her away when a rock like the one she kicked over the edge earlier comes bulleting back up from the inky depths. Monique's lips begin to move over rushed words. "Eclipse of light. A heart prepared. Harken loud ye woeful cries. The Eye aligns the blade of rite. And the wolf stands at the gate where it all began."

She collapses in my arms, blood draining from the corners of her mouth. "Monique!" I shake her, checking for a pulse.

Keela's shadows engulf us, her voice a dark whisper against my skin. "Are you the wolf at the gate, little one?"

I recoil, dragging Monique's body with me. Keela's darkness crawls over my skin, an army of prickling cold spiders covering me head to toe. "Stand wherever you like, little wolf." Her voice rakes against my ears. "When the time comes, we will *all* return to that place where it all began."

# ~11~

I walk away from my bedroom door and pace back across the sitting room. Monique is asleep on my bed, where I brought her after Keela disappeared from the cliff edge. I used the mindspeak to call out for help, telling Collin what was happening and that I needed him to find me. Follow me back to the castle to be sure Monique and I arrived safely. He did, but ever since we determined as best we can that Monique isn't on the doorstep of death, Collin hasn't spoken to me. Most of the time, he's keeping his back to me, staring out the window at absolutely nothing.

I scrub my hands over my face. I told Collin everything that happened on the chasm's edge and now I wish I hadn't. The disturbing way Keela spoke to me...touched me... Her shadows aren't just shadows. There's something in them, and with the blood of the Seidr coursing through Monique's veins, I wonder if that's what she was listening to out there.

I sit down in a chair where there's a view of my bed and the sleeping witch. *Did Abhartack's death hasten this change in Keela?* I ask Collin. *Or do you think it was his mating with her?*

*His death or their mating.* He finally answers me. *Or maybe even Dökkbraek itself. This place is alive in ways no other castle and forest are. Which is why you shouldn't be sticking your nose where it doesn't belong. Keela told you to stay away from the chasm so stay away from it.*

A chill rolls down my spine. I'm grateful for the mindspeak so we can communicate privately, which is important when these castle walls might literally have ears, but him chastising me from within my own head is so much worse than just having him yell at me.

Collin abruptly turns away from the window. *We've been here too long. We need to figure out what Monique's vision meant and then get out of here.*

I like his plan, but the obvious question is where would we go? The Vasilis are powerful and their influence is far-reaching. Throughout all of Yggdrasil's worlds, they have some form of treaty. Some level of control. Even their enemies have been slow to cross them. *Your will is mine, alpha. I'll go when and where you tell me. Maybe Monique will wake up with more information about the wolf at the gate.*

He stares at me. Silent again. I want to scream at him. Force him to say everything he's been holding back. To rebuke me. To send me away. To tell me what it is he really thinks whenever he bothers to look at me. I want my brother. But we're nothing like what we used to be and fighting will gain us nothing.

A knock cuts through our silent vigil. It's Caroline. Collin's human girlfriend. The amount of time he's spent with her disqualifies her from being only a fling. Even now, her scent on him is strong. He crosses the room and yanks open the door, his shoulders more tense than they were a few seconds ago. Caroline's are too. Seems the lovers are in a fight. Not enough of one, though. Her smile is tentative but spreading. Collin's shoulders relax and he strokes his fingers over her arms as he takes the heavy stack of books from her and presses a kiss to the corner of her mouth. Their closeness makes my heart ache. Collin deserves all the happiness he can find, and I hope he's finding more than a small amount of it with Caroline, but I can't help but feel the weight of my own losses even more acutely when I see the two of them together.

I look away, staring back through my open bedroom door to where Monique still hasn't moved. Caroline strolls across the room and peeks in on Monique too. "How is she? I ran into Harlan in the village just before I set out to come here, and he told me the witch had passed out. I brought these herbs for her." She removes a satchel from her wrist and places it on the table in front of the sofa. "I'm not great with herbs but one of the human healers is, so I went by her shop and grabbed this pouch. Virginnia swears these herbs will cure anything. Says to just brew them into some tea and have a cup a day."

I dip my head in gratitude. "Thank you, I'm sure Monique will appreciate them."

Collin places the books next to the herbs and rifles through them. "Are these for Virginnia or are you studying to become a healer now?"

Caroline's brows scrunch, teeth sinking into her lip as if she's not sure how to answer. Or maybe she doesn't want to. "Most of them are for Virginnia. I mentioned to her that I was coming to Draugrkeep to talk to you about what we...discussed earlier. She asked me to go by the library while I was here because..." Frown lines frame Caroline's mouth. "The bloodthorn that grows around our village is beginning to die. Virginnia is hoping one of these books will help us save it. Or at least figure out why it's suddenly dying off."

Collin's eyes dart to mine and then drop back to meet Caroline's. They go silent, staring at one another, as if they too can communicate using mindspeak. I clear my throat. "Are the humans worried about the bloodthorn dying off?" As in, do you keep a supply to stave off the vampires in case they decide you're no longer family, but food?

Caroline looks away from Collin, her sigh heavy, voice low. "No. It's just…well, the bloodthorn goes through seasons but it hasn't ever died off this severely before." She gives me a weak smile. "Abhartack surrounded my village with bloodthorn so that whenever the humans saw it, we would remember his promise to treat us as equally and fairly as he did the Vampir. If it's true that Abhartack sacrificed his own blood to the aurora as a promise to the Vampir and an omen to those who would dare to harm them, then we believe the changes in the aurora and the bloodthorn are linked to Abhartack's death."

Harlan has said as much to me, regarding the aurora growing darker. Bloodier. He hasn't mentioned the twisted vines of crimson leaves, though. Maybe because the highly toxic bloodthorn is poisonous to all supernaturals so he's glad to be rid of it. I give Collin a quizzical look. He slips his hand onto Caroline's back and ushers her into his room. I lean forward, elbows pressing into my thighs, a jolt of surprise rippling over me when his bedroom door opens and closes again. Collin comes to tower over me and I brace for the impact of his words, but they're soft. Troubled. "I'm trying, Leah. It's just…"

I brush the sudden rush of tears from my eyes. He's speaking to me like a brother talking to his sister. Not an alpha to an inferior wolf. "I know. I'm trying too. I've *always* been trying."

He crouches down next to me. "Why Sean? Can you at least answer that for me because you could have just left him alone and this..." His jaw flexes. "Things would be easier if you would have just left Sean alone."

I drop my eyes and focus on the floor beneath me. If Collin wants an answer, I'll give it to him. "You're right. It would have been easier. For everyone else. And maybe for me too, but you have no idea how hard it was for—"

"Don't," he growls.

My teeth grind. "You *don't*, Collin. You *don't* get to rewrite my history just because you *don't* know what it was like to lust over someone your entire pack would have shunned you over. To lust over someone while in the presence of wolves who could smell it on you. I had to date other guys and throw myself all over them to keep any of you from smelling my desire whenever Sean was around, which was all the time, thanks to you." I wipe the tears from my cheeks and meet my brother's stare. "It was hardest trying to hide it from Dad. The alpha. Now that you're one, you understand how heightened your awareness is when it comes to what I'm feeling. Now imagine me feeling *anything at all* over Sean. Happy, sad, turned on..." Collin looks away and I'm not surprised. He doesn't want to hear how hard it was for me to be around Sean while we were growing up because knowing that changes everything. "Imagine how I felt knowing Dad thought I was a tramp. That I was a boy-crazy idiot who needed to be exposed to every wolf in Midgard as soon as possible so I would find my true mate and not disgrace our pack. Imagine all the ways I disgraced myself because I was *trying*. For the pack. *Always* for the pack."

He looks up at me. "Dad didn't think you were a—"

"Yes, he did." I stand and move away from Collin. I don't need his pity. "It's what all of you thought. Even Sean. He, at least, had the courage to say it to my face. And I'm only sorry that I can't be as good at hiding my true self from you now as I was back then. I'm *trying*. I've even considered giving myself to Harlan to see if that would change things back to when you only thought that I was a tramp instead of a traitor. But it doesn't really matter what I do because it will never be good enough. I'll always do a poor job, and you will always be disappointed in me. The same way Dad was."

I lean against the wall beside my bedroom door, sagging in shame. Relief. Exhaustion. Collin moves nearly as fast as the Vampir, his arms closing around me as he pulls me into a hug. "You're no more of a disappointment than I am. We both have our issues and we'll work through them, Leah. Together. And then we'll find new things to irritate each other with." He leans back and tucks a hand under my chin, making me look into his eyes. "Dad adored you. *I* adore you. And Sean…"

"Is missing." My voice breaks.

Collin pulls me back to his chest, his arms even tighter now. "Everyone is gone and there's nothing we can do about that. We have to move on. I need to talk some things over with Caroline so I'm going to walk her home. When I get back, we'll start mapping out our plan. Figuring out what's best for our pack. *Together*." He lets go of me and pinches my nose like he used to do when we were kids. "No to the vampire. I've yet to meet anyone who is good enough for you and he's definitely not."

Collin disappears into his bedroom and I try to smile but I can't. I'm not sure I'll ever be able to smile again. I turn through the doorway to my bedroom and shut the door lightly, so I don't disturb Monique. I just need to be in here when Collin and Caroline leave because it's bad enough that I let my tears fall in front of Collin. I don't want Caroline to see how pathetic I am.

I hear Collin's bedroom door open and listen as their footsteps cross the sitting room floor. When the suite door closes, I take a deep breath, wiping my face and trying to tame my tears. "What kind of plan do you think Collin has?" Monique's hoarse voice startles me.

I tug up my shirt and use it to dry my face. "Whatever it is, Keela has helped us, and that's forcing us into a dangerous alliance." I move to the bed and sit down beside Monique. "How are you feeling? You really scared me out there."

Her cheeks tinge pink. "I'm okay. Just tired. The spirit channeling through me is draining. I really wish she would warn me."

I nod, turning to stretch out next to Monique, facing her and keeping my voice low. "Especially if she's going to channel when you're on the edge of a cliff. What happened to you looked painful, and what happened after was terrifying. I carried you here to my room because it seemed like the safest place, and we need to be *safe* right now."

Monique shifts, lying on her side to face me. She reaches underneath the blanket and pulls out that circle of sticks, whispering a few words as she places it between us. "This will block anyone from eavesdropping. My magic is drained though, so it won't last long. This place, Dökkbraek, is older than what anyone thinks. There's ancient magic here, woven into the earth. Into the stone. The land of the Norns felt this way too, like it was made of magic instead of only holding it. I think it's why the Seidr was able to channel through me so easily there and here. She's somehow using the enhanced magic to hijack the control I should have over whether or not I *want* my body to be used for a spirit-call."

I swallow my ever-rising dread and send a comforting vibe to my wolf. "Do you remember what the spirit said on the cliff?"

Monique sighs. "Yes. I can hear everything. I just can't...move or talk for myself. Let alone kick her out of me."

I reach out and clasp Monique's hand in mine. "That must be scary."

Her fingers close tightly around mine. "It is. But seeing you angry is worse. Almost as bad as seeing you upset about Sean. I don't know if he's a good guy or a bad one, or even if he's alive. I don't even know what the ramifications of a life like his would be if he's alive and somehow you found a way to be with him. But I overhead you talking to Collin just now. I never knew how you felt about Sean but I did see the way you looked at him, and that last day, before Odin took Sean away, I saw Sean look at you that very same way." Her fingers give mine another tight squeeze. "In light of what Sean did to you, I don't know if that helps or hurts."

I let go of her hand to combat the tears that don't want to stop because her words only make the pain surrounding Sean so much worse. "Your vision said a wolf stands at the gate. What gate? What wolf?"

She sighs. "I don't know. Sean could be seen as a gate, so maybe him? Maybe you or Collin are the wolf?"

I roll onto my back. "When I was with Sean, in that rotunda, there was a room with all of these runes carved along the ceiling. I couldn't read most of them but..." I think of how the runewisps drew my attention to certain ones. Showed me what seemed important right up until the Fossegrim attacked. "There were runes for bonds of past and present, and a warning to prepare one's heart. You mentioned bonds of the past and present before, and today you said a heart prepared." I turn my head to look at Monique. "Is it possible the Seidr was talking to me today?

There was a rune in the rotunda that I thought either meant star or eye but I couldn't remember which. And today…"

Monique's brows scrunch. "She said the Eye aligns the blade of rite."

Tears sting my eyes. "A heart prepared, and a wolf standing at the gate where it all began." I take an unsteady breath. "There was an altar in the rotunda. The sword Zara used was near it, and inscribed with runes about dragons. I didn't think it connected to Sean but what if… What if I was the wolf at the gate and I was supposed to save us by sacrificing Sean? Because if I'd slaughtered him in that room, none of us would have faced what happened afterward." Tears begin to roll down my cheeks. "Abhartack would still be alive. My entire family would still be alive… Am I the reason the Vasilis murdered my entire family? Am I the reason the Norns didn't release us until Keela's mate was dead? Am I the one who broke everything?"

Monique shifts closer to me and wraps an arm around my waist. "No, Leah. The Norns may chart a course but like the spirit who speaks through me, many things work outside the will of the Norns so it doesn't matter what they wanted. All that…" Her hand clamps onto my waist with bruising force. I try to pull away but she latches onto me tighter, her body seizing. Her mouth opens, her eyes widening. A sharp, painful light bursts in front of my eyes. Nausea climbs up my throat, my body weightless and fractured, weaving through time and space until I'm no longer in the bedroom with Monique. I'm alone, sitting in the middle of a narrow hall. Stone above me. Below me. All around me. A tunnel. I rake my hand through the layer of leaves and dirt covering the stone. No one has been here in a very long time.

I get up from the floor. "Hello?" My voice echoes down the endless corridor, no doubt the only sound this abandoned place has heard in years. But if that's true, why do I feel like a predator turned into prey? Every hair on my body rises. I spin around, sensing the eyes of a hunter on me. Nothing is here but darkness. Still, I tremble, calling on my wolf for comfort. She doesn't answer. I try to shift but she's too far away, bound and subdued deep inside of me, a void as deep and wide as the one behind Draugrkeep separating us.

I begin to walk, breaths coming heavier. Shallower. The cool air in front of my face misting with each stunted exhale. A low, feral growl rumbles through the tunnel, followed by the sound of stone breaking, as if something is clawing its way into this corridor with me. To hunt me. I take off running, hard and fast, lungs burning as I race away from the sound of those claws tearing over stone. The predator barrels toward me and all along the corridor, tiny pricks of light dislodge themselves from the wall, circling and darting around me, wild and frantic. The runewisps. They're here, urging me forward. I follow them through an intersecting hallway, running down the branch they rush into, focusing on their movements instead of the snarling, rabid beast closing in behind me.

I slam into a wall, the runewisps darting away at the lest second, floating high up into the ceiling of this dead-end chamber. It's no larger than an elevator box and the only way out is back the way I came. Where the beast has already passed through the intersection. There's nowhere left to run. Sean was right. I shouldn't have befriended the runewisps.

I press on the wall, trying to find a weak spot. A hidden door. A broken chunk I can use as a weapon. Anything. The runewisps spin around me, pricking along my arms and face. I swat at them. They increase their speed, making me spin around, blinking and swatting as I scream at them. They swarm an object standing alone on the opposite side of the chamber. It's tall and thin, and so covered in grime that it's hard to make out the mirror's glass. The runewisps light up all around it. "Fine," I growl at them, approaching the filthy mirror whose surface twists, distorting what little reflection I can see as I approach. I lift a shaking hand and swipe away the grime. It's not my reflection in the mirror. It's my mother's.

Tears spill over my lashes and I reach out, stroking my fingers over her smiling face. My stomach somersaults and the world once again falls away, my body tugged into the mirror, transported through time and space until I'm standing inside my family home. What's left of it. Crumbled walls and burned-out rooms. And the mirror, still in front of me.

I search for my mother in the reflection but all I see is myself. Face pale and hands covered in blood. I look down. The blood is only in the reflection. "This is my fault," I say aloud. Acknowledge what my own reflection is telling me. I did this. I brought death to my family.

The mirror contorts. Collin now stands in its reflection, flanked by wolves I don't know and doused in a fury I've never felt from him before. Next comes Sean, wreathed in light and flame, and bound by chains of gold and silver. Then Keela, cloaked in shadows, her blood-red eyes rimmed in a darkness that makes even my trapped wolf howl in fear. I stumble away from the mirror. "What do you want from me? What do I have to do?" I drop to my knees, wracked with sobs. "Please, tell me how to fix what I've done."

The floor opens up, swallowing me back through time. Back into the tunnel. Back to where I began. A savage, thunderous snarl sounds over my shoulder, so close the creature's hot breath scorches my neck. I dig my nails into my palms and turn, scooting over the stick-strewn stone to cast my eyes on my end. To see the magnificent, ravaging jaws of the great wolf before it takes my soul, trapping it here in this forgotten place for all eternity.

My chest burns. The creature begins to speak, using a language I don't understand. Still, I understand his rage. See it in the rabid face of the great white wolf. His thick fur is tipped in ash, as if he's been dipped in the fire burning behind those glowing yellow embers that are marked by two black ash-colored strokes under each eye. War paint for a warrior wolf. His teeth snap in my face, saliva splattering and spewing as he yells into my head. "Release me!"

I scramble backward, away from him, that spot in my chest growing hotter. The wolf advances, great paws cracking the stone as they pound against it. His face presses forward, his great gleaming teeth an inch from ripping into me. *Release me!* His snarling order bleats into my mind. Over and over. *Release me! Release me! Release me!*

I scream, the pain inside my head only diminished by the one in my chest. His teeth snap, his roar deafening. The world twists, the tunnel dissolving into mist. I scream harder. Louder. Reaching for the beautiful beast, coughing and choking, all the air being sucked out of my lungs in one painful rush. Light pops all around me, the last vestiges of his image shattering. "Leah!" Collin's shout grates over my senses. Brings me back to Dökkbraek. To my room.

"No!" I scream. Clawing and fighting.

Collin's arms hold me in a death grip but his isn't the only presence here. My eyes fall on Sean and seeing him here, in the flesh, only makes me cry harder. I kick against Collin, fighting to get back to Monique. "Did you see?"

Collin pulls me away from the witch who only stares at me, blood oozing from her nose and mouth. But I don't want to be away from her. I want to go back to her. To my wolf. My throat is raw, voice caked with agony as I fight Collin, eyes on Monique. "Did you see?" Bloody tears spill down her cheeks, making her look all the part of the possessed girl that she is. "Did you see?" I scream again. She nods, collapsing into Beatrice's arms. The old witch's frantic eyes meet mine and I give myself over to Collin's will. Monique saw him. I don't know his name or where he is, but the white wolf is my mate. My own wolf howls the truth of it. He is our mate, and he's out there. Somewhere. Trapped. Hurting. And he needs our help.

## ~12~

# Sean

Collin holds onto Leah like a bear protecting a cub, and Leah fights him like a wildcat, tooth and nail, doing her best to get to Monique. Beatrice rushes to the bloody young witch and I try again to get to Leah. To help Collin. But my best friend is no longer Collin. His eyes are dark and his canines long. Gray fur spreads over his arms and his face distorts, a snout growing long while his sister's screams rip through the room. When the portal snapped shut behind me, there was this brief moment when I was happy. I walked through Beatrice's portal of my own free will and this time, I didn't feel sick. Not until I heard Leah scream. The agony in the sound churned my stomach. I raced toward that agony to find Leah here, screaming bloody murder while Monique bleeds from her eyes like some witch in a horror show.

Queen Sóleyva digs her fingers into my arm, pouring her comforting magic into me. "This is a private matter. Let's give them space, and figure out what we have walked into once everyone has calmed down."

Her words and her magic freeze me in place. Whatever is happening here, Collin doesn't want me involved. He no longer sees me as family. Right now, he only sees Leah. She gives up her fight, going limp in his arms. I turn away, allowing the queen to pull me from the chaos. We march out of the bedroom and through the suite, followed by King Riktr and the only two royal guards they were allowed to bring with them: pointy-faced Vigmund and my braided guide Toreyn. I tug free of Sóleyva's grip once we're in the hallway. A vampire is waiting for us, hands folded casually in front of him. "I am Kythos. My queen sends her regards. Follow me and I will show you to the rooms she has prepared for you."

Queen Sóleyva hesitates. "How gracious of your queen. Accommodations *and* the privilege of having only two guards attend us. What a magnanimous display of affection for this Fae delegation."

Kythos inclines his head. "I will give my gracious queen your regards."

Riktr moves to Sóleyva's other side, cutting me a harsh look as he sandwiches her between us. A look that says this is my fault so I better be ready to protect her. But he's wrong. Beatrice is the one who had all of this planned out. The instant she opened her portal and said she had gained permission from Keela to bring me here to see Collin and Leah, I regained enough control to stop my magic from trying to burn her alive again. Queen Sóleyva and King Riktr followed me to the portal and it was Beatrice who put an end to their calls for their guards. She claimed Keela only gave her permission to bring the four of us and two royal guards into Dökkbraek. Any others who attempted to enter would be killed by Dökkbraek's wards. Sóleyva seemed to believe that was true, and there was no time for debate even if she didn't. I was leaving, with or without them. They chose to come and now we're all together in this dark, foul-smelling castle, and the longer I stand here with Leah only on the other side of that wall, the more likely I am to tear this place apart, stone by stone.

"Fine." I flick a hand at the vampire, faelight mixing with flame on the tips of my fingers. An involuntary threat. "Get on with it. And tell Keela I need to see her because if the hell I just witnessed in that room is what's been going on around here, she has a heck of a lot of explaining to do."

---

I sit on the edge of the bed in the smallest room of the three Kythos gave us. We're one floor down from Collin and Leah, tucked into the back end of a hallway with a suite similar to theirs, only smaller. Riktr and Sóleyva are in that suite with their two guards. I left the next largest bedroom for Beatrice and took this one, waiting here ever since for a vampire queen who hasn't shown her face yet.

Beatrice's cane scrapes over the stone in the hallway and I jump from the bed, swinging the door open. "Is Leah okay? What was that up there? Why was Monique—"

Beatrice lifts a finger to her lips. "Why don't you invite an old lady inside? I'm tired and need to sit down for a few minutes."

I open the door wider. "There's not much space in here but there's a chair or you can sit on the bed. Whichever is more comfortable for you."

She shuffles past me, her strained laugh cutting through the room. "You look as frayed as I feel."

I shut the door. "Frayed is an understatement, but probably for you too. How's Monique?"

Beatrice pulls a palm-sized wreath of dried branches from the folds of her dress and places it on the windowsill. "Monique will be fine. She's resting now. As is Leah. They want to stay together after Monique's vision somehow allowed Leah to participate in viewing whatever it was the two of them saw. Neither of them is ready to talk about it yet, so we'll give them time and a little space." She turns from the window and studies me, her old face not as pinched as it was when she entered the room. "These dried herbs are gathered together in what we call the Circle of Roots. They're meant to ward off evil spirits but more importantly, the herbs are spelled to give us privacy. We can speak freely now. Without even the worry of prying eyes. My magic will shield your window the same way it shields our words." She sets her cane aside. "Monique told me you encountered the dragonless dragon during your time with the Norns. By chance, have you been in contact with her since?"

I watch Beatrice move with ease. She doesn't need the cane. It's all an act. "Dragonless dragon?"

She smiles, a glint in her aging eyes. "Zara. A sacrifice for a sacrifice. Not one willingly given, but a sacrifice all the same. Her dragon a small price to pay for the greater good."

"Greater good," I repeat the words, remembering Zara's promise to return if Beatrice wasn't dead in some kind of dragon time frame. "Who gets to decide what the greater good is? You? Is that why the Völva had a hand in Aether's death? Trapping his soul in a stone so that his magic could be taken by someone else?" I move past her and snatch the dried branches off the windowsill. "And isn't that something Keela might be interested in knowing about? Zara sends her regards, by the way, she just forgot to mention that you stole her dragon the same way you stole Aether's soul."

Beatrice waves her old wrinkled hand. Only, it's not quite so old and wrinkled anymore. "Don't be a fool. Put the circle back before I have to use more of my magic to keep up this old weakened woman façade." She grins up at me through lashes that are much thicker and younger than they were only minutes ago. She's still older, but not as ancient and broken-looking as she was when I saw her walk into Sóleyva's throne room. "Zara's involvement in you having what belongs to me isn't that surprising. The dragon never could tell the Seidr no. Not even when it mattered most."

I cross my arms over my chest, keeping the dried herbs. "It seems the Völva have a lot of things to hide, and I'd rather not get mixed up in whatever you're here to do. Especially if you're here to do to me, or anyone else I care about, the same thing you did to Aether. Or Zara, apparently."

Beatrice sighs deep and long, her features transforming with the breath, returning her to the decrepit woman who has no choice but to drag the cane to her and lean on it heavily. "Zara's fate was recompense for the betrayal dealt to the Norns. By her, and others before her. Others *using* her. Zara paid the price for all of it because that's what the Norns demanded. Her dragon was forfeited to them, not me. I'll admit to having played a part in her fate, because the Norns left me no choice, but I did not betray Aether. I *saved* him."

I snort. "By sentencing his soul to live trapped inside of a stone? Don't you think saving him would have been to tell him about his impending death rather than sitting by while it happened?"

Beatrice rubs her hand along the windowsill, lips pressed tightly together. I slam the roots back onto it and she nods approvingly. "I could do no more than a simple intervention into his fate for the very same reason I intervened in Zara's. The choices were made for me, the same as yours have been made for you." She hobbles to the bed and lowers herself onto the corner, her aging features softening just a little. "Good and evil have always battled. The righteous and the corrupt. But no one speaks of the truth of those absolutes. Of morality's true murkiness. It's easy to say murder is wrong, for instance, but there are terms under which many would feel justified in taking a life. Stopping a mass murderer would certainly be justified, but whether or not one believes ending their life is then justified is a moral debate."

Frustration tightens my jaw. "Hardly."

She props her cane against the bed frame. "Odin and Loki. The gods of enlightenment and the ones of chaos. The ones considered good or bad, though the deeds of both can be placed in each of those categories. Yet they are still pitted against each other as absolutes. Two halves who stand in stark contrast to one another. Every other creature counted for one of their sides or the other, in the end."

I cross my arms back over my chest. "Put me down for Loki."

She nods. "I feared you would be pushed to such lengths, though Loki is no better than Odin. Then there are the Norns who consider themselves righteous, and the original Seidr who seems to have had a god complex all her own. Only now are pieces of her old prophecies becoming clear. And to me, this clarity only proves that the beings of fate are no more pious than the gods."

I glare at her. "But you aren't compromised or self-serving? You don't kiss little boys and lie to them while stealing their innocence? Take away dragons? Create soulstones even when you know trapping someone is the equivalent of sentencing them to life without parole? Solitary confinement? You helped Odin with me, didn't you?"

Beatrice frowns. "My path was written into your fate long ago and if I didn't assist the Norns by taking Zara's dragon away, Zara would not have played her crucial roles. She would have helped no one but herself, and if she did not release your dragon soul, none of us would be standing here today."

I lean against the wall. "Then why did the Norns put Leah through all that trauma in their land when they could have just trapped me in the rotunda with Zara and saved everyone a whole lot of trouble?"

Beatrice's eyes scan the corners of the room. "A test, perhaps. But the question you should be asking is why did Aether give you the Eye?"

I don't answer her and she smiles. "From what I've pieced together, Aether found out the Fae were uniting—his Unseelie with the Seelie, to once again challenge the Álfar. He was a peacemaker and did not want the war. Maybe for Keela's sake. That part, I don't know. But Aether was not as power hungry as most of his kind are. Nor half as arrogant as his father. The Fae believed the Eye would amplify their power and allow them to defeat the Álfar. So, he took it and ran. But the Fae sent Draugr to hunt for the Eye." She motions to me. "They found Aether, and from what I understand, they also found you. But the Vasilis were there to protect you from them. Aether was not so lucky."

I think back to that day when Gelby first introduced me to portals, dragging me into one right after telling me the creatures ripping his magical barrier apart were shapeshifting zombies. Draugr. But it was those *things* materializing from the swirling mass of darkness that slithered over the walls that he said I should fear the most. The Jötnar—creatures who could devour me soul and all. "Arsenious let the zombies tear his son apart?"

Her laugh is soft. Pained. "I suppose they are nothing more than zombies, and I suppose Arsenious might have wished for his son to meet another fate." Her eyes pierce mine. "But Queen Sóleyva demanded the death. A severe and ancient punishment for a crime she hoped Aether would confess to. Explain every detail of, so she could find the amulet."

I drag my hands down my face, remembering all too well the day Keela found out about Aether's death, the way he was left mutilated. "Queen Sóleyva ordered the death and it was done at that ritual site where the big slabs of black stone form a triangle. Right?"

Beatrice nods. "The Draugr were allowed entry so the royals could claim that their hands were clean in the death. They used that site because no Fae would dare go there without permission from the queen." She eyes me. "No ordinary Fae, anyway. It is a place meant for rituals of such secrecy that only the highest degrees of Fae royalty know about them. Aether's father being in league with Queen Sóleyva, and after such a hard lineage of fighting between the Unseelie and the Seelie, made Aether's betrayal all the worse. They were finally working together and then the Unseelie king's own son becomes a traitor to their cause. If Arsenious did not go along with the demands of the Seelie queen, he would have brought death upon himself instead."

She shakes her head before continuing. "He valued his own life more than his son's, and that earned him only death at the hands of the Vampir instead of his countrymen. But you need to know that King Riktr was against the slaughter of the royal son. If Arsenious couldn't get a confession from Aether, King Riktr agreed that Aether should be tried for treason and given a reasonable punishment, but one befitting a royal. I know this information to be fact." Her eyes drop to my pocket as if she can sense the stone's presence there. "After I heard how Aether's body was found, I had my doubts about the success of the stone. I created it, but it was in the Seidr's possession after that so she could ensure it was placed when and where it was needed. I had hoped it would work, but I also hoped that a father would not murder his son over an artifact no one knows the true power of." Her eyes lift back to mine. "Death was not the only possible outcome for Aether. King Riktr is Fae and riddled with their self-importance, but he is not so cruel as to demand blood the way his queen does."

"You're here to lobby for him? You want me to give Aether's soul to King Riktr?"

She stands. "What I tell you today is only to prepare you for what you will face. The Seelie are no better than the Unseelie. Had Queen Sóleyva not demanded it, Aether would still be flesh and blood instead of merely a thought trapped inside of a stone. And had the other powerful heirs in her lineage supported her ascension to the throne, they would not be stone husks littering her gardens."

I plop down in the only chair in the room. Beatrice sighs. "I know, boy, this is a lot to take in, but you must understand that King Riktr is not a true mate of Queen Sóleyva, although he is fiercely loyal to her. And he is powerful. Though not enough to challenge her rule, so if she were to ever deem his silent strength at her side to be a detriment, either in might or will, she would hollow him to a husk and make him yet another addition to her garden."

That old fairy-tale-type song that said a queen of the Seelie Court turned a man back into his true form after a witch cursed him for denying her advances rushes into my head. I think whoever wrote that down got it backwards. Then again, that's exactly what Bishop's yearly dose of magic does to the humans. Makes them believe a murderous maniac is only a jolly old elf bringing them gifts.

Beatrice picks up her cane. "Aether's bloodline traces back to the first Fae court—a time before the Fae split into the two courts of the Seelie and Unseelie. He is also the rightful heir to the Unseelie throne. Simply possessing his soul could give Queen Sóleyva leverage, where matters of Fae politics are concerned." She shakes her head. "Then again, Aether died to save Midgard from ruin, because he knew that's what would happen if the Fae were in charge. The Vasilis may need new management, but none of us need Fae rule. Though, you aren't exactly Fae, are you? You just happen to have the power of a very accomplished and very old Fae royal inside of you, and now the soul of another very powerful Fae lineage in your pocket."

I study her changing features, watching her grow older. "How do you know which Fae lives inside of me?"

Her eyes roam over my chest. "The power you have stems from the long-reining queen's own family. I suspect she's realizing now that it disappeared from her bloodline because it never passed from the soul inside of you back into their lineage. I imagine she's thinking that hollowing you out will give her that power back."

Footsteps sound in the hallway. Beatrice leans her weight onto her cane. "If there is to be war with the Vasilis, we need the Vampir. Their numbers added to those of the Fae are the only way we stand a chance against the Álfar army. Remember that when dealing with Keela. Right now, she blames Gelby for her king's death, but she also knows that your actions put Abhartack in Gelby's path. If she finds that reason enough not to help us, I thought offering her the soul of her longtime friend might compel her to change her mind."

There's a swift rap of knuckles on my door. Beatrice leans forward and takes my hand in hers. "I'm afraid our fate is resting on your shoulders. Those powers who orchestrated both the Eye and the soulstone falling into your possession are not ones I can argue with." She pulls her hand from mine. "Aether's magic and birthright are yours now. Choose his fate wisely. You may not want to rule or accept your place among the supernaturals, but Ulfr are dying, and I know you care about that."

# ~13~

King Riktr didn't say anything to Beatrice but the searing glare in his eye when she opened my bedroom door told me what I needed to know. Beatrice is a walking conspiracy. And she's right about him not being fully on board with every move Queen Sóleyva makes. Riktr can't override his queen though, and he'd rather live at her side doing everything by her rules than not live at all.

    He shoves open the door to their suite and strolls into the room ahead of me, having come himself to extend her summons. I shoulder my way past the guards standing on either side of the door and follow the king. The queen is sitting straight ahead, along the back wall where a plain gray chair has been centered in front of a wide window. I notice the same privacy-giving wreath that was on my windowsill is now on the windowsill behind the queen who is still in her layers of sheer fabric. The glow of the aurora filtering through the window makes Sóleyva look more like a bloody bride than the vision of a goddess that she was when sitting upon her throne.

The king moves to stand beside her chair, burning eyes instantly connecting to mine. I stop in the center of the room and hope that my eyes are delivering back to the king the exact sentiment he's trying to convey to me. If he thinks I'm afraid he'll tattle to the queen about Beatrice being in my room, he's going to be very disappointed when he pulls that trigger. I wasn't conspiring against the queen when I talked to Beatrice, but he was. That's how she knew his feelings about Aether's death and why the emasculated king has stayed quiet about my run-in with Zara. He's loyal to Sóleyva, he might even love her, but he's only pretending to be okay with sitting quietly by her side, a pretty face to be seen and not heard. Whatever leverage he thinks he has on me, I hold the keys to his death. And I'm pretty sure he knows I also hold Aether's soul in my pocket.

I manage not to bow to the queen this time. "You rang?"

Her dark sculpted brow rises. "I shouldn't have had to. You see the situation we're in and surely after that display earlier you see that you are not among friends out there. Now is not the time for us to be divided. We need to be here, together." She motions to a chair off to her left. "Sit. There is much to discuss."

I plod to the chair and drop into it, crossing an ankle over my knee. My loss of control in her throne room was enough to let her know that I'm not hers to order around. But after what Beatrice said about needing the Vampir to join the Fae against the Álfar who killed Leah and Collin's family, I shouldn't make a sworn enemy of Sóleyva. "I may not have a people to belong to, but I'm not completely isolated out there in the big bad world." I rest a hand over my pocket, eyes moving to the king. His jaw is so tight I'm surprised his teeth aren't broken.

Queen Sóleyva flicks her fingers at him. His jaw ticks but he lifts his shirt, untying a black leather sheath from around his lean waist. He presses it into her waiting hand and breaks eye contact with me. She pulls a dagger carved of bone from the leather. "That's why I wanted to speak with you. We are your people. Your *family*." She emphasizes that last word, her eyes holding an intensity that I haven't yet seen from her.

I stare at carvings running from tip to hilt along the dagger. "And you're going to use the king's fancy dagger to do what, exactly?"

The queen sighs and the muscle feathering in the king's jaw works overtime. She places the dagger back in the sheath. "This is a family heirloom, carved from the horn of a Skarthorn. Nasty creatures, but prized for their horns." She extends the sheath to me. "The dagger is more ceremonial than useful, but it's a gift befitting my best champion. And that's what you are. A champion among warriors."

Now I understand the king's hostility. I don't take the dagger from the queen's outstretched hand. "I have fire and faelight. Speed, strength, and the ability to heal almost before I ever get injured. I don't need a dagger."

She lifts from her seat and kneels beside me, leaning forward to find the waistband of my pants. She holds my eyes, her fingers sliding under the hem of my shirt and along my skin, taking their sweet time as they wrap the leather straps around my hips and secure the dagger. Her eyes dip, a soft smile on her lips as her hands linger too close to where they shouldn't. "You do not need this dagger, Sean, but you are my family, so I am most sure that you are the one to have it."

I look up at the king, his queen on her knees before me. He gives me a tight-lipped snarl. I hold his stare and lean forward, kissing Sóleyva's cheek. The suite door opens. Collin stomps in. Followed by Leah. I jump out of my seat, the knee of my crossed leg ramming Sóleyva in the chin.

She yelps and her guards rush in, the king already lifting her from the floor. I try to help him but he shoves me away. I meet the queen's eyes, running my hands through my hair, taking in the chaos I've created—all because Leah is standing five feet away and I've graduated from being an idiot and arrived at arrogant idiot.

I turn and face her. Leah's eyes are wide and fixed on where I was sitting. Where the queen was on her knees in front of me and I was kissing her. All to get a rise out of Riktr. "That...it's not what that looked like—"

"Shut up!" Collin roars. "You do not speak to my sister."

The guards draw their weapons—the swords they were wearing at the palace. Monique shoves her way past Collin and spreads her arms wide, separating the Fae side of the room from the wolves, all of us too crammed into this small space for anyone's comfort. Beatrice slowly makes her way to Monique's side. "This is a time for diplomacy, not swords."

I look over their shoulders to Collin, mouth opening and shutting again. He has that look on his face. The one he always got when some jerk said something terrible about Leah. It was the last look they ever saw before his fist found a home in their face. I look past him to Leah, whose eyes are diverted and focused straight ahead now, avoiding me altogether. A soft growl rumbles in Collin's throat and I should heed the warning, but I'm more concerned for Leah than myself. "Collin, I'm sorry...I just...please, Leah—" Collin punches over Monique's shoulder, his hand clamping around my throat, squeezing so hard my windpipe would be crushed if I was human.

"Enough!" Sóleyva shouts.

Leah turns and storms out of the room. Collin lets go of me. "Stay away from her."

There's no chance of me staying away from Leah. Especially now. I need to talk to her more than ever. I need to talk to Collin, too. I hold my palms open in front of me, using the universal sign that I don't want any trouble. "Col, I'm so sorry. For your family. Everything. All of it…"

He ignores me, his hard eyes fixing on Sóleyva. "You wanted to see me?"

"Indeed," she answers him, the word curt as she gathers her skirts and moves back to her chair, dismissing her guards. "Now that we are all here, let us begin with civility. We don't need to be friends but surely you can see the benefit of our unity in this *situation* we have found ourselves in, alpha? Fraught with uncertainty as it is."

Collin's eyes are canine. Not the human ones I've always known. Nothing about him is the boy I remember. "You mean the situation you just found yourself in. I've been here. Because unlike other people, I don't abandon those I claim to love."

I lose my voice. And a little of my courage. Collin is talking about me. He thinks I abandoned him on purpose, which I did. But not for lack of caring. I left with Odin that day because if I'd stayed, he would be dead. All of them would have died that day. "I'm on your side, Collin. You and Leah—"

"He's on everyone's side." The queen's voice cuts mine off, tinkling through the room with a sound I now recognize as being laced with her soothing magic. She's trying to calm everyone. Defuse this situation before Collin's smothering anger reaches the point of no return. I've never felt anything like this coming off him before. It's overwhelming. "That's why we insisted upon coming here as soon as we heard the news of what happened to your pack. It's simply mortifying. So, we're here, putting ourselves in *your* delicate situation, to stand as a united front upon the threshold of war. One that will find us sooner now that we've all convened here. Once Bishop finds out, which he will because the Vasilis are powerful, he will insist that we've gathered to conspire against him, whether we do so or not. So, let us do so."

Collin bares his teeth at her and Beatrice moves to stand in front of Sóleyva, dipping her head—the first to show deference. "You speak truly. Bishop has lost his way, and bitterness over those things which have happened already will not help us stop his wrath."

"Says the coven leader who is responsible for the conspiracy that got my family slaughtered and my pack imprisoned." Collin's thick-coated voice is more wolf than man. "The innocent paying the price for the guilty."

Beatrice turns a cold eye on Collin. "The Ulfr were targeted by Bishop because they were working for the Fae, and now you are here with the Vampir. Two kinds in your good graces that he sees as direct enemies. Are you so young that you know nothing of the last war?"

Stone grinds against stone in Collin's throat. "What I know is that you orchestrated the attack on your own coven."

Monique's head shakes furiously, her long braid whipping against her back. "No. That was a mistake. Beatrice made a deal with Abhartack so that he could come and get Keela—"

"What?" The word unglues my heavy tongue, a pang of jealousy cutting through me at the mention of Abhartack's name. Visions of him kissing Keela one of the many reels in my head that I wish I could get rid of. They only serve to open the door for Erik's own memories to rush forward, tying his visions of Keela to my own. Giving me his lust. His love. And his regret. He was Keela's rebound guy. One who thinks that if circumstances had been different, he would've been her second and last love. "You set up that whole attack just to—"

"No!" Beatrice slams the bottom of her cane into the stone floor. "I did *not* know Abhartack was bringing an army. He was supposed to come alone so he could meet Keela in person. He felt strongly about their meeting and so did I. She never belonged with the Vasilis, so I allowed him entry to my coven lands. But the Fae got involved and Abhartack brought an army with him, and I could do nothing to stop what happened because of what you did to my witches and our home before the portal opened."

"What *I* did?" Rage as hot Haldir's dragon breath explodes behind my eyes. Haldir was ready to burn down the whole world for Keela that day and so was I. I still might. I call flame to my hands and cast a burning ball into the stone at Beatrice's lying feet, leaving a smoldering ring of fire around her. "You mean what the *witches* did to *me*."

King Riktr steps forward and holds his hand out to the flames. Dirt wiggles and writhes from between the stones in the floor, slowly covering the smoldering circle until all that remains is a ring of dirt. Queen Sóleyva stands, giving him an approving nod. "Are all of you quite finished now? Because it's so very convenient that we're standing here fighting like vermin when the vampire queen in question is nowhere to be found. Curious, is it not?"

"Not as curious as the Fae working with the vampires," Collin answers.

The queen places her possessive hand on my shoulder. "Something we would not have been driven to do had the *Ulfr* found our artifact. But we have it now, so your incompetence in the matter is forgiven. Now we can all focus our attention on how the missing Vampir queen was *Vasilis* up until just moments before Abhartack's long-lived life ended. Should I continue to spell out your predicament for you? Or are you beginning to understand that the great deal of power you have inherited will do you no good because as we stand here squabbling, the Vasilis do to you what they have done to us. They are pitting every other Ulfr pack against yours. Against your allies. That is how they broke the Fae, severing our great kingdom in half, Seelie in the light and Unseelie in the dark. Where magnificence one stood, the Vasilis sowed seeds of doubt and mistrust, bringing down our unity and raising walls of enmity. They flit about, committing atrocities in the name of Odin and finally, now, we have a chance to stand against them."

Collin's features smooth. In a dangerous way. I can feel his rage coiling tighter and King Riktr's straightening posture tells me he feels it too. "If it's bitterness you're worried about, you came to the wrong place. Keela meeting Abhartack was the end of her loyalty to the Vasilis. Her mate being murdered was the beginning of the holy terror of bitterness she's now become. She's going to serve her bloody retribution upon their heads, and I will be right there with her every step of the way." His head slowly turns in my direction, eyes locking onto mine. "My sister and I will fight with the Vampir against the Vasilis, and against anyone else who decides to align against us because once I'm back in Midgard, I will call to *all* the Ulfr packs and they will race to my side because *I* am the most powerful alpha Yggdrasil has ever dreamt up. If someone crosses one of mine, I will cross them into the afterlife."

Sweat beads over my forehead as I stare into his eyes. I have the urge to look away but I don't. Queen Sóleyva's delicate fingers caress my shoulder, her body moving closer to mine while her comforting magic pours into me. "And here I thought Keela's greatest accomplishment was figuring out how to disappear after becoming queen. Instead, she has earned herself the undying loyalty of the most powerful alpha known to all of Yggdrasil. A wolf without a pack." Collin's eyes cut to Sóleyva and she laughs. "Surely you are not so naïve as to think Keela is giving you safe haven for free? The vampire will demand a cost that's worth much more than you fighting at her side. And you will pay it, if you haven't already."

Beatrice shakes her head. "The kinds represented in this room must pledge to stand together. Not just against the Vasilis but in unity with one another because if the Vampir join us, there will be no bond of faith. If they march with us, they may very well turn against us. But we *cannot* destroy the Vasilis without them. We need the Vampir much more than they need us." She curls her hand over the top of her unneeded cane, casting her stare around the room, meeting each one of us in the eye. "Monique and I have done our part to conceal everyone in this room from the prying eyes and ears of those Vampir whose castle we are in, but Queen Sóleyva is right to question why it is that Keela allowed us to enter Dökkbraek but has yet to greet us." She motions to Collin. "Monique tells me you know something of Keela and her horde?"

Collin's jaw works. He stares at Monique, who fidgets with the end of her long braid. "Dökkbraek is larger than what anyone could guess. Keela has strength in numbers."

I press the heels of my hands into my eyes, trying to stop Erik's Keela-loving reel from playing. Of all the heavy chambers of memories continually opening inside of my head, his are the worst. He had good intentions when he decided to pursue her. Good intention to heal the wounds left on her heart by her first love. Good intentions that meant something right up until push came to shove and the reality he'd been trying to avoid came for them both. "Keela is strong on her own too," I mutter, lowering my hands. "She's deadly."

Collin's brows furrow. "There aren't that many Vampir in Midgard or anywhere else outside of Dökkbraek because they don't *need* to be anywhere else. Their food source is here. Compliments of the Vasilis. Did all of you know Bishop was breaking his own treaties?"

Queen Sóleyva barks another laugh. "You seem scandalized to learn that the high Álfar of Midgard would stoop so low as to play us all as fools, but it is only in Midgard that the memory of his past cruelty has long been forgotten. In Yggdrasil's other worlds, Bishop is remembered for exactly what he is." She moves forward, sweeping her hand around the room. "The Fae have always done what is necessary to secure victory for our people, but these Vampir whose castle we most certainly do not cower in have no such claims. They didn't even fight in the war. Not on anyone's side anyway. They feasted on the dying whenever they had the chance and I dare say they took the opportunity to cause some of those dying states to begin with, but they did not enter the war in any official capacity." She nods to her king.

He steps to her side once more, taking her hand in his. "Since the death of Arsenios, the Unseelie king, my queen has had the privilege of speaking for the Unseelie as well as our own Seelie Fae. An advantage we did not have in the last war because the Fae were split back then. Now we have highly trained armies from not one, but two Fae courts. Without us, Keela and her coalition of wolves and witches stand no chance against the Vasilis."

Queen Sóleyva smiles at me. "And we have a weapon designed by Odin himself, and an artifact that was only ever meant for the Fae." She looks back at all the others. "You stand in the presence of legends. So, the question isn't if we will join you, but whether or not all of *you* will be joining *us*."

A muscle in Collin's jaw twitches and the witches both stare at me. I glance at Sóleyva and Riktr. This was their play all along. Blackmail. Without them, Collin is locked into a losing side and they know I won't allow that. They know I'll give up the Eye to save him. But what they don't know is that I *can't*.

I raise my hands, coaxing the tight coil of faelight to the surface of my palms. Within that light, tiny flames flicker, their warmth spreading over my body. Through it. I glance at Beatrice. Her eyes are wary. I look back at the queen. "Legend. Singular." The flames grow larger, licking up my hands, over my wrists and forearms, burning away the tunic because I will it to. Turning it to ash so that the queen can see for herself what I am.

Everyone in the room backs away from me, gasping as all along my body, everywhere the flames flow over my bare skin, runes appear, like trenches of burning gasoline dug into my skin. The leather of the queen's dagger melts away, the carved bone falling to floor beneath me. I train my flames to the lines and strokes, my body a map of whatever magic the Eye has decided not to give back to Odin. "I heard this rumor that the Fae amulet Collin was looking for was the Eye of Odin. Well, he couldn't find it because I don't just have the Eye, I *am* the Eye."

Sóleyva's head shakes. "No, that's not possible."

I release more faelight, letting it blaze as bright and wide as my flames. "This is what happens when gods mess with fate. The amulet is gone. Dissolved. Running through my veins and doing a heck of a job of using its power to create *me*. A new kind of destiny weaver. So let me tell you how yours is going to go. Your armies fight with us, or I take your throne. *Both* of them."

## ~14~

The light inside the castle is dim but the emotions racing through me are bright. Sharp. Almost as sharp as my vision. It clears with each step I take, focusing like a set of binoculars being dialed in. It's creepy to see so clearly when my brain knows I shouldn't be able to. Creepier to be inside a castle full of vampires. The smell in here is too pungent to be anything good.

I turn the corner leading to the stairwell. By the time I finished making my point to the Fae, Collin was gone. He's probably thinking the same thing about me that I thought about him. I'm not the boy he remembers. I can only hope that I'm someone Leah still likes. I take the stairs two at a time, rushing up to the floor where Leah and Collin are staying. I charge out of the stairwell and come to an abrupt stop. Collin is leaning against the wall straight ahead, arms crossed and eyes feral.

I heed his warning and stay where I am. "You saw me down there, Collin. The Fae are on board to fight against the Vasilis because they don't have any other choice. And you know that I love you. I love your whole family and I will go to my grave doing everything I can to make sure the Vasilis burn for what they did. So tell me what you need me to do and I'll do it. I'll beg. Apologize until you're sick of hearing it. But the one thing I can't do is promise not to let you down again because that's a promise I don't know if I can keep. Every day feels like an alternate reality. A new life." I take a step toward him. "There are all these new people manifesting in my head. Their personalities and powers creating these different versions of who I am. It's exhausting. But the worst part is trying to figure out how to explain all of this to you and to Leah."

His low growl slips under my skin. "Keep her name out of your mouth and stay away from her, or I'll be the one going to *my* grave making sure *you* burn."

His words cut deep, which is what I deserve, but the threat is empty and he knows it. "You're right to be angry, I didn't expect anything less. But think about how angry *she* must be." I slide a hand down the back of my neck, trying to calm my nerves before I explode again. "I doubt she still feels anything for me, but I've had a lot of time to think about all the reasons why I fell for Lea—"

Collin launches off the wall, his fist connecting with my face. My head snaps back and he heaves a tense breath. "She's my *sister*."

I wipe the blood from my nose. There was a time when that punch would have hurt a lot more, and I regret that the crunch of cartilage and bone isn't something I'll still be feeling tomorrow. "I know who she is. Leah's be—"

His fist connects with my mouth. I swallow down the trace of blood and run my tongue over my teeth. He's so much faster than I remember but maybe that's because the last time I saw him punch someone in the face for disrespecting his sister, he was pretending to be human. "I messed up. Trust me, I know. And I hate myself for what I did more than you could ever hate me. More than Le—"

He swings on me again but this time I duck out of the way, showing him how fast *I'm* getting. "I deserve a beatdown from you and I'm not here trying to make excuses for myself because there's not a single good excuse for what I did to Lea—"

His fist grazes my jaw. I spin around him and put my back to the hallway, already moving before her name finishes rolling off my tongue again. "I feel the same way about Leah that I did the night I finally went from being *No Shot Sean* to being the guy who got to make her smile. You can hate me for that and so can she, but I am talking to her."

The tension rolling off him follows me as I back down the hallway toward their door. He's a livewire, the air around us so charged that one tiny spark is all it will take to make this a death match. "Please, Collin." I reach their door. "You know I would never intentionally do anything to hurt either of you. Even when I thought she hated my guts, I was always there to defend her. But the day I arrived at Merrymont, everything changed. I thought I was going crazy, and then I thought I'd already gone crazy because I *stalked* Keela. I wanted to. *Had* to. Then her brothers…and the magic…" I take a breath. "I don't know who I am anymore but I do know that I love your sister. I'll deal with her hating me the best I can, but I need to tell her how sorry I am. She needs to know that I didn't use her…" My voice breaks. "It's important, Collin. She needs to know how I feel about her. *Me*. Sean. The guy who only ever wanted a shot with her."

He stares at me, some of the tension between us diffusing. "She doesn't want to talk to you."

I press my hand against the door. "I wouldn't want to talk to me either. I can barely string a coherent thought together so there's no doubt I'm going to blow this. That's pretty much my record. Every time I see her, I do something stupid." I lean my head on the door. "That thing with the queen today, I was just trying to tick the Fae king off. It was dumb and petty. I don't know what's wrong with me. The one girl I've always been embarrassed of wanting so badly finally gives me a shot and these freaking people holding me hostage inside my own body screw it all up."

He lets out an annoyed huff. "Spare me the pity party. Leah's not even in there. If she was, do you think I would have let you get by me, moron?"

I rip my hand from the door before I incinerate it. "You wouldn't have been able to stop me, *moron*."

His upper lip curls. "You want to bet?"

I ball my hands into fists at my side. "You know what, Collin, the day when you get forced to have a whole bunch of other people inside of you, messing up your head, that's the day you get to judge me. Better yet, the day Odin puts you in prison and plays slice and dice because he's trying to get back his little magic game piece, *that's* the day you get to judge me."

Collin freezes. "Odin had you in prison?"

I unclench my fists, dragging a hand down my already healed face. Collin is the last person I want to lose my cool with. "Yeah, Odin's as much of a dirtbag as the Vasilis are. He had me locked up until one of his Einherjar people helped me escape. She sent me to the Fae queen. I didn't have a choice in where she made me go, and I didn't know anything about what was happening with you until Beatrice showed up." I swallow. "As soon as I heard, I made them bring me here. If I'd known sooner... What happened to your parents and siblings..."

He holds up a hand between us. "Don't. Words can't bring them back."

He's right. So, I take a chance and put my arms around him because that's what friends do. This is what he did for me in the past—he hugged me like a brother would and let me feel that I wasn't alone in my sorrow. I hold him tight. "I wish I'd been with you. I should have been with you. I'm so sorry."

Slowly, his arms find their way around me, the gesture saying more than either of our words ever could. "Why did you leave us?"

The brokenness in his voice sends a crack straight through my heart. "If I didn't, all of you would have died. The Norns showed me the carnage. Showed me what I was. So, when Odin came, I went with him. To give you and…your sister a fighting chance." My throat works. "I didn't know what was going to happen to your family. If I'd known… I'm sorry, Collin. You were there for me when my parents died, and I hate that I wasn't here for you."

We hold on tight, tiny needles beginning to mend what's broken between us.

Collin finally pushes me away, wiping at his eyes. "You still can't talk to my sister."

I sigh. "Even if I say *pretty please* and go find you a cherry to put on top?"

He groans. "I don't know why I was ever friends with such a dork."

I shrug. "Probably the same reason I was best friends with a pompous jerk."

Collin stares at my chest. "You're a weird hybrid with the Eye of a god inside of you. What does that even mean?"

I tap his chin. "It means my eyes are up here." He growls and I shrug, lightening the mood a little more with some humor was worth the shot. "It means that what Leah taught me in the land of Norns has helped me to unlock more of my power." He lets out a hoarse, angry snarl and I smile at him. "I can't not say her name forever. Everything I thought she was that summer she became the face of my nightmares, she's all of that. And more."

"Dude, stop." He groans. "She's my sister."

I rub my temples. "I know. But isn't that a good thing? I mean..." I bite the inside of my jaw. "You always trusted me with your sister before, so if I could figure out how to just be me again, would you be okay with..." His face pinches and I sigh. "The wolf thing. Unless I'm a wolf it doesn't matter, and the one soul Odin didn't harvest for his science experiment was an Ulfr."

Collin's hands flex at his side. "How many souls are there?"

I lean against his door. "No idea. Right now, the strongest is the Fae, but it used to be the dragon. Until Zara stabbed me. Her sword was some sort of dragon blade and it took the dragon soul with it."

Collin's jaw ticks. "I guess that's my fault. I should have trusted my instincts and never let her tag along with my pack. Then she wouldn't have even been there."

A frustrated breath breaks over my lips. "I wish that were true, but the Norns meant for her to be there so she would have been, regardless."

Collin shrugs. "What about Haldir? Where is he?"

I push off the door. "No idea on that one either. But Zara doesn't have her dragon anymore. Beatrice took it from her. I don't know all the details but I saw..." I hesitate. I wish I could tell Collin everything about Zara, Aether's soul, and even Keela. But I can't. Not here. "Everything is pretty messed up. We should hang out in my room later and catch up." I nod toward the door. "You swear you're not lying to me about Leah being in there."

He snorts. "If she was in there, she would have already been out here kicking both our tails." He stares at the door. "Leah...she's not doing good so if all you're going to do is make it worse, then stay away from her. She's been through enough." He looks back at me. "It's bad, Sean. As her alpha, I can *feel* her agony. And it's worse now that..."

My gut sinks. "Now that I'm here."

Collin shrugs. "I don't know. Leah won't talk to me but that thing you walked in on with her and Monique, something scared Leah. She won't tell me what really happened and Monique says she can't, that it's Leah's place to talk about it. I could force Leah to tell me the truth, perks of being her alpha, but..."

But if he does, making Leah talk before she's ready will only hurt her more. *Me* making her talk when she doesn't want to can hurt her more too. I let out a curse. "This is why I'm so ticked off all the time. I don't think the souls Odin stuffed inside me even knew what happened to them until Odin started unravelling his spells, but I still lost all my independence the second he shoved them into me." I lift my hand, showing Collin the flames flickering along my fingertips. "There's this one soul who has the hots for Keela and some of the others are stuck on her because of her allure. It influences them so much that when the dragon first sparked to life, it flew into a rage when I saw Keela kissing Aether. It wanted me to kill him but at the time, I thought I was going homicidal."

I douse the flames and pace away from him. "Now I really am about to go on a murder spree. You know me better than anyone. The actual me.

And you know I would never disrespect anyone the way I disrespected Leah, and I especially wouldn't do that to my best friend's sister." I punch the wall. Cracks splinter out through the stone, my fist the epicenter.

"Holy…" Collin inspects the wall. "What kind of juice did Odin put in you? If the dragon is gone, Fae aren't this strong."

I lean against the stone beside him. Defeated. "It's the Eye. It's doing some kind of piecemeal science experiment of its own, ripping off bits and pieces of Odin's coveted souls. I'm becoming some new kind in real time." I drag in a reluctant breath of air. "It's hard to explain. The souls are still inside me but there are no hard lines between where they end and I begin. The Eye is kind of attacking them, making them less *them* and more me. But the stupid souls can still influence me. I'm getting stronger, though. Better at being what I think is the new me. Which is a whole lot of nothing but ticked off."

Collin is still staring at the cracked stone. "I'm not going to force Leah to talk to you any more than I'm going to force her to talk to me. She gets to make those decisions and we're both going to respect whatever she decides. But good luck. If you can explain all of this to her, maybe she'll finally talk to someone other than Monique."

I lift off the wall, a smile breaking over my face. He rolls his eyes at me. "If she hits you, you're going to take it like a man because you deserve a heck of a lot worse."

I rub my hands together. "Terms of your permission to pursue accepted. Where is she?"

He turns, a threatening growl stalking down the hall ahead of him. "I didn't give you permission to pursue anything. I'm hoping Leah will play her own game of slice and dice with you so come on, she's down in the library where she's been spending her time since you got here. Hiding from both of us."

I follow him into the echoing tomb of the stairwell, palms sweaty. It won't be as easy to talk to Leah as it is Collin. She won't feel better after slugging me a few times. She'll feel worse, and so will I. "I meant what I said earlier. The Vasilis are going to get the reckoning they deserve. Bishop will meet the same fate he gave your parents and siblings."

Collin huffs as we trudge down the stairs. "You get a little magic and now you think you can take on the whole Álfar army alone?"

I cast a ball of faelight above us, letting it grow bright enough to light up every corner of this dark stairwell, chasing all the shadows away. "I don't just have a little magic, I have a lot of it. And I won't be alone."

He jerks me to a stop, looking above and below us. "My…contact in the human village says Abhartack always disagreed with what Bishop was doing to the humans. And my contact also says that humans have started going missing. I don't know what that means but Keela isn't herself. And you're not yourself. Leah is lying to me, and I'm…a freaking alpha now. *The* alpha." He blows out his breath. "I'm the most powerful alpha there is and I'm stuck here in this creepy vampire den. Just look at this place. We're all screwed if we don't get out of here."

I scan our surroundings. "I've been thinking the same thing. This place is Dracula on steroids."

We stare at each other, both our throats working as I try to ask him if he's telling me he thinks Keela will side with Bishop against us, or if he's saying the Vampir are siding with themselves and turning us all into their next meals. His shoulders lift and he nods for us to keep going. "It gets worse. The library is down another four flights and talk about creepy…"

His head shakes. "It'll be a good place to hide your body if you make the rift between Leah and me worse."

"Ha," I mock him. "Weren't you listening? I'm invincible."

His eyes narrow. "Believe me, I can find a way to kill you. There are a lot of spelled blades out there and I'm sure one of them is specially made to kill a god's hybrid who has a gross old rotted Eye inside him. No way my sister is going to forgive you. Odin somehow managed to downgrade *No Shot Sean*. Who would have thought that was even possible?"

# ~15~

I wind through the labyrinth of shelves in the library. Collin wasn't kidding about this place being creepier than the upper floors of the castle. It's below ground, windowless, and the shelves are pillars of carved stone stretching from the floor all the way up to the vaulted ceiling, as if they're what's holding it up. Maybe holding up the entire castle. The air down here is colder than it is above, and it's heavy with the scent of leather. I scan the books as I pass by the rows of volumes that go on and on in every direction, the shelving fitting together like walls of an inescapable maze. Some of the books have cracked spines and others are bound in hides, their textures ranging from smooth to spotted to scaled. My breathing shallows. Leah shouldn't be down here. The candles flickering from grooves cut into the stone aren't providing much light and most of the books are only marked with runes, if they're marked at all. She said she isn't good at reading runes so finding anything down here is going to be impossible for her. Some of the books are even locked behind metal cages, and missing from every shelf is a ladder. Unless you're willing to climb these towering shelves, there's no way to know what kind of disturbing books are all the way at the top.

The scent of earth hits my nose and I follow it through the maze, hoping I don't find a fresh grave dug down here. Voices are whispering from deeper in the library. I focus on the sound, stomach tightening when I recognize one of them as Leah. I pick up my pace, the seams of Collin's shirt pressed to their breaking point. I told him I'd stretch it out but he insisted I be fully clothed when I talk to his sister.

I home in on the male voice mixing with Leah's. "Hang tight, I'll grab the other one for you."

I emerge from the end of one of rows, turning left into another one where I spot Leah standing near the next bend. She's looking up at a vampire who's close to the top of the shelf in front of her. He uses the stone lips as hand and foot holds, shuffling along the edge. He tugs a book from the shelf and jumps back down, landing beside her like a crouching cat. He straightens to a height a few inches above her and hands her the book. "Thanks," she whispers to him.

"No problem." He smiles down at her, watching as she opens the retrieved book.

I don't like what I'm seeing. He's way too close to her and much too smiley. I let my steps fall heavy as I walk toward them. They both know I'm here but neither of them is bothering to acknowledge me. "Leah." I say her name as she thumbs through the pages. She ignores me. The vampire leans closer to her, pointing out something in the text, his free hand feeding around her back and his fingers brushing against her waist. I clear my throat, magic surging. "Yeah, this is going to be a problem for me so how about you two put some space between you?" I let out a ball of faelight, casting a bright glow around all of us. The vampire's dark eyes come up to meet mine. I hold his stare. "What? Scared of a little light?"

He hisses, baring his teeth. Leah snaps the book shut. "Ignore him, Harlan. And give us a minute. I'll catch back up with you in a few."

He dips his head and disappears in a swoosh of air, leaving my too-long hair sticking out in every direction. I pat it down. Leah rounds on me. "The next time you see me, go in the opposite direction."

I cut off my faelight and move closer to her. "You underestimate how impossible that's going to be for me. Especially if I see you with some other guy. I've watched that my whole life and I'm done with it, Leah. I already know what it feels like to see you wrapped in someone else's arms and after finally getting that for myself, I can't let you go. I'm nuts about you."

The growling rattle in her throat catches me off guard. "Is that anything like how Queen Sóleyva was *nuts* about you earlier? Because I'll pass on whatever it is the two of you are offering. Or is it the three of you? Four of you? Two queens, a king, and a liar."

I study the hard planes of her face. Leah is just as angry as I am, and for reasons that are two sides of the same coin. "I promise you there is nothing going on between me and anyone else. The Fae queen probably wants to separate my head from my shoulders right now, and I know her king does."

I don't bring up Keela's name because it isn't fair that Leah doesn't have the same kind of allure the demon has. It isn't fair that I can't have one of those mia mel bonds with Leah like Rohan got with Jofir. I don't have a full understanding of the mate bond but I do know it kicked out Keela's influence, overriding Rohan's pull to her in favor of his loyalty to Jofir. Plus, Collin is right—Leah is hurting and dredging up every detail of the past will only hurt her more. I snatch her book, flipping it open. "What language is this?"

She yanks the aging brown leather from my hands. "It has nothing to do with you. The same way *I* have nothing to do with you. Whatever you have to say, say it to Collin."

I'm not as fast as the vampire but I use what speed I have to close the distance she's putting between us, the back of my hand resting on her cheek stopping her dead in her tracks. "I've already talked to Collin, and you have every right to hate me, but please don't leave. There's so much I need to tell you..." I turn my hand so that my palm is against her warm face. "I'm so sorry for what happened to your family. I wish I was there to help them. Here to help you. I wish more than anything that I would never have let you walk away from me that night. In the most perfect world I can think of, we're together, and we always have been. You're it for me, Leah. You've always been it for me."

She shakes her head, a tear streaking down her face. I wipe it away with my thumb and press my other palm to her other cheek, wiping that tear away too. "It's true, and I'm not trying to upset you, I just need you to know this part. The rest can wait." I lean closer. "I have *always* chosen you. When the choice is left up to me, it's you. Every. Time. Always."

She bats my hands away from her face. "Stop. Your words are *not* true and I don't need to hear anything from you. Not anymore."

I lean back against the stone pillar, trying to hold myself up. I feel her rejection deep inside me and it's making my knees shake. "Leah, my parents were married for a long time and never left each other's side. Why would I want anything in my life other than that kind of steadfast love? I didn't intentionally let anyone come between us. I wouldn't do something like that to you."

"You did!" she screams. "*Everyone* knows what you did with Keela ten seconds after saying all this garbage to me before, so just shut up. I don't want to hear it anymore!"

I taste Leah's bitterness. It's as thick as my own. "You don't understand, Leah—"

"I find that she's a bit slow," says a voice I haven't heard since the day I gave Erik exactly what he wanted and ruined my life in the process. "Maybe I can help the little wolf understand what it is you're trying to tell her."

I can already feel Keela's pull, Erik leading the way to grow the swell of yearning for this reunion with Keela. I want to run. Take Leah with me and the two of us hide away somewhere together. But whatever the Eye is doing to these souls, it's making them more aggressive. Frantic. Desperate to feel the rush of life again. A thrill that only Keela can give them. Not Leah. *My* Leah. The sound coming out of her is savage. Broken. I lower my head, a war raging inside me. A battle of wills.

Keela moves closer and I lift my head, meaning to send her away. To keep the demon away from Leah. But Keela... Her dark hair is longer and streaked through with the blonde from Erik's memories. Tears prick the back of my lids as I stare at her, Erik's memories of her on the day she was taken away from him as fresh and vivid as the wind crashing against the castle outside. He didn't save the human Keela from her fate and for that failure, he gave up his throat to this demon wrapped in Keela's skin. I feel myself reaching for her, the allure so much stronger now than it was before. A slash of fur the color of Leah's hair cuts through my periphery. I pull my hand back but Leah is gone, her wolf disappearing into the labyrinth and taking the scent of earth and sunshine with it. She smells like memories. Dreams. It's no wonder my favorite vacations were always the ones when my parents and I camped or hiked. How could I have ever grown up around Leah MacKenzie and not developed a love for the outdoors? She's the soothing scent of life and I hope when she kills me later, she buries me on a sunny hillside where I can be surrounded by all the things that remind me of her.

A tear slides down my cheek. I rip my eyes from where Leah disappeared and focus on Keela. Her eyes are sharper than before. Darker. Colder. Familiar in a way I wish they weren't. "You look different, Keela. I remember a time when your hair was blonde. Long. And you were human."

Her soulless eyes trace over me. "Then it's true. You are a prison of souls and they whisper untold secrets into your ears."

Tension knots in my shoulders. Not so long ago, I was ready to do everything within my power to be whatever and whoever Keela needed. Anything to be her home the way she felt like mine. The Dearg Dua may be wrapped in one of the most beautiful of human skins, but she's still a bloodsucking demon and I no longer want to fall on my knees in front of her. Leah is the only one with the power to bring me down and she's the only woman whose feet I'm going to grovel at. As much as necessary, because Leah is the sanctuary I've always wanted and never deserved. I push away from the stone and stand up straight. "I'm a lot of things, and one of them is busy."

Keela's too-red lips turn up into a tempting smile. "We are both quite busy. Which is expected. After everything Odin did to bind us both, we are finally emerging. Stronger than we were. And after all this time."

I work to steady my heart rate. Being this close to her makes it spike in an unnatural way. "Odin bound you?"

She brushes her fingers through the ends of her lengthening hair. "He betrayed all of us. But even without memories and an altered appearance, those on the Isle of Misery knew me as Death. *Dauði*." She moves her fingers from her hair to my throat, a long sharp point piercing my skin as it trails along my jugular. "Thanks to the power of my Lilitu, I will once again look how Erik prefers. Will you like that?"

A shudder runs through me. The allure she possesses draws men to their death. Makes them eager for it. As eager as I'm becoming. I glide my knuckles over her cheek. "Bishop rescued you from that island and you became his loyal soldier. Are you still his?"

She lifts herself toward my mouth. "I am a *queen*. I no longer live in darkness. No longer live on the brink of starvation. And no longer abide by any treaties of Midgard." Her lips caress mine, soft and teasing. "Even the ones insisted upon by their High Álfar."

I run an arm around her, unable to stop myself. "Did he know who you are, Dearg Dua?"

Her lips curl up into a grin, showing off the needlepoint sharpness of her canines. "My king knew. My *mate*. Erik's poor rival. But how does Erik feel now?" She slides her nose along the column of my neck, mouth trailing up to the shell of my ear. "We are lovers, bound by the shackles of eternity. Do not fight what you feel. I can hear the unsteady beat of your heart and smell the lust on your breath. Erik is happy his pathetic human life was upgraded and you are powerful. Take what you want, Sean Winkle."

I pull my arm away from her, alarm shooting through me. Fast as a viper, she strikes, sinking her teeth deep into the vein at the base of my neck. Sucking. Her hand clutching the back of my head, holding me to her. Ecstasy shoots through me. Pure, raw desire taking hold. I hoist her onto my hips and walk her back against the bookshelf, body rocking against hers. She clamps down harder, sending chills exploding over my body. A groan slips from my mouth and I try to hold onto the sound. To follow it back to sanity. But there's only... "Keela." My voice is pure gravel, body lost in the bliss of her bite. Her *venom*.

My hips thrust into her and I fist my hands into both sides of her hair, sweat pouring down into my eyes as I struggle to keep myself from stripping her down and doing exactly what she wants me to. I slam her head back into the stone. Her fangs rip free, taking a chunk of my skin with them. Fury slithers across her features and I back away, heart beating out of my chest. "Erik might be fighting with everything he has, but he's nothing more than a soul hitching a ride and I'm not a prisoner to his desires anymore."

Dark lines form under her eyes, the gem at her throat pulsing against her smooth, pale skin. "Erik isn't the only one who wants me. The greedy Fae inside you wants me too." Her tongue sweeps the blood and skin from off her lips. "*Mmm*, I can *taste* his desire. He craves power, and he knows that compared to me, the Fae queen is weak."

My mouth waters at the idea of her feasting on my flesh. *Sick freaking demon venom.* "What the souls inside of me want doesn't matter. It only matters what I want and that's not you. If Collin and Leah weren't here, I wouldn't even be here."

Shadows bleed from her eyes, running down her face like tears. "You stand before me so cavalier. So sure I won't finish ripping out your throat. Much like my king. He never believed I would slit his throat."

My eyes go wide and her shadows crawl toward me, claws scratching over the stone floor. "Did you know that I can feel you across mountains? Across oceans? That even the shadows long for us to be together?"

She smiles, the inside of her mouth like an oil slick. "Before I came to Dökkbraek, the shadows knew me. They knew you. But it wasn't until my king returned me to this homeland that I realized how important you are to me. So, tell me, who do you submit to, Sean Winkle? The Norns? The gods? Those forces greater than even Yggdrasil?" Shadows morph around her, draping over her shoulders to form the wide, flowing tail of a royal cape. Above her head hangs a dark crown. "I am the queen of Endless Night. Do you submit to me?"

I summon my fire, mixing it with enough faelight to cut through her shadows. They pull away from us faster than even Keela can move. "I don't submit to anything other than the love I have for my family, and that's not you."

She cackles, a loud piercing sound that follows me out of the labyrinth. "Leah will reject you, and when she does, you will be at my feet, *begging* for a *bite*."

# ~16~

My hands shake with anger, jaw clamped so tightly that my entire face hurts. Everything I thought I was, and everything I thought I valued, changed the instant I set eyes on Keela. My parents raised me in a loving home and taught me values that were supposed to help me navigate whatever path I found myself on. Only they never expected I would navigate myself into being seduced by a demon in a basement. Or that I would like it.

I rip out of the stairwell, leaving the heavy metal door leaning sideways on its hinges. My nostrils flare, filling my nose with the scent I want to spend my life waking up to. It's ironic that I never realized Leah's scent of earth and sun was what filled my nose when we were in the land of the Norns. Once we made it to the rotunda, I just thought the air was fresher. Cleaner. And that I was finally able to smell again after being neck-deep in mud and muck. Now, I'd give anything to be stuck right back in that muck so long as she was at my side because the possibility of never holding her in my arms again is growing brighter by the second. After what just happened, I can't look Leah in the face and make promises about loyalty. The souls in me are fighting. Trying to save themselves. And because of that, I can't give Leah the one simple thing she deserves. My heart is devoted to her but that does me no good if the rest of me isn't. I'm a terrible choice for her. But that isn't stopping me from hunting her down, and it won't keep me from begging her for one more shot.

"Freaking Odin!" I yell, curling my shaking hands into fists and punching my way through yet another door, still following the scent of pure joy through this stupid freaking castle and remembering all the reasons Leah has to hate me. All the reasons why Keela might now decide not to help the MacKenzie pack anymore. Beatrice warned me and I still couldn't keep my hands to myself long enough not to screw up everyone's life.

Monique is up ahead of me, standing in front of a door that leads outside. The way Leah went. The witch holds up a hand to tell me to stop but I shake my head at her. "Move. Now."

Her hands shake, a faint red glow warming them. "Please, Sean. I know you're upset but so is Leah. You need to let her go."

I call on my fire, tracking the fear in her eyes as I barrel toward her. "How about you move, or I'll remove you. *Permanently*."

Her lips begin to move. "Halls of honor, old and bound, inscribed by fate and forged by fire. The heart once shattered becomes the blade. Wary be he who threatens both glory and ruin."

I let my flames lick higher. "I've heard all this crap before and I'm not in the mood, witch. *Move.*"

She backs against the door. "I can't. There are things here. Spirits..." Her eyes trace the hallway behind us. "I cast a silencing spell before you got here but there's no telling what I might have trapped in this bubble with us, so I need you to listen. We don't have much time left. You may be right to curse Odin, but if you don't get your emotions under control, it is *you* who will curse the rest of us."

I stop in front of her, Keela's venom still burning through my veins. "I'm aware of what kinds of *things* are lurking in this castle. And I'm tired of everyone acting as if I have some great power to control situations I never asked to be put in the middle of when I can't even control who I kiss. So spare me your lecture, and *move*. I don't want to hurt you, but I will."

Monique heaves a sigh, her hands still glowing. "I'm sorry you're the one who has to carry this weight but you're the collector of souls. The *fulcrum*. And the fulcrum makes choices for all of us. Like it or not, you alone have the power to change *all* of our fates."

I can feel the veins popping all over my body, every muscle I have tensing as my magic swells. "I. Don't. Care. If you can take these souls from me, then do it. If you can take the Eye, *do it*. If you can't—*move*. Because changing Leah's fate is the only thing I care about."

Pity cuts across Monique's face. "This isn't about you anymore, Sean. We're well beyond that." She thrusts her hand into the space between us and begins to trace symbols in the air. They sizzle to life and instead of looking at her, I'm suddenly staring into a hearth. Into the flickering fire inside of it. I see flashes of myself in the flame. Haunted eyes. My hands blazing with power. A great rattling glow erupts from my chest and behind it, something ancient prowls, devouring flame and spark, until there's nothing left. Only ash in a dead hearth.

The present comes crashing back to my vision and I suck in a gasp of air, my magic snapping back inside me like a rubber band, coiling down tight and low in my stomach. Monique's runes crumble away, as dead and dark as that hearth. "What in the heck was that?" I yell.

She winces. "That's you…destroying everything. And everything includes Leah." A tear streaks down the witch's face. "*Keela* is your key. Right or wrong, and no matter what any of us want, Odin has been manipulating us into position for a very long time. Keela was supposed to be *your* mate, not Abhartack's. But the Norns intervened and now Abhartack's death has untethered the dark queen. Instead of you binding her, you have created fractures in every bond Odin worked to forge. Your pursuit of Leah has driven Gelby so mad that the Vasilis may never reconcile with us. Even if Odin commands it."

I lean into her face. "Good. Because I'm not interested in reconciling. Gelby can blame anything he wants on Leah, but that family of oversized elves are the reason their precious god is going to lose his war. If Odin wanted an advantage in Ragnarok, he should have worked on cutting them down to size and left the rest of us alone."

Monique chews her lip, staring at me as if she's never seen me before. "Odin's Eye walks in the flesh. The source of the god's fear." Her eyes glaze over. "Wrath is rising. Salvation's end. Seek those things hidden by endless night."

Keela's words stick in my mind. "Endless night. What does that mean?"

Monique slides down the door, eyes refocusing on me. "You and Keela have the power to sway the outcome. The rest of us will face what happens once you make your decision. Each path will come with its own downfall but if you want your burden to be lifted, then you must choose a path. For all of us."

I eye the door. The escape. The path to Leah. "I already have, and I'm sorry it isn't what you want but I will never realign myself with Odin. Or Keela." I look down at Monique. "I'll beg her to help, but only so the world can be a better place for Leah. For Collin and his pack. I'm not in this for the greater good. I'm in it for the good of the people I care about."

Tears slip out of Monique's eyes. "Power is seductive. You already don't know what it is that you possess, and therefore you can't yet imagine what you will become when coupled with the dark queen. And you also have Aether. I'm afraid of what this all means for you, but more so, I'm afraid for the rest of us." She lowers her eyes. "Leah was in the library today because she was looking for books on Ulfr lineages. She's trying to pinpoint the pack her mate belongs to."

My body tenses, senses painfully sharpening. "What did you just say?"

Monique curls her knees up to her chest. "Leah is devastated. Broken. She's been losing her will to go on. To fight. That's why the spirit who speaks through me gave her a vision. Allowed Leah to see that she has a mate. That's what you walked in on when you first arrived. Leah learning that she has a reason to live. I'm breaking her confidence telling you this, but you need to understand that fate has taken this one choice out of your hands. Now you can focus on who you were destined to love, before Keela kills us all."

---

My hands are still shaking, but for a whole new reason. The sound of Leah screaming keeps replaying itself in my ears. Followed by Monique telling me Leah is lost to me for good, snuffing out the tiny flame of hope that refused to die even when Keela's fangs were deep inside my neck. But Monique is wrong about one thing. The choice I have to make isn't between Leah and Keela. It's between me and myself. What I want and what the conglomerate of souls want. Keela offers power that's nearly as seductive as she is. With her, we could rule everything. Eldemar would even settle for ruling both Fae courts via Aether's added magic. But he and Erik and all the others don't deserve second chances at love or crowns. Not when their crusades kept me from my own happiness for even the smallest amount of time. They turned me into a terrible, horrible person and now they get to live inside a body hellbent on finding a way to put them inside of a cage like the one Aether is in now. Odin subdued them once and with the Eye stripping them bare, it won't be long before they reap their own rewards.

I stop in the center of the path and take in the view of Leah. She's sitting on a wood-hewn bench nestled into the frosty foliage, her arm resting along the back of the bench and her eyes fixed on nothing. She looks lost in her own thoughts, and she's beautiful. Perfect. How could I have ever thought for one single second that she was the arrogant brat she worked so hard at pretending to be? No one who smells this good can be anything but pure joy. I open my mouth to say something but I don't know what that something should be.

"Think of all the truth we would've missed out on had we stayed together," she says, breaking the silence. "This way has been much more enlightening."

I walk closer to her bench, moving slowly. Being grateful that my healing abilities have rid my body of the effects of Keela's venom. Thanks to Monique's delay. The witch spent the dregs of her magic trying to erect a wall between us in case I decided to kill the messenger. I didn't, but I wanted to. Just to erase the words I'd rather die than hear.

I sit down on the opposite end of the bench from Leah. "Is this okay?"

"No." Only her lips move. "I'm waiting for someone who isn't you."

My gut has a violent reaction to her words. I don't want her waiting for anyone *but* me, and even knowing her mate isn't here, I want to dismember that vampire she was with earlier. "I'll wait until someone gets here. You never know when a Fossegrim might pop out and try to steal you away again."

She shifts her body away from me, lowering her arm and pushing up from the bench. I lunge for her hand, cupping it in mine. "Please don't go, Leah. I'll leave when whoever you're waiting for gets here. I swear. But there are some things I need to say to you." I can already feel my waves of emotion breaking over the dam I've tried to erect. "Please, Leah. Give me this one last chance to talk to you and then I promise I won't bother you anymore. Because..." My grip tightens on her hand. "Monique told me about your mate."

Leah's hand goes limp, her mouth gaping open. I gently guide her back to the bench, taking advantage of her shock even though I know I'm a dirtbag for doing it. She's practically sitting on my lap. I brush her hair away from her face, letting myself feel her skin this one last time. "I know you're hurting, Leah, and I'm sorry for every time you've felt bad because of me. You never deserved it, and I wish more than anything that we had the power to change our fate because I would cut out all the souls inside of me if I could just keep this one. Me. The Sean you've always known. The one who wants nothing more than to tell you all the things I should have said a very long time ago."

Her jaw snaps shut and her eyes harden. I slide my hands over her cheeks, staring into the scathing look she has every right to give me. "My parents used to fight sometimes. My dad even made Mom cry on occasion, and there were other times when she said things that really hurt him. But they never gave up on one another because that's what love is, never giving up. And I need you to know that I never gave up on you, Leah. I never gave up on there being an us, because I'm not capable of it. I've loved you my whole life."

She pushes me away, tears clouding her eyes. "Stop. Just *stop*."

I drag in a painful breath of Leah-scented air, capturing her legs so she can't run away from me. "None of this is my choice, Leah. There's a battle inside me and it's only getting worse. Odin turned me into a weapon, and I can't control my actions most of the time because I'm at the mercy of all these other people he put inside me. So, all I have are my words. They're all I seem to always be in control of." I run a thumb under her eye, catching her tears. "I hope you can feel my sincerity because I'm not here to make excuses for myself. I just need you to go to your mate knowing that I love you, too, and that I would count it as my greatest honor to be in his place. To fight with you. Make up. Live with you, laugh with you, and fight again just so we could make up over and over again."

A shiver runs through her and I wrap my arms around her, calling my fire to the surface to warm her up even though I doubt the cold is why she's trembling. "For the rest of my life, Leah, I'll wish I could fight with you about you spending too much money on clothes, and about how you don't need manicures when you have claws half the time and run through mud. I'll wish that after I caused those fights, I could be there to make it up to you by holding your purse and carrying your bags while you shopped in Rome. That I could pay for a spa membership where you could get as many manicures as you wanted." I rest my forehead on hers. "I'm going to spend my life wishing I could get down on one knee and beg you to take my last name."

A sob breaks out of her. I slide my hand up her back, letting it get lost in her silky hair. "You deserve my honesty, Leah. You deserve to know that I like you for *so* many reasons. Some of them aren't good reasons, but most of them are the ones I've always had. You're fiery. Strong-willed. You never back down, even when you should. And you never ease up, even after you've won. You're an unyielding mountain of courage, as fierce in your spirit as you are in your heart." I slide my cheek down to hers, whispering in her ear. "The time we spent being tortured by the Norns were some of the worst days of our lives, but you managed to turn them into some of my favorite memories. I'm so grateful for those days, Leah. I love you, and I'm so grateful that you showed me your heart." She cries harder and I don't bother to hold back my own tears. "I'm grateful you chose me even when I was too stupid to choose you back. And most of all, I'm grateful you're giving me this time with you now because there's nowhere else I'd rather be than wherever you are, and if it were up to me and only me, I would be your mate, Leah. Gladly. Happily. For all my days."

She turns her face away. "Do you say these things to her? Because I don't need you to say them to me. I have...a mate."

I pull her body closer to me, cupping her cheek and bringing her eyes back to mine. "Keela has never had me the way you've always had me. You pull me in naturally, whereas for her, it's allure that pulls me in. Odin put a cocktail of souls inside me and they amplify her allure. I hate it. I hate that I have always been the common denominator when it comes to your pain."

She touches my face, drawing her fingers away to look at my tears on her fingertips. I take her hand, pressing a kiss to her palm and placing it back against my face. "If anything in this life was my choice, it would have your name all over it and I would be able to tell you every day, rain or shine, good or bad, that I love you, Leah. That I always have, and that I always will."

She crumples against me, her own mighty dam breaking. I feel the explosion inside me, chunks of concrete and twisted rebar plummeting into my depths. "They're dead," she sobs. "I was supposed to watch over my siblings and now they're all dead."

Her pain tears through me. I hold her tight, pulling her onto my lap and curling myself around her. One way or another, the stages of grief demand we live them and Leah is too drained to stop every single emotion she has from bubbling to the surface. Her hands fist in my shirt, nails digging into my sides as she clutches me tight, hiding her face in the crook of my neck. I rest one hand on the back of her head, holding her there, the sound of her pain sending sharp blades stabbing through my heart. She shouldn't have to experience this kind of sorrow. "I'm so sorry, Leah. You were a great big sister, even to Collin, and I'm so sorry you've had to live through such evil."

The sound of her tears breaks through the heaviness of all the things still left unsaid between us. All the things that will stay left unsaid. I've done enough damage, so I sit here, holding her, letting my own tears pour out. For her. Her family. Us. For all the years I wish I hadn't wasted. This is the place, sitting on a little wooden bench underneath a bloody sky in a strange world, where I get to hold her in my arms for the very last time.

As awful as that is, I want to commit everything about this last bit of contact with her to memory. Her head on my shoulder. Her body curled on my lap. The quiet darkness that makes me feel like this isn't as wrong as it probably is. But Leah having a mate doesn't change anything for me, so if there's a chance that me holding her will ease the ache inside of her even a tiny fraction, I'm going to sit right here and hold her so tight that the shape of her will be a permanent imprint on my skin. "I'm going to make them pay, Leah. I'm going to make every last Álfar pay."

She lifts her head from my shoulder and a pang of fear stabs its way through my heart. I hoped to take away some of the pain of her regret, letting her know that she meant so much to me even when I never knew how much. But I've only managed to make this harder for both of us, and each passing minute brings us closer to that time when she's going to pull away from me for good. I press my lips to her wet cheek. I can't help myself. It's strange how violently my feelings for her clash with my pull to Keela. What I have right here and now with Leah feels so raw. Real. This isn't a god's game. It's nothing more than a man desperately wanting to love a woman. To take away all her pain and sorrow, and spend his whole life trying to put a smile on her face. "Consider all of your enemies dead. I'll be in your shadows, making sure no one ever hurts you again. Just promise me that when you find this mate of yours, you'll spend the rest of your life happy. Laughing like you did in the rotunda. Spinning around carefree when you were playing with those stupid little lights, letting them swirl all around you. I'll never forget the way you looked then. It was the most beautiful thing I've ever seen."

Tears spill from her eyes. "Runewisps. I call them runewisps."

My laugh is bitter and I wish it weren't. "Of course you named them. They sensed the good in you before I was willing to let myself see it. All

I saw was the beautiful person you are on the outside. But you're terrific on the inside too." I tense my jaw. "Maybe one day I'll get to thank the Norns for giving me that time with you. And then I'll kill them for letting us out of there."

"Sean," she whispers my name. I meet her eyes. Fat heavy tears drip from her lashes. I adjust her on my lap so her knees are pinned on either side of my hips. Holding her like this is a need. Not a want. I know that as certain as I know that saying goodbye to her is going to hurt as badly as it hurt to say goodbye to my mom. I would give anything to rewind time, to go back to that summer when I had no shot and force both of us to make different choices. I would have fallen all over myself to be everything Leah deserved, and my mom would have been able to know Leah in a deeper way. And I would have all those years of memories. Knowing Leah's every quirk. Like. Dislike. Everything that makes her smile. Big or small. If I was lucky enough to spend those years with her, I would have been taking notes, so I could be the one to tell her mate all of the things that make Leah wonderful. I brush my hand along her face, wiping away her tears, touching her something I'll dream about every time I close my eyes. "The thought of never being this close to you again is ripping me up inside, but I'd sign up for a thousand more heartbreaks just like this one if it meant I could have more memories of you. Of *us*." Her breath shudders and I lean into her. "How sure is this mate thing? Because I remember you marked me once and announced to a room full of people that if I was turned into Ulfr, you'd mate me. Any chance we can still make that happen?"

She extracts herself from my body with such force that my world spins. I blink at her. "I'm not going to stand in the way of you mate—"

"My *mate* is in trouble," she shouts, flagging a hand at me. "The bond hasn't kicked in but I *felt* him. He's hurting and I'm sitting here with you, dishonoring him before I even..." She runs her hands up through her hair, tugging at it. "Don't tell Collin. He doesn't know anything. He has enough to worry about and if I leave here to find my mate..." She yanks her hands from her hair. "He doesn't want me..."

I get off the bench. "Of course Collin wants you. He loves you, and if I didn't heal so fast you'd see the evidence of that on my face."

"Not Collin!" She slaps my hands away. "My mate. I need to help him but..." Her hands shoot back into her hair. "If I leave here the Vasilis will find me and then Gelby is going to..."

I grip her wrists and pull her hands from her hair before she rips it all out. "Slow down. First off, your mate is going to want you—"

"No, he won't!" she screams, yanking her arms away. "He already doesn't! He's angry and he blames me!" A torrent of sobs rips out of her. "Gelby probably has him and if Harlan helps me escape..." She looks around. "He's supposed to meet me here. Help me get out of Dökkbraek. Monique can't open a portal and—"

"Leah!" I pin her face between my hands. "I'll help you. Just calm down and tell me—"

"Gelby is going to kill me." Her teeth grind. "Slowly, he said. *Slowly*, Sean. So what do you think he's doing to my mate?"

Ice cold rage pulses through me. "Gelby threatened to kill you?"

Grief threads through her every feature. "I used him. The same way I used so many others, because of you. And now my family is gone. Dead! And I'm helpless to do anything for my mate, who won't want me even if I do rescue him because there's no one left to convince him to be proud of my last name." She slams her fists into my chest, bringing them back to slam against her own. "I killed them! I killed them all! Because of *you*. If I go after my mate, I abandon my brother because Collin can *never* leave this awful place. All because I'm in love with you!"

## ~17~

# Keela

This land is a tapestry threaded together not by fate, but the chaos that created fate. A land where streams glow with destiny's harbingers and the sky is painted with pledges. Dökkbraek is the epicenter of primal energy. A place where winds whip with secrets for all who can hear their whispers. The gem at my throat grows warm. I kick Harlan's body over the edge, into the void, returning him to the domain of chaos. The place where my lifeforce is harnessed. Abhartack hunted my sisters and he paid for that crusade with a bond made to Chaos. One that led him to me. Not to rule at my side but to bow at my feet. A servant to cherish. A mate to love. Roles that must now be filled with my new choice of mate. Sean Winkle will feed my ravenous appetite or I will feed his blood to the void.

    A cold wind rises from the depths of the Primordial Void, spraying over my face. I close my eyes, savoring the approval of Chaos. A smile strokes over my lips and I turn to face my gathered horde. Slowly, I've filtered them. Sorted their ranks. Took out those whose minds are not so easily swayed. I am the queen and this land will once again bring life from the Void. We will celebrate the old rites, honor those creatures woven from the night, feasting blood upon them. *Raising* them. Releasing the Lilitu upon Midgard once more.

"Another sacrifice earned," I tell my horde. They pound their fists as one, beating them over their silent hearts in one solid thud.

"The Norns will not stop us," I tell them, basking in the sound of their pounding fists as they echo my words back to me.

"The Fae will not stop us." My heart races to the tempo of their building frenzy. Their pounding fists and echoed words.

"The *Vasilis* will not stop us." Rage pours through my veins, feeding their ire. Bishop will pay for his many betrayals. Starting with his lies about retrieving me from the Isle of Misery. It was Odin who exiled me there. Odin who cloaked me. Changed my appearance. And drew on dark magic to suppress my demoness. Magic the Void is slowly unraveling, returning the Dearg Dua to her rightful position. Bishop did not merely stumble upon me. Odin held me captive on the Isle until the memory of the Dearg Dua was forgotten. Then, when he was ready to test me, to *use* me, he sent his faithful Álfar servant to fetch me.

"The *gods* will not stop us!" I bask in the growing hunger of my army, sending shadows into their ranks, brushing against their rabid shoulders and running down their hungry spines. A testament and a promise. Those who have not bowed to me, sworn their loyalty with their own blood spilled into my mouth, will meet their end the same way Harlan just did. The same way those Vampir and humans who came before him have. Compulsion or not, I will have their loyalty. In life or death.

I raise my hands, gathering the shadows to me. "I am the queen of endless night. Given by your king and crowned by the Void. I. Am. Your. Queen."

"Dauði," they chant in unison.

"You will hunt for your queen."

"Dauði," they answer.

"You will kill for your queen."

"Dauði." Their fists pound.

"You will *die* for your queen."

"Dauði!" they shout, dropping to their knees, fists pounding like war drums. I feed the shadows to them, darkness growing around us, passing over them. Whispering. Screeching. Searching for any hint of one who may be disloyal. I glance to the wrecked body of the witch on the ground beside me. What an interesting find she was. Abhartack treated her well, kept her hidden and tucked away, pampering her to buy the loyalty of her coven. When Kythos revealed her to me, I decided not to reward her greed.

I run my fingers through her matted hair and tug her head back so I can see the fear in her blue eyes. She casts her spells for me now, because she has no choice. The witch only knew to defend herself against the basic mind-bending tricks of the Vampir. She has no idea how to defend against me. And when I compel her to cast for me, I always compel her to remember how badly she hates it. Her spells are sweeter that way. Like the one she's cast over us now. My horde is free to celebrate me without anyone outside of our ceremonial clearing hearing or seeing, and the witch knows the death she witnesses here is all her fault. I crouch and scrape my teeth against her throat, forcing her pulse to race. Faster and faster, so I can hear the swish of terror in her veins, always wondering if today is the day when I silence her heart forever.

I lift her arm to my mouth, pulling it up so she can watch as I take a long, thick draw of her warm blood. Today is not the day I end her miserable life, but my last feeding was unsatisfactory. Sean is now able to resist my seduction. Barely. But he is growing stronger and if I do not rid us of Leah MacKenzie, his resistance will continue to grow. Odin may have created him with this power to resist, should Odin need Sean to oppose me, but the *Void* created Odin. As it created the Lilitu. And the Void does not desire me to rule and care for Dökkbraek as Abhartack did. The Void wants its demon to reign throughout *all* of Yggdrasil's worlds.

I release the witch, tossing her arm into her pathetic lap. I stand and face the horde, ordering my shadows to go as still as the fists against the chests of my Vampir. "Rise," I call to them, scanning the faces of my army as the Vampir reclaim their footing, darkness all around them. "War is coming to Dökkbraek—the land of all beginnings. Even now, our enemies gather in our castle, preparing for a great battle. One fought between the gods and their pawns. But we prepare for the real battle. One where our side is not aligned to one god or another, but to the *Creator*, because it is the Void who spawned the Lilitu and the Lilitu who spawned the Vampir." I slice my hands through the air, drawing runes and filling them with shadows for all to see. Gelby Vasilis spent many years teaching me to draw on the natural magic of Yggdrasil's worlds, and those lessons will be his undoing.

My shadows fade and a window opens. One revealing the interior of the Álfar domain in Midgard. Gelby Vasilis sits in a chair, staring at the wall, face pinching as if he can sense my magic. I crush the window in my fist and smile at my horde. "We may not have the magic of other kinds, but we do not need it. Nor do we need the blessings of their gods. We are the spawn of Chaos. Your queen is a spirit of the night. Woven from the very darkness of the Void. It is my sisters and I who are written about on the ancient runestones embedded into the very earth upon which we stand. We are the spirits you honor in sacrificial feast."

I meet the eyes of my faithful Vampir. Send my desires through the bonds of the bite I have given each of them. "Your king was made powerful through the blood of the Lilitu and he used that power to slaughter my sisters. But your king spared your queen. He *revered* your queen. He became *one* with your queen." I spread my arms wide, allowing my shadows to fill in the spaces behind me where my Lilitu's dark wings once spread. A sacrifice to the broken rage of the body I now inhabit. "Your king gave himself to this land and to your queen. For *this* purpose. To restore the rites of celebration to our great chasm. To offer it blood in place of the mead." A high-pitched wail rises from the Void. My sisters—being pieced together by those whose blood and bones have already been sacrificed. When the slaughter is complete, all of them will live again.

I flick a hand, causing my shadows to coalesce. Forming a writhing obsidian statue of my demoness. "I am the Dearg Dua. The Red Bloodsucker." My statue tips its head back and answers my sisters in a screeching wail. "I am the beginning. And the end!"

"Dauði! Dauði!" my Vampir shout, their voices rising up to join those of my sisters. Those who are the Void's will. I glance down at the upturned face of the witch, tracking the tears streaming down her wrinkled face. "Don't worry. You will live to rejoice in our victory. And I will then personally congratulate your coven on the success of their leader's spells."

Defiance trickles through her, mingling with the hot stench of her fear. "You're evil. Abhartack would never have condoned this. He didn't want to raise demons from the Void."

I disperse my shadows, wrapping them around her and letting them slam her face into the ground. Had Abhartack lived, he most certainly would not have condoned sacrificing the humans. He may not have even condoned changing the strongest among them into Vampir. But his wishes would not have mattered. In the end, he could never have stopped what the Void ordained. I leave the witch crumpled at my feet and move past my enthralled horde. They will stay here, stroked and encouraged by my shadows, fed by their whispers and ministrations, so that when the time comes, my horde will only know the fiend who created them. They will not remember the weakness of their king.

I rest my hand against the jeweled collar Abhartack placed around my neck. He thought the Void offered the precious stones upon this very ledge so that our natural powers could be increased. So the rulers of Dökkbraek would have the strength to protect and defend the materials of Chaos. So that we would never stray far from our duties in Dökkbraek. But the Void only wanted that from him. From me, they want to raise their angels of death once more. Because the Void did not give birth to the Norns. The gods did. And the only true balance there will ever be is when that which resides in the Void. Chaos itself.

I stop at the edge of the forest where Kythos waits. As one of Abhartack's most trusted advisors, I was not surprised by his loyalty to his queen. It took very little persuasion for him to bring humans to me, even knowing I would drain them. Kythos didn't even waste time when I asked him to serve up his fellow Vampir. He recognized what his king did not. That once I reconnected to the power of this land and my demon rose, she would be wide awake with need and want. Ravenous with revenge. Kythos's fist lands on his chest. "Gott Koldv, mi Faugr Dauði."

I rest a hand along his jaw. "Good night to you too, my beautiful Kythos. The Álfar will be here soon. When you smell them, release your newly transformed Vampir. Take them into the village and let them feast. Take the army and let them gorge on the willing and the unwilling. The Vampir will need their strength for the battle." I curl my fingers and rake my claws through his skin, burrowing down to the bone. He doesn't so much as wince.

I smile. His eyes meet mine. "When the Vasilis breach our soil, your Vampir will feed, mi Dauði. We will slaughter the invaders and feed their blood to the Void." His hand draws forward, touching my waist, a pleading in his voice. "Who shall I send for your next feast, my queen? I am here for you now."

I pluck my nails from his skin, licking his blood from my fingers. His eyes dilate and I run my tongue up the wounds on his face, his skin sowing itself back together faster than it used to. Compliments of his gracious queen feeding her blood to her horde. They all have a taste for me now, blood and bite, but Kythos is as unsatisfying as Harlan was. I sigh, moving away from him. Harlan had to be sacrificed. I ordered his attachment to Leah so she would come to consider him a friend, if not more. So I could hurt her more in the end, when she realizes that I took yet another adoring male away from her. "I will source my own meal, Kythos. My Lilitu desires a hunt."

I leave him to command the horde. He will disperse them slowly, and to different ends of Dökkbraek, so none of our esteemed guests will become curious. Not more so than they already are. They believe

Abhartack's death has unleashed my darkest power. That I mourn his death to a terrible fault. But there is no folly in my vengeance. He was my promised king, by Void and rite. Sworn to me as he was sworn to this land.

The wind shifts, blowing from the forest to disappear into the void, bringing me the scent of the one Odin intends to be my undoing. The god wants me neutralized, but Abhartack's faith restored me to my true form, and the power roiling beneath my skin says I alone will choose how Yggdrasil falls.

# ~18~

# Sean

Blood drips from my closed fists, knees and legs aching, curls of guilt spiraling through me as I clamp down on my need to go after Leah. I don't know how it's possible for me to feel so calm in her presence when I have the exact opposite effect on her. The screaming...the haunted look in her eyes before she left me standing here alone in front of our bench...blaming herself for what happened to her family. Blaming me. A rightful accusation. Without me in their life, Leah's whole family would be surrounding her right now, probably admiring her wedding dress and celebrating her big day with her mate. I took all of that away from her. Took it away before I even knew what was happening between us. And now all I can do is promise to stay away from her. As painful as this is, it's the least of what I owe her.

Pricks of agony bubble through my chest, briars of sorrow forming a cage around my heart. If I can't be in Leah's life anymore, I can still help her. I can clear the way for her to find her mate. I can keep her from running away from Collin. He loves her, and if I didn't heal so fast, she would have seen the evidence of that on my face.

I turn away from where her wolf disappeared into the forest, anger rising red-hot from my depths. My wrath won't make Leah whole again but if she's united with her mate, he might be able to piece her back together. He might be able to keep me away from her so I don't break her apart all over again.

I walk into the wind, letting it pull her scent from my nose. I was created to be a weapon, so I'll be one. Gelby Vasilis is a dead man walking and if the Vasilis have Leah's mate locked up, I'll burn their man-eating prison guard to a crisp and feed him to Bishop's jolly old soul.

I stomp through the woods, heading for the faint sound of crying ushered to my ears by the bite of this cold wind. It's Keela. And her pain is real, because not all of the ancient demon is darkness. She has a human soul inside her, the same as me. Together, we could be the most honest lie. Two halves of the same curse. One of us reanimated and used a demon to rip out our lover's throat. The other was born for that demon and used her to rip out Leah's heart.

Keela stands with her back against a gray tree, vines of half-dead flowers hanging down from its branches, sprinkled around her like shimmering stars. The ground beneath her is littered with the frosty husks of those buds who have already given up. They're just as pale as she is, and they crunch under the soles of these soft-soled Fae shoes as I walk toward her. She's wearing a thick crimson cloak lined with black fur, its hood pulled down low over her face, her gloved hands resting against her stomach. I'm not sure when she decided to look the part of a little girl off to see her grandmother in the woods, but the locks of sun-soaked hair spilling out from underneath the hood complete the look. The Dearg Dua is back. *All* the way back.

I rub a strand of her hair between my fingers. It looks like a patch of warmth against her cloak but it's as cold as she is. Touching any part of Keela is so much different than touching Leah. "Are you finally remembering to be in despair over Haldir? The dragon who would've laid down his life for yours."

She lifts a gloved hand and rests it against my chest. "You have not been here. You do not know who I weep for, and how often my miserable beating heart breaks."

I slide the hood away from her face, this fiend of nightmares who is supposed to be my balance. Haldir was her confidant, that was easy enough to see. She trusted him more than the others. And Rohan loved her just as much as Haldir did before Jofir came along. I wonder if that's why she kept Rohan at bay and fed from Gelby. Because deep down she always knew what she was and since Gelby wasn't influenced by her allure, his was the heart she needed to find some other way into. "The time to strike the Vasilis is now."

"I see," she murmurs, face losing its pallor of grief. "I remember my first death. The weakness of my human flesh. The cruelty it endured until my Lilitu rescued it from ash and decay, only to have the gods twist us into powerlessness." Her voice is cold. Detached. "They took me away from my people. My king. My birthright. Bishop deceived me and Odin set you against my own desire to defend my land. And now the beggars have come to my doors, pleading for help. For *my* power to be given to their cause." Shadows warp and churn behind her, growing thick and translucent, like I'm seeing the forest through layers of liquid glass. "I have cause for my revenge, but it is her, the little wolf who even now is looking for a way to escape, who has caused this. She is what brings war down upon all our heads."

I fail to keep the bite of anger from my voice. "You were there. You know the Vasilis caused this, and you know *I'm* the one who brought wrath down upon your king's head. The Norns let it happen. *Chose* to let you watch him die and *chose* to let Zara take Haldir away from you." I lean into her. "Now I'm all you've got. You said I would come begging and here I am. But I don't want your body and I don't want your bite. What I want is your lust for revenge. You know exactly what I am and I know exactly what you are. Deny me, and you're going to end up like your king. So let's go kill everyone *else* who's responsible for Abhartack's death, and for the deaths of Collin and Leah's family. You brought them here as bait. You knew I'd come for them, and that I would give you exactly what you want to save them. But you're not getting it until this war is done and they're safe."

She removes her hand from my chest, plucking the glove from her fingers, revealing talons of thick obsidian nails, sharp and long. "You are weak. Still clinging to virtue. But you have no honor, Sean Winkle. It died the day you reunited with me." She curls a nail against my lip, dragging its sharp point down over my chin and along my neck, leaving a thin burning line its wake. "I can force this bond on you, but it will be much more fun if you participate in the rite willingly."

Collin

I put my nose to the air, locking onto the unseen pull of my prey. The sudden fight with Caroline felt like something that was always there—anger waiting for the right time to strike us both. A warning to wake up and face our reality. She belongs to Keela and when I leave here, I'll never see Caroline again. A terrifying thought. One made worse by Sean's presence in Dökkbraek. His musk is strong, and growing stronger. Ordinarily, my wolf wouldn't be bothered by the scent of any other kind. The human part of me can be jealous but being who I am, the girls I want to mess around with usually want to mess around with me, so I've never had the need to be anything but confident. And Sean isn't challenging me for Caroline. But still, his scent is driving my wolf into a frenzy, making us want to mark what is ours. Caroline. The human who is never far from my mind. Or my heart.

Caroline stands underneath an archway of bent trees and coiling vines, staring off down a path leading to a cul-de-sac of crude stone huts on the outskirts of her village. From the look and smell, this is one of the oldest parts of O'Dearg. I shift, walking on human feet to stand beside her. She doesn't speak. I run my arm around her back. "What are you doing out here?"

She nods to the end of the path where a man in his seventies is bent over, tending to a patch of flowers beside his porch steps. "It's been a very long time since a human has been changed and normally when someone has been granted permission, it's something the rest of us know about. Becoming Vampir is considered an honor."

I scan the hunched shoulders of the man. Now that she's pointing him out, I can smell that he's a newer vampire. He doesn't have that musty closet smell that most of them have. "Maybe he didn't want the fanfare, he just wanted to live."

Caroline's eyes are molten amber, her lips thinning as she glares at me. "He's one of the first who went missing and he shows back up here this morning acting as if nothing has happened. Nothing has changed."

I look away from her and back at the vampire. He's sitting up, leaning back on his legs and watching us. I turn Caroline away and start walking, arm staying firm around her waist. "I'll find Keela later and see what she says about all of this."

Caroline steers us toward a little-used trail that circles away from the cul-de-sac and out onto a path that meanders around the outskirts of the village. She doesn't speak until we're in the thick of the forest. "If you're right, and Keela is turning humans to build up her army, then why not change me? Why take our elderly and our healers, and not me? It doesn't make any sense." She stops and turns to me. "Keela *knows* how I feel about fighting. About being like her. But she's never here so I went to Kythos. I told him that I volunteer for the change if it means I get to help defend my people."

I grip her arms. "No, Caroline. You don't want to be one of them."

She lifts her chin. "Then you change me. Let me be one of *you*."

I pull her to me, my wolf making me a natural heater. I've never seen Caroline dress in anything more than short-sleeved tops and long pants, her feet tucked into a pair of fur-lined boots. It's like she's forcing herself to be conditioned to the temperature, so she can fit in more with the vampires. She respects them and I respect her loyalty to those who have been her family, but a life as a bloodsucker is no life at all. "The Fae queen is here. She's promised her armies for our cause, so we're going to be fine now. You don't have to make such a brash decision. That's probably why Keela hasn't taken you up on the offer. She's probably only being liberal with the older people to help them escape death. And granting immortality to a doctor for the humans can't be a bad thing, right?"

Caroline's knee slams into my thigh. "You don't believe that any more than I do so stop trying to sugarcoat this. I'm not stupid. Keela isn't choosing me the same way *you* won't choose me. It isn't fair! I've been training for this my whole life. Always ready, the way the Vampir are. And before Abhartack died, Keela said she would help me! That she would train with me."

I rub the spot on my thigh that was way too close to the family jewels. Caroline is passionate in her convictions. Courageous. But she's also fragile. She was born into this world and though it seems harsh to me, she's survived because so many other humans paved the way before her, with the help of whatever magic holds this place together. Caroline has never known another way of living. She doesn't even realize that to the everyone who resides outside of Dökkbraek, her home is mostly a myth. A place so rarely heard of that even if I took her to Midgard and she survived, no one would ever believe she hailed from the mysterious land of vampires. "We have things under control. You don't need to give up your life, but I do have to leave soon. Do you still feel safe in the village? I'm going to have a hard time concentrating on what I need to be doing if I'm preoccupied worrying whether or not you're okay. When we leave, most of the Vampir should be going with us. But many of them will come back."

She stares at me. "If I asked you not to go, would you stay here with me?"

Her eyes tell me she already knows the answer, so I give it to her. "No."

She nods. "Then let me come with you. Even if Keela doesn't want me for her army, let me come with you. I'm good with knives and you don't know if the Fae are going to follow through. We're insulated here but the Vampir have always told stories about how horrible the Fae are. How they lie and cheat."

I run a hand over my face, thinking about how Sean looked standing before Sóleyva, a candle of flame, carved and cut with runes. I had to get out of there. My wolf wanted to challenge him and if I did that… I shake my head. "Fae can't lie. So they omit, conspire, twist words, and weave webs that amount to deceit that's worse than telling a good old-fashioned lie. But Sean…my friend, he's one of them. Partly. The Fae can't be trusted but Sean can be."

I slide my hands into hers, choosing my words carefully. If I wasn't so ashamed, I'd be honest with her. Tell her how much her presence in my life these past weeks has meant to me. Tell her that my wolf and I have fallen for her. "I can't make you Ulfr. Keela won't allow it and she has jurisdiction here. I'm in no position to go against her on this." I kiss the tip of Caroline's cold nose. "I'm already touching you, which is something else Keela doesn't want me to do. But how can I be near you and not want to touch every single inch of you?"

She pulls away from me. "So, it isn't about going against what Keela wants, it's about what you want? You want my body and nothing else, and that's fine, Collin. I'm not asking you to marry me. You don't even have to choose me for your pack. If Keela won't change me, you *can*. Because we're allowed to choose what we're willing to give for our families, and this is what I'm willing to give. If I'm not good enough to fight as a human, then *change* me. Let me fight as a wolf at your side and then when this is all over…" She looks past me. "If you don't want me and Keela won't let me come back here, then I'll just go somewhere else."

I reach for her and she backs away. I sigh. "I *can't* change you. Not because I don't want to. There's a big difference in me coming to see you, and me making you Ulfr. One Keela can get over but the other she won't. Besides, there's no time to change you now anyway, Caroline, and it's a supernatural war we're entering. Even if it doesn't explode the way the last one did, you would still be in too much danger as a human. There's not a single scenario in which you can come with us."

She rips the bracelet off her wrist, throwing it at me. "Then here, take this. I have memories of you to keep me from forgetting you, but I'm only human, so I don't have as much time ahead of me to forget about people the way the rest of you do." A tear lands on her cheek. "When you look at that, remember you left me here to die."

I snatch the bracelet from the ground and chase after her. A strong scent cuts through hers. I stop and look around. "Sean?"

He stumbles out of the woods ahead of Caroline. She yelps and I race to her side, putting my body between her and him. "What is wrong with you? And why do you smell like... Whose blood is that?" I grab his shoulders, shaking him. "Where is my sister?"

He touches his bloody neck, eyes glazed and distant. "Gone. Mate. I said no."

Caroline steps around me. "What wrong with him?"

I guide Sean to the ground. "I don't know." I snap my fingers in front of his face. "Maybe I need to punch him again."

Sean's eyes zero in on mine. "Change me."

Caroline snorts. "Yeah, good luck with that."

I growl at her, shoving her stupid bracelet in my pocket before taking a big whiff of Sean. No trace of Leah. The blood smells like...his. "Snap out of whatever you're in and tell me why you look like you just popped out of a bathroom mirror at a little girl's slumber party."

Sean looks at his hands, shaking his head. "I can't fight her. I did it again. I did it again..."

I jerk his chin up. "You did *what* again?"

His hands go limp. "I didn't let her finish. I broke her..." His eyes go distant again. "For Leah. Stopped so she... Leah has a mate."

"What?" My shout is half roar. "Leah has a what?"

Sean's eyes go wild. "Leah's gone. She's going to leave. She's going to find him, he's in trouble and she's going after her mate. You have to stop her but you can't tell I told you or—"

I deck him. Caroline screams. I fist the collar of his ripped and bloody shirt, pulling him up and hitting him again. "That second one was for you destroying my shirt. Now get yourself together and tell me what you know about my sister before I rip your rambling head off." I toss him to the ground. "I'm her alpha. If Leah had a mate, I would know. I would *feel* their bond."

Sean falls onto his back, spreading his arms wide. "There's no bond yet. Monique showed Leah a vision and now he's all Leah wants. I love her but she has him. And I have this *sickness* inside of me. It won't go away." His eyes slide to mine. "But if you change me, you can order me to stay away from Keela. That's how your alpha thing works, right? You can tell me what to do and I *have* to do it. I need you to keep me away from her. Change me." Tears slide out of his eyes. "If you don't, she's going to use me to kill Leah."

Caroline gasps. "No...Keela would never do that. Why would she..." Her voice falls flat as she meets my eyes. She looks down at Sean. "Why don't you already have a wolf? Everyone keeps saying that Odin gave you all of the most powerful kinds, so why would he leave out the Ulfr?" She looks at me from beneath her lashes. "It's a valid question."

She's right. Too valid. I look past her into the memory of my buddy Lance talking about his Greaty G, the ancestor who claimed that Odin was sending demons into his bed at night, using them to try to steal his soul. The old man refused to retract his outlandish stories and Odin struck him dead for the blasphemy. Since that day, Lance's bloodline has been devoid of alpha spawn. They were folded into the MacKenzie pack and no one has thought much of their misfortune. But what if their bloodline wasn't cursed, but diverted? What if Odin knew which wolf would have received their alpha mantle and he used some form of manipulation to steal that mantle? After all, my great grandfather never fought for the alpha mantle and that's usually the only way to take power away from another pack. And as strong as my lineage is, my great grandfather probably would have thought there just wasn't much of a power bump to feel when it came to conquering a weaker pack. "Holy shi—"

A sharp metallic sound booms across the sky, repeating over and over. My wolf whines at the shrillness of it. I cover my ears. "What's that?"

Caroline draws a dagger from her boot, clutching it in her fist, eyes wide. "It's the alarm Abhartack put in for the humans. Our senses aren't as good as the Vampir so the king put in a magical alarm. He said it would be our warning if...if Dökkbraek was ever invaded."

# ~19~

## Sean

"Álfar." I shout to Collin, running alongside his wolf as we race toward the castle, my body still weak and trembling. My mind not fully tethered to the present. It's the blood. *Her* blood. Keela fed me her blood and since then, I haven't been able to smell anything else. Nothing but blood. Keela. She ripped into me with paralyzing ferocity. I was too stunned to stop her. Too on the brink of just letting her drain me to remember that I could never help Leah and Collin if I gave Keela what she wanted. But then she spoke Leah's name, letting me know what we would do to the wolf...and I nearly killed her. If I wasn't already delirious with the fever of her blood, I might have managed to get the job done.

I try again to drag in the scent of earth and sun. Leah is out here somewhere, all alone. I was looking for her when Collin found me but I can't smell her. All I can smell is Keela, and *them*. A minty smell I now realize I first picked up on when I walked through a fireplace into a pocket world of elves. The Álfar aren't close, but they're here. "There are a lot of them."

Collin answers me with a throaty growl, his head down and eyes up. Ears alert. Every forceful exhale is laced with that quiet rage I've felt in him since arriving here. Something that I'm certain filled him once he learned that his pack was slaughtered. He sent the girl he was with, Caroline, to the village, telling her the humans were vulnerable and needed her there to protect them. She seemed to believe him, but I knew what he was really doing was sending her to what he hoped was her own safety because if Dökkbraek is under attack, Draugrkeep is the target. Something I hope Leah realizes. So she can run in the opposite direction.

Flames flick along my fingertips, the sound of Collin's enormous paws tearing over the ice-crusted earth tangling with my thoughts of his sister. Maybe Leah found her way out of here. If she did, then she's safer now outside of Dökkbraek than in it.

Mid-stride Collin's wolf raises up on its hind legs, fur shedding as his limbs contort back into his human form. "Stop," he orders, low and menacing, canine nails raking over my arm as her pulls me to a halt. "Listen. What do you hear?"

I turn toward Dökkbraek. Toward the silence. "Nothing." Now that our feet aren't crunching over the ground, I don't hear anything.

"Exactly." He crouches low and I do the same, both of us moving quietly through the last patch of heavy limbs along the forest's edge. Draugrkeep is three hundred yards away and Collin puts his nose to the air, inhaling deeply. I focus on the rigid set of his shoulders. The tight clench of his jaw. "Anything? All I can smell is candy canes."

His brows crease, a flick of his eyes making me think the Álfar don't smell like Christmas to him. He moves forward another two feet. "What are the Fae doing down there, and why can't I communicate with my sister? I've been calling to her wolf but she's not answering. I can't even feel her."

I move to his side and look down at the group gathered in front of the castle. The Fae queen stands at the front, the sheer folds of her gown billowing out behind her. Riktr is beside her, both of them looking off into the forest opposite where Collin and I are crouched. To their right, Beatrice is on her knees and to the left, Monique kneels, both witches bending forward with one palm flattened to the earth and another raised high toward the sky. Behind them all, Leah stands in her wolf form, safe and alive. I blow out a breath, a rush of tears pricking my eyes.

"Get yourself together," Collin growls. "There's no crying in war."

I wipe my eyes, wondering how long it will be before I have to give him those same words. "Do you think Caroline reached the village yet?"

A deep growl stirs in his chest. "If I know Caroline, she's there, and already has everyone heading toward safety."

We both stare at the unchanging scene in front of the castle. The one devoid of Vampir. "Magic," I say to Collin. "Monique cast some kind of bubble thing around her and me so she could tell me about Leah's mate. I bet that's what the Völva are doing down there now."

He stands. "And they're strong enough to block my connection to Leah. Who does *not* have a mate." He spits, stomping out of the forest.

I follow him. Leah's big furry head swings in our direction, her mouth opening in a heavy pant. She shifts, shouting something to the others. Monique's eyes dart to us and she lowers her hand, picking the other up off the ground. Beatrice does the same and my nose is suddenly full of Leah. A deep, shuddering sigh of relief works through me. What I feel for Leah is undeniable. It's always been there. Strained and battered, but she was the first girl I ever liked and somehow that like grew into love, despite never being watered or cared for.

Leah runs to Collin. He bares his teeth at her. "We need to talk. *Later*."

She turns accusatory eyes on me. I lift my hand to pull her in for a hug but she moves out of reach. "I'm sorry, Leah. I was upset and it just...slipped out."

"Shut up," she grinds. "I'm tired of hearing you say how sorry you are. The Vasilis are here. Focus on that before we all find ourselves apologizing to the ends of their blades."

My heart sinks. I've brought Leah nothing but pain her whole life and even knowing that, I keep right on hurting her. I walk past her, following Collin to where he's confronting Sóleyva. "Where's your army?"

Her eyes narrow on me. "Ask your friend where my army is."

My brows pinch. "How should I know where your army is."

Her hand balls into a fist, faelight glowing brightly around it. "You brought us here, dared to blackmail me, and now not even the Völva can open a portal. You brought us into this nest of vipers and now we die alone. The Vasilis will pillage and lord over all our lands and it is *all* because of *you*."

I look around at the drawn faces of the witches, Collin's presence heavy beside me. Between him, the Fae royals, and Beatrice, a victory for the Vasilis means even more power and control for Bishop. For Odin. "We still have Keela and her vampires. We let them take the lead and we—"

"Look around you!" Riktr shouts. "They are gone. Left. Run off and abandoned us to these Álfar. It was a trap! One you led us straight into."

"An ambush," Collin mutters.

I shake my head, turning to Beatrice. She's the reason I jumped into the portal to come here. She puts up her hands and backs away. "I did not do this. I only knew to bring you to Keela. To Collin and to Leah."

Monique rushes to Beatrice's side, that red glow burning around her hands. A shield she already knows I can break through. "The castle is empty. We sensed the Vampir leaving but by the time we realized they were abandoning the castle, it was too late. They were gone and the Álfar were here."

I turn in a circle, the wind whipping at Sóleyva's dress stirring Leah's hair into a frenzy that's as wild as the one building in my chest. Draugrkeep is the location of the Vasilis attack, and Keela ordered her vampires to abandon us. Because I didn't mate with her. Or because this was her plan all along. Bring Leah and Collin here so I could watch them both die, either by my own hand or that of the Vasilis. She doesn't care either way.

I face the ravine that cuts behind the castle, following it to where it disappears into the forest. "The Vampir are that way."

Sóleyva's voice is cold and flat. "We assumed you were with them. Considering your affinity for the dark queen."

Anger spikes in my gut. "And I assumed you would have already slit your king's throat, considering your affinity for what I have in my pants."

Leah gasps at the inuendo and the queen's eyes fly wide. I tuck my hand against the soulstone that somehow stayed with me during Keela's brutality. My clothing isn't intact, but the pocket holding the stone is solid against my skin. "Where are your guards?"

"Inside," Beatrice answers for Sóleyva. "They're searching the castle for relics or anything that might be responsible for the disruption that keeps us from using our magic to open a portal. That's why we erected the shield. To keep our enemies from learning what we were up to."

"So they wouldn't rush in and stop us from leaving," Monique finishes. "If there's an object that can be destroyed, we'll open a portal and get us to safety. The guards…"

"Sacrifice for their queen." Sóleyva gathers her skirts and stomps past me. "Fae loyal to the crown. *Real* Fae, not traitors who drag us all to our deaths."

---

Draugrkeep's dining hall is massive and feels even more so with only a few of us to inhabit it. Collin is still off with Monique, searching the floors and rooms Sóleyva's guards haven't reached yet. Beatrice and I came back from searching our assigned rooms five minutes ago. Sóleyva and Riktr were already here, sitting on one side of the room with Leah on the farthest side away from them. Beatrice headed for Leah so I chose a spot in the middle and plopped down to stew over my life. To stoke my anger over Sóleyva's accusations. I was always going to come here. Leah and Collin are the only family I have left, even if neither of them wants to claim me. But Sóleyva had a choice. Riktr and her being here is their own fault, not mine.

"The magic here is too deep. Too entwined with the land," I hear Beatrice telling Leah. "Keela gave me permission to portal us all here before and unless she does that again, I fear we are on our own."

"Thanks to Sean's newly blonde girlfriend letting the Vasilis into Dökkbraek," Leah growls.

My head snaps in her direction. "I know you're ticked off at me but like you said, *now* is not the time."

Leah lifts from her chair. "*Now* is exactly the time. Keela wanted you here and because of that, the Vasilis are also getting the head of the Völva coven, the Seelie royals, *and* my brother."

Beatrice stands up beside Leah, her cane as abandoned as her little old woman charade. "The Vasilis have strong magic. They may have been able to break the wards on Dökkbraek and let themselves in. It's possible Keela didn't allow them to enter."

I like this explanation better than the one where Keela is as good of an actor as Beatrice and is joining the Vasilis to kill us. "There are only nine of us. If Keela wants to take us out, she doesn't need the Vasilis to do it. So instead of blaming me, consider the possibility of this trap being set for the Vasilis, not us. Keela could be using us as bait and once the Vasilis surround Draugrkeep, she'll bring her horde from the forest."

"That would give her the upper hand," Collin agrees, walking into the room wiping sweat off his forehead. "Not every vampire can move around in daylight and Keela's been making new ones. I thought maybe to leave them behind when the oldest left with us to march on Midgard, but maybe she never intended for any of us to leave Dökkbraek. She brought the battle to us, where the vampires have home field advantage."

"Then it's settled." Sóleyva's voice tinkles through the room, filled with her magic. "We make our stand here. The castle is ours and should Keela return with her horde, they will help us defend it. Together, we will free the Ulfr and rid Yggdrasil of the corruption of the Vasilis. Then the Fae will inherit the vacated seats of power in Midgard, because it is with our army that the Vasilis will be broken. As soon as our dear, trustworthy Keela returns and allows our portal to open."

Collin snorts, unaffected by her influence. "The Fae will rule Midgard over my dead body."

"That can be arranged," Riktr threatens.

Sóleyva grins. "When I break the Álfar and their magic fades from that realm, who do you think the humans will prefer to rule over them, Collin MacKenzie? The Ulfr who have blindly lived among them? The witches who knew what was happening and yet said nothing? Or do you think they will choose me?"

I get out of my chair. "Queenie, you have the same problem Odin does. You keep forgetting that humans don't want to be ruled over by any of you. So let's get this straightened out one more time. I'm going to help Collin and Leah save what's left of their pack, and the first step in doing that is dealing with the Vasilis. *Together*. Because this infighting only benefits Odin. This is his play, right? Use the Vasilis to keep us all segregated, so no coalitions will ever be able to grow strong enough to stand against him?"

"Then why do you sit here like a helpless fool while the rest of our worlds fall apart?" she challenges. "The eye can usurp the will of the gods *and* the fates."

I pull Aether's soulstone from the pocket that must have somehow been protected by my magic. Or by Aether's. "You and these witches keep saying that I can override fate but so far, since Odin gave me this upgrade, my luck has been terrible. Except for maybe getting my hands on this." I hold up the gem. "Given the choice, do you think Aether would rather his magic stay trapped right here, or do you think it wants to be set free? I don't particularly care, but I do know that I would rather toss this down into the bottom of that ravine out there than hand it over to the queen who *murdered* Aether."

Sóleyva's eyes fly wide. I shove the soulstone back into my pocket. "The days of everyone in this room started being numbered the second you decided to dethrone the Vasilis, so spare me your righteous indignation. You aren't doing anything out of the goodness of your heart. You only care about putting power in your own pocket and that's why you started this war. The Vasilis are here because of *you*, not me." Her glare cuts straight to my bone. I smile at her. "Eldemar is glad he didn't have to stick around long enough to see you ruin our family." I slide my eyes to Riktr's. "And he has no respect for a king who lets his queen make a fool of him. But neither of you need to worry. Eldemar will be gone soon, because *that* is the fate the Eye rewrites. All the souls Odin collected will be gone soon. Drained. And dead." I let my own glare cut through Sóleyva. "I'm all that's left, and I'd love for you to try to make a statue out of me."

Her eyes brim with rage. Riktr takes her arm and she pulls away from him, storming out of the dining room. He shoots me one last glare before silently following after her, the sound of their heavy footsteps slowly fading away.

Beatrice lets out a sad laugh. "The Eye among thorns. The fulcrum, upon whose shoulders the fate of Yggdrasil rests. A beacon of hope. An omen of doom. Bishop always did somehow manage to end up with the most curious collection of children."

"You think Bishop knew what Sean was the whole time?" Leah asks.

Beatrice lifts a shoulder. "Haldir and Keela are not the only non-elf kinds Bishop has taken in over the years, and the gods always claim those things that matter most. And it's no secret that Odin favors Bishop."

Monique walks in, stopping just inside the shadow of the door. "And it's true that we do need unity, but if the gods interfere—if Odin returns—you *must* act first, Sean. You have the power to save us, or to hasten us all to our deaths. But you must choose."

"Choose what?" I yell. "And how? You act like I know what I'm supposed to do but I didn't get an instruction manual so if you have one, hand it over and I'll be glad to *choose* for you, Monique."

A bead of pity spills across her face. "None of us got instructions, Sean. And it's certain that any choice of yours means many will die in this war. But when the strike comes, it will be your mercy that decides who remains."

"A gate opened by memory's blood." Beatrice moves to Monique's side, both of them staring at me like they've never seen me before. "Aether is of the first court, his soul is gone but his magic does live, and it cannot live in your pocket forever. It wants a vessel. So, start with making that choice." She looks to Leah and Collin. "Maybe the two of you can help him decide. Monique and I will be outside, seeing if there is a way to shield the castle from attack. Our magic is inferior to that of the Vasilis, with there only being two of us, but we will do our best to aid you in this fight."

Beatrice dips her head and Monique waves goodbye to Leah like it's the last time she'll ever see her friend. I've heard Leah's wolf before but this time, the sound it makes cuts off my air supply. Collin walks over to her and places his hand on her shoulder. "It's okay, Leah. I'm going to get us through this." He looks up at me. "With Sean's help, we're all going to make it through this."

Her expression is haunted but in typical Leah fashion, her voice is strong. "I have a mate. In a vision, he chased me toward a mirror. Monique thinks the mirror was only a symbol, that it meant I was supposed to see something, but I think it means I'm supposed to go home because that's what the mirror showed me. *Home*." She looks away from Collin. "But I was never going to abandon you. Ever. No matter what Sean told you, if I'm forced to choose between my mate and my pack, I'll choose my pack. Every time."

"Which is what I would have told Collin if the conversation ever got that far." I approach her slowly. "You've spent your whole life fighting for your pack. Trying to protect everyone, even when that choice hurt you. Even when it kept all of us from seeing your true heart. It's time for you to let the rest of us step up to fight for you because you aren't the one who deals in death and destruction. But that's what I was created for, Leah, and I'm sorry I brought so much pain into your life."

I stop on the far side of her table, making sure to keep a physical barrier between us because if I don't, Collin is definitely going to punch me again. "Let Collin take you away to hide, and if you're both able to get through a portal, go. Find your mate and live happy, Leah. All I ask is... Odin stuffed a very specific combination of souls inside of me so they would force me to choose Keela. He created me for her, so that she would be on our side. I've messed that up but I'm going to do everything within my power to fix what I've broken. To make sure—"

Leah lunges across the table, her fist hitting me dead center in the jaw. I jump away from her. "Whoa, wait a minute—"

"No, *you* wait a minute!" she screams. "Keela is going to use me as bait to get Gelby and if she misses, well guess what, then *Gelby* is going to kill me. All because of you!" She throws her hand toward the door. "They're here, Sean. They're going to kill us all, so just shut up!"

"Fine!" I yell back. "I'll stop telling you how to save yourself."

"Don't yell at my sister!" Collin roars.

"Then tell *her* to shut up," I yell at him. "Unless she's picking a fight with me just so we can make up, but I doubt she's going to let me kiss her because of all the things your sister is good at, she's best at denying me the one thing I want for myself."

I head for the door. Collin's hand wraps around my bicep. "Where are you going?"

I yank free of him. "I'm going to go be this weapon everyone keeps telling me I'm supposed to be, like I was given some sort of blueprint on how to save the world when all I've actually been given is a whole lot of misery."

He follows me. "You don't have to do this alone. We all just need to calm down and start making a plan. The Vampir are to our east and the Álfar to the west…"

He stops walking. I turn toward the window he's staring out of and find out why. A cloud of mist is rising above the trees to the west, blades of light sparking within it. Sizzling strands of crackling blue vines and explosions of bright red piercing the darkness like a tempest in the middle of an even greater storm. "What is that?"

"The Álfar," Collin whispers. "The Vasilis didn't come here to fall into a trap. They came with their army…expecting war."

# ~20~

The wind outside Draugrkeep rushes back to us, away from the coming storm, turning warm where once only its icy fingers blew. I stand shoulder to shoulder with Leah and Collin, Beatrice and Monique out to the side of us, and the four Fae stringing out beside them. All of us facing the sharp promise of death that blows our way. Death coating the wind with the thick scent of candy cane as it tears past us, retreating back to the safety of the void it came from. "I need to tell you something, Sean." Collin's voice is hoarse as we watch a series of streaks break from the eye of the storm, embers of lightning and fire shooting across the haze of the darkening sky.

"Can it wait?" I ask, tracking the three Álfar barreling toward us, their bodies wreathed in blue vines of crackling magic and the long beaks of the creatures underneath them flickering like Rudolph's nose.

"Yeah, I guess," Collin answers. "Probably not important anymore...considering..."

"Don't go there," I admonish as the Álfar thunder toward us, riding those avian beasts I saw them on at the Völva compound. The ones whose crimson wings are covered in iridescent scales. "This isn't the fairy tale we die in."

Leah's fingers brush against mine, startling me almost as much as the army hovering just off to our west. I look down at her but she pulls her hand away, her focus straight ahead. I turn to Collin. "Take her. Take everyone and run. Go to Keela and tell her to let you out of here. Tell her that if Leah dies, she's next. But if she lets all of you get to safety, then I'm hers. For good."

"No," Leah chokes out. "Bishop is sending a delegation so maybe we can negotiate—"

"I'll hear his demands." Sóleyva moves around her guards and heads out into the yard to meet the Álfar. "The Fae can accommodate whatever it is that he wants."

Collin rushes toward her. "More like the Fae will strike a deal to save their own hides and feed the rest of us to the Vasilis."

Riktr and Vigmund head for Collin, Toreyn drawing his sword as if he's standing guard to stop the rest of us. I hit him with a blast of faelight and send another bolt blasting into the ground at Sóleyva's feet. She jumps and spins on me. I walk toward her. "We don't have time for this, and without Keela, not even *you* have anything to negotiate with. So, leave. Run. I'll hold the Álfar off for as long as I can but all of you need to go. *Now*."

"We're not leaving you by yourself!" Leah screams, tears in her eyes. But even she knows the touch she just gave me was meant to be our last. A parting gift. One I won't accept if it means parting in death.

"Take. Her," I growl at Collin. "If Leah gets hurt—"

"It will destroy us both." He snatches his sister around the waist, keeping her from getting to me.

I turn away, letting flames bleed from my palms, Fae magic skimming along my fingertips. I move past everyone, meeting the three riders descending from the sky, banners of blue with three interlocking triangles marked in gold unfurling behind them. It's the same symbol Merrymont uses for their logo. One day, I'm going to find out what that is and what it means, but for now, I'll just give the Vasilis the reunion they're looking for.

Beatrice and Monique begin to chant, their voices low. A faint red shimmering wall pulses out behind me just as Rohan lands, the clawed feet of his giant bird digging into the earth as it comes to a running stop a dozen feet away from me. Gelby lands next, flanking Rohan's left side while Jofir lands to Rohan's right. They're each clad in armor, their chests protected by breastplates adorned with intricate engravings of mythical beasts and ancient runes—imagery that reminds me of the mural I saw in their house. Rohan dismounts, his armor moving like skin stretched over muscle. Gelby jumps off his ride next, eyes looking past me. I don't have to follow that narrow-eyed stare to know it's Leah he's locked onto. I send my flames higher, drawing his attention. "See something you like? Because everything here is *mine*. But I'm happy to fight you for it."

"Come to me, Leah," Gelby calls out to her, his vines of magic popping against his skin. "I'll shield you from our march on Draugrkeep and let you watch them all die from the comfort of my arms."

"You're sick!" she screams.

"Because of you," Rohan defends, looking at each of us. "*All* of you. Your sedition has pushed my brother to his brink and it has brought my father here, to march against the whole of Dökkbraek. Against *Keela*." He zeroes in on me. "Odin could not break the bonds of this fate because you would not follow orders. But it is not too late. Odin has revealed all to us. Submit to our authority and those gathered here will live to see another day."

I pull my flames down to a simmer. "If Odin sent you to fetch me, then guarantee the safety of everyone standing behind me for a lot longer than one day. Make it safety for the rest of their natural lives and you've got a deal."

"No!" Leah shrieks.

Gelby smiles at the sound of her fear and I send a bolt of faelight spearing for his head. "Right after I kill him."

Gelby breaks my magic apart with the flick of a finger and Jofir jumps off her mount. "Do not be a fool," she hisses through clenched teeth. "This is madness and you have the power to stop it."

"Don't do it, Sean," Collin calls out. "They're as bad as the Fae when it comes to deals. They'll find a way to break the pact and without you…"

Gelby tsks, walking forward. "You choose your bosom buddy over your pack, alpha? And here we brought them all with us to make a trade I warned my father you would be too stupid to make."

The storm cloud they broke off from splits open behind him, a great white beast stomping from its center. Bishop's horse strikes its eight legs against the air, its wings beating downward in heavy strokes. "Sleipner," Sóleyva breathes, her voice full of reverence and awe. The horse turns, giving us a view of the rune-etched sleigh he pulls, the heavy iron body hovering midair. The back of it is full of familiar faces. People I've known as Collin and Leah's extended family of aunts, uncles, and cousins.

A whiff of agony hits me, Collin's jaw snapping as he rushes forward, fist hitting against the red haze of the barrier the witches erected between them and me. "What did you do to them? Why can't I talk to my pack?"

"Your mindspeak is blocked," Rohan answers while I train my eyes on Sleipner's rider. Even from this distance, I can feel Bishop's red-eyed stare on me. With another member of his army pulling out in front of him, it's no wonder human minds so easily believe Bishop's lies of Santa's sleigh being pulled across the sky by magical reindeer. From here, they almost look the part. A grotesque rendition of a winter tale.

"Let them go," I say to Rohan, eyes still locked on Bishop's red gaze.

"Make us," Gelby challenges. "Come on, Sean, show me what you've got."

"Cut it out," Jofir scolds. "Your stepmother is coming and you know we are not to engage until Sihoma gets here."

A bolt of lightening strikes behind them and a woman who looks as much like Mrs. Claus as Bishop does Santa, lands just off to Gelby's right. And she's not alone. "Lance!" Collin and Leah shout in unison.

"What have you done to him?" Collin's snarl is guttural and wet, a bull foaming at the mouth, ready to charge.

Lance's head is down, his hands in front of him, bound with rings of sizzling blue light. "They..." he rasps, trying to speak. Gelby backhands him. Lance falls to the ground and Leah screams for Monique to drop the wall.

"No!" I send a line of flame moving out behind me but it does no good. The red wall comes crashing down and it's all I can do to restrain Collin, relief flooding through me when I see Leah stuck to the ground, her face red and sweat beading across her forehead as she fights the unseen force, trying to take a step.

Something hits my foot and I swing around. Sihoma walks toward us, my oversized blue and gray duffle at my feet. The one I haven't seen since I was in her big white house. "All of your personal belongings are there, and you will have a place in our home, as one of us, if you come with me now." She gives Collin a sad smile. "Your call is powerful enough to override even that of another alpha, so you understand that we had to take precautions."

"Let them go," he roars.

I kick the duffle that holds the blanket my grandma quilted for me when I was thirteen, sending it skating back toward her. "Do what he says. Send Lance to us and let the rest of the Ulfr go, and I'll consider not ripping Gelby's ugly head off his body until tomorrow."

"Why wait?" Gelby drags Lance up off the ground. "The Vasilis don't cave to demands, we break bones."

Lance's body begins to shake and Collin breaks free, racing for his friend. His packmate. Gelby throws Lance forward and Collin skids on his knees, scooping Lance's head into his lap. "You're going to be okay, I've got you—"

Lance's hand shoots up, wrapping around Collin's throat. "Or do I have *you*, alpha?"

Leah breaks whatever hold Collin had on her and runs for him. I intercept her, arms around her waist, holding her back as Collin rips Lance's hand from his throat, glaring at Gelby. "I'll kill you for whatever you did to him."

Gelby laughs. And so does Lance. "He didn't do anything but offer me what you're too stupid to take." Lance rolls to the side, away from Collin as he climbs to his feet. "All you had to do was turn yourself in, but you've always been too far up Sean Winkle's backside to be the leader our pack needs. So, I *challenge* you, Collin MacKenzie. It's time you give back what your family took from mine."

"What?" Leah's screech rakes over my ears. "Are you crazy? He was going to make you his second!"

Lance's lip curls up at her. "And I was going to make you my mate, but then you turned into a sloppy—"

Collin decks him, shifting mid-punch and bowling Lance over. The sudden explosion of fur sends the birds the Vasilis rode in on into a squawking, screeching frenzy. Lance shifts and the creatures go airborne, feathers and scales darting around the two massive wolves who are ripping each other apart.

"No! No, no, no, no, no." Leah shouts the word she's been screaming a lot lately, horror-stricken as she watches her brother fight a long-time friend who just went from hostage to traitor in less time than it took for these birds to begin pecking at us. The Fae fight them off, the queen's magic streaking through the air in radiant bursts of light while her king sends roots hurling up from the frozen ground to wrap around the clawed feet and wings of the creatures, bringing them crashing to the earth where Vigmund and Toreyn slice off their heads. I drag Leah backward, out of the building pandemonium, sending my flame coursing over my body and out along hers, letting it shoot high enough to deter the birds. More and more of them swarming us, Bishop's army arriving in organized units to back up his sons and his wife.

"What are you doing?" Leah kicks and claws as I pull her back toward the castle. "Let go of me. Collin!"

"Stop it," I growl into her ear. "He'll hear you and get distracted. Let your brother fight. He's strong, so just let him fight."

"But," she whimpers.

"I know," I whisper, holding her tight and secure against me. Lance challenging Collin means Lance becomes alpha if he wins...and Collin will be dead. It means Lance becomes Leah's alpha, and then her pack will fight against me. *Leah* will fight me...on the side of the people who murdered her family.

I run my nose along her ear, filling up on her scent. "We can't stop what's happening so let it play out. The Vasilis won't fully attack until it's over because that would make Lance's win null and void. He wouldn't become alpha if they help him win, right?"

She nods and I plant a kiss behind her ear. Lance is fast. Faster than Collin. But Collin is stronger, and he's smarter. His blows are fewer in number but they're doing more damage than the ones Lance is giving to him. Collin will win this fight...if he can hold on long enough. "I'll intervene if I need to. I'm not going to let your brother die today."

"Stop." She squirms in the only arms she's ever had any business being in. "What are you doing? Sean, *stop*."

I lift my eyes to where Gelby is watching us and tighten my hold on her, not giving her an inch of space, my mouth working over her neck. I didn't even realize I was trying to devour her, but it makes sense that in a time like this, I would crave her. Only when I touch Leah do I feel like I'm settled in my own skin. Like I know who I am and exactly what I want. I nuzzle her earlobe, an urge to bite her gurgling up through my belly. She goes still in my arms. I melt around her, eyes still locked onto the purple-faced Álfar enraged with envy. The Seidr Collin spoke to was right about one thing—bitterness is going to destroy us all. "The only peace I ever have is with you, Leah. But I'm not meant for peace. I'm meant for war. And I'm going to kill Gelby for you." I bring her mouth around to mine. "You are my pack. Never forget that." I sweep my tongue over hers, getting one small taste of her lips before she bites down hard enough to make me bleed. I spin her around. "I hear the death rattle, Leah. *Run.* And don't look back."

I shove her toward the castle as hard as I can. She skids and stumbles, tripping over her own legs to land hard on her knees in front of the castle doors. I turn and race toward Gelby, catching sight of Lance's now human body lying on its back, blood pouring from the open wounds all over it. His palms are up, mouth pleading with the gray wolf standing over him. "Mercy? Mercy, please?"

Collin shifts back to his human form. "No." His bare fist plunges into Lance's chest and Gelby lifts his arms over his head, bringing lightning down from the heavens. The ground shakes and the Völva shout words that tickle a spot in my memory. Old words. Ones that represent the past, present, and future. Life, death, and rebirth.

A pulse of red light ripples across the battlefield, striking against Gelby's magic. Shattering it. I launch myself at him. He flips away, twin vines of blue magic tearing from his hands, crackling like whips as they slice through the space between us. I veer off to the left and they slam into the ground where I'd just been, earth erupting in a shower of frozen shards. I throw a spear of faelight at his throat and Gelby retaliates with a blistering boom of magic that rips skin from my face and arms. We're too close to each other now. Every burst of magic is going to hit its mark and like Collin, I'm just going to have to be strong enough to hold on.

I sweep Gelby's legs out from under him and he throws a magic bomb straight into my gut. I slam my hand against his breastplate and send a pulse of faelight into it. He bucks forward and rams his foot into my bloody jaw, following the blow with an uppercut of sizzling hot magic. The vine grabs hold of my chin, snapping and burning. I throw magic into my hands, ripping the vine free, Gelby's magic shattering into sparks under my grip. He gets to his feet and spins, sending another direct hit into my face. I charge, using some of Ilda's brute force maneuvers to smash a burning elbow into the side of his skull. He buckles and our next blows meet in a violent collision, light detonating outward in a shockwave that stuns us both. Him more than me. "That's what arrogance gets you." I knock him onto his back and kneel on his chest, covering his nose and mouth with my hands, willing my magic to pour inside him. To cook him from the inside out. His eyes go wide, his daddy's army descending from the sky all around us. One. Four. Seven. Eighty. All of them too late to save him now.

Vines of Gelby's magic crawl out of his hands, striking against me like vipers. I force my faelight out of my pores, leaving his vipers to hiss and die. I smile at him. "I'd love to give you the slow death you promised Leah, but there's no time to enjoy that now."

A ball of brown fur slams into me, Leah knocking me off Gelby. I twist back around. Her massive jaws clamp down on the arm Gelby has his wand buried in. He yells out and she shakes her head, his bones crushing underneath her bite. His magic flares wildly and Leah's body jerks like she's having a seizure. She's trying to enact her own revenge and she's getting herself killed in the process.

Rage sears through me. I yank Leah's body off Gelby's, breathing fire out of my mouth like there's still a dragon inside of me, spewing it over the Álfar coming to Gelby's aid. They flail, my fire burning through their armor and turning their winged beasts into bonfires. I drag Gelby from the ground, bringing him to stand with his back in front of me, my own magic sizzling and sparking. Just like his. I lean into his ear. "I'm not just Fae. Odin gave me one of you too." I pull his back flush against my chest and wrap my arms around his throat, feeling his magic leak from him and into me. Meant to harm. But Gelby has nothing left. My flame is inside of him and the more I will it to burn, the sooner this ends.

I turn us with cruel precision to where Sleipner's hooves thunder overhead. Magic bleeds from Bishop's staff, rolling down like a dark red fog of death, charging over the ground to save his son. I hold his stare, Gelby tight in my arms, his body thrashing where his father can see the fruit of his own choices. Power corrupts, and Bishop did everything he could to get more of it. So did Gelby. And this is how that's working out for him. "I hope you make it to Valhǫll, Gelby. If you do, tell Natalie I said thank you, and tell Odin that he can still kiss every inch of my backside." I squeeze Gelby's neck harder and harder, tightening on him like a python. I don't let go until his body crumples to the ground and his head falls off to the side.

I point at Bishop. "You're next."

## ~21~

All around us, the air is thick with ash and sulfur. Earth and blood. So thick it coats the back of my throat. That, and guilt. But not regret. I ease down to kneel beside Leah's healing wolf, eyes tracking out over the silent battlefield, watching the trees with the same rapt attention as everyone else. The echoing howl of bloodlust is growing louder. The scent of death stronger. It's everywhere. Coming at us on the cold wind that's once again rising from the void. Seeping up from the soil. And settling down onto us from the sky above. The trees rattle and creak, the forest groaning as a lone figure breaks from its grip, racing into the open with long, wild strides. Her hair is matted with dirt, clothes torn, and face splattered with blood. Behind her, the forest swells, limbs coming alive with a swarm of bodies. Thousands. Crimson-eyed, and looking out into our frozen silence.

"Collin!" Caroline's scream cuts through the hush like shattering glass. His wolf howls in answer, the sound overwhelmed by the vampires now beating the rhythm of death upon their chests. Their fists slam as one, the trees shaking. Ground quaking. More and more of them pour from the forest, forming row after row…line after line.

Collin tears across the frozen earth, a phantom of gray fur as he rushes for Caroline. I lift Leah to me, holding her still as her brother races toward the wall of darkness billowing over the treetops. It grows across the sky, blotting out the aurora. Spreading. Widening. Turning the battlefield into the pitch of night. The Fae send up orbs of light, illuminating the patch of ground around them—where Toreyn's body lies twisted and broken.

Collin reaches Caroline just as another lone figure peels away from the forest, walking out beyond the lines of Vampir, her cloak of shadow flowing behind her and a dark crown tall upon her head. "The queen of eternal night," I whisper.

"She came," Leah breathes. "Keela came to save us."

I press my hand to Leah's soft cheek. She winces, curling an arm around her middle. "Go, Sean. Go to Keela." She pulls my hand from her face and sits up. "Save my brother, like you promised."

I wipe a blood-soaked tear from her cheek. "You cared about Gelby—"

She slaps my hand away. "I… You did the right thing. Gelby would have killed us. So, just go. I'm fine, but Collin isn't."

I tilt my head toward the castle. "Hide in the library. No one but me will ever find you down there."

She gingerly climbs to her feet, turning toward the castle. I watch her take three steps before I turn and take three steps of my own, toward the darkness. Away from Leah. "Sean," her voice is raw. I stop but don't turn around. If I do, I won't make the choice that's best for all of us. "You're my pack too."

I bite down against the inside of my cheek and walk, opening my senses up to Keela, but all I can feel now...all I can smell...is Leah. Leah *everywhere*. I pass by Monique and Beatrice, the two witches holding hands while we all watch my dark queen lift her hands. The first wave of her Vampir surge forward, frenzied with bloodlust, ripping into the Álfar with the remnants of the people Caroline called family still smeared across their faces.

The copper stench of death meets the screams breaking out across the battlefield. A band of Álfar take out a trio of Vampir only to then turn their fire on the Fae who are now fighting two enemies. I run toward them, heading straight for the axis of darkness beyond them, surging fire from my hands and letting it mix with the golden hue of my faelight that now sizzles with faint blue vines. My Álfar magic isn't strong because Odin didn't want to weaken his favored kind, but whether that Álfar wants to lend me his magic to use against his own or not, the Eye has taken it from his poor soul and now it's mine. I tear into his kinsmen's ranks, clearing my own path, and helping to keep the remaining Fae alive. Keela isn't here to save them. The Dearg Dua came to destroy.

"Eyes up!" Riktr's voice roars above the screeching clamor of battle, the warning nearly lost beneath the thunder of wings and hooves. Sleipner circles above me, Bishop's staff pointed down at my head. A thick band of red magic hits me full force, throwing me back. Driving me down into a crater of exploding earth. I sling a sizzling ball of fire toward his horse but Sleipner evades it, shattering the ball against the iron sleigh where Collin's pack huddles together.

Bishop comes around on my other side, hitting me again. His magic wraps around my throat in a tight, smothering bow. Constricting. Burning. Another thick band leaps around my chest, tying my arms to my sides as his magic chews into me, crushing the breath from my lungs. "You don't get to walk away from fate," his voice booms. "And you do *not* get to live after murdering my son."

His magic crushes my windpipe, lifting me into the air and throwing me out behind enemy lines. Right into the thick of his raging army. My magic surges, healing bones and bruises as it flares bright. I tackle the first Álfar dead center, driving everything I have into him—body and magic alike. His armor hisses and another band of magic snaps around my ankle, yanking me off the downed elf. A third blow hits me in the side of the head. Blood flings out of my mouth and I follow it around, spinning with a spray of magic and fire, willing even the frozen ground to burn. Some Álfar and their feathery scaled fiends catch fire while others succumb to the strength of my magic, but still, they keep descending. More and more to fill the spots of those they've lost.

The darkness above us moves, the sky as alive as the pounding crimson-eyed forest. Spears of midnight slice down into necks and arms, another great wave of Vampir swarming over the ground and launching from treetops. The Álfar surge forward, the battle cry on their lips adding to the erupting chaos as they beat back the bloody swarm. Vampir hang from the warriors' feathered mounts, dragging them and their unlucky riders down to disappear beneath a waiting pack of frenzied fangs. More Álfar pour their magic into their front lines, vampires exploding all around them like gorged ticks. And around me, shadows swarm, crawling up my legs and arms, a form solidifying in front of me. Keela smiles, whipping around to send her blades slicing into Bishop's back.

Sleipner turns, hauling his burdens out in a wide arc. Bishop's eyes land on Keela. Her shadows wrap around him like chains, throat and chest, squeezing Bishop they same way his magic buckled me. Light bursts from his body, his magic hurling her shadows back to the dark folds of sky they came from. He counters her next strike and my head snaps to the sound of Collin's wolf, yelping and snarling, lashing out at the ring of Álfar descending upon him and Caroline from the sky. They hit his body with throbs of magic and drive the beaks of their mounts through his fur. Caroline kicks and punches from beside him, sobbing as he does his best to keep her from being killed. A furious roar spirals down into my gut, from Leah's mouth to my ears. She's on her back, ten yards behind Collin, pinned down by two Álfar and their pecking mounts. Bishop is killing them slowly. The way Gelby promised.

I race for Leah. Keela's claws rake across my back, her words cold and brittle against ears that only care to hear Leah's voice. "Hopeless fool, you run to your death."

"Erik is dead," I tell her lingering shadows. "He was a coward. You killed him for it and so did I. The end. Romance over."

I weave through torn and wrecked bodies, jumping over mounds of feathers and scales, the ground littered with Álfar. Vampir. And Vigmund. Riktr and Sóleyva have fallen back to the castle doors, Beatrice and Monique with them, a wall of brittle protection around them. Protection Leah should have been behind, safe in the belly of the castle. For however long she would be.

Fire surges from my palms and I lift a blazing hand to the sky, launching a volley of shots as I dodge incoming strikes. Leah rakes a claw through the soft underbelly of one of her attackers, bloody entrails spilling down on her. Caroline screams and Collin's snarl rips out of him again, but this time, the sound is desperate. He's hurt. And Collin can feel that Leah is too.

I clear the air around the wolves, magic quaking out of me and snaking off in every direction, striking the Álfar down and setting their birds ablaze. A band of Vampir blur across the battlefield, swarming over the dying Álfar. Diving for Collin. Caroline. Racing for Leah. I strike out again and my magic dissolves against a growing cloud of shadow. It billows down from the sky, hanging low over the battlefield. Beatrice screams, the sound cut off in a wet, spluttering gurgle. I keep moving. Leaving Beatrice behind, her body to lie in rest with Toreyn and Vigmund. Relieving Zara of her oath to come back to witness the old witch take her last breath.

Sparks of blue tint my fire and faelight, crackling over the shadows. Penetrating the darkness only to be covered over again. Sóleyva's bright magic joins mine and Riktr's roots crash up through the ground, ripping through the holes we create before the shadows regroup. He grabs Leah first, yanking her back through the darkness while another root twists around the head of the vampire lunging for her. Sóleyva hits the darkness in the same spot as me, creating another gap for Riktr to see through. He guides his roots to Collin, whose wolf is curled around Caroline. He yanks them both from the swarm of Vampir, hurling them out of the darkness and back toward us. I hit the dirt, arms shoving underneath Leah as Riktr pulls her to me. I tilt her wolf up to my chest, my feet already regaining ground, our whole group banking right as the cloud of darkness dissolves only to reform at our backs, the sound of it chewing over the ground more terrifying than the Vampir charging at us from the left.

Leah shifts back into her human form, her body slick with blood. "He's coming," I tell her, knowing she's looking at where Collin is back on his feet and dragging Caroline along with him as they race hand in hand toward the same place we're heading. The edge of the cliff behind the castle. The only place not full of death. Sóleyva and Riktr are with us and I can hear Monique's sobs trailing behind them, her tears only fueling the intensity of the pressure building behind my eyes. This isn't a war. It's an extermination.

"Rohan!" Jofir screams. I spin around and see the eldest son of Bishop fall onto his hands and knees, three vampires on top of him. Jofir races for her mate, swinging her longsword as more vampires race out from the wall of darkness. Monique stops and begins to chant, her thin red magic joining with Rohan's as he fights back to standing, sending the vampires crashing backwards into their brethren.

"Help them." Leah struggles to free herself from my grip. "Please, Sean." Her voice breaks. "*Please* help them."

I set her on her feet, pushing her behind me as I take aim, shooting a pillar of fire over Rohan's head. An assist as much as it's a warning. My fire billows out along the dark cloud and I fling my hands downward, willing it to dig into the ground. To form a wall of my own making. Sóleyva adds her magic to it, strengthening the barrier. Rohan spins around and does the same, his magic pouring into it reminding me of the attack at Merrymont, where Gelby put walls between us and the Draugr. The same as they did then, tendrils of darkness begin to bleed through.

I take Leah's hand and we fall back to the cliff edge, all of us huddled together in the glow of my faelight. Leah leans against me and Collin brings Caroline to his chest, holding the trembling body of the only human allowed to survive the slaughter. Allowed, at least, to live long enough to see the end.

I move to the lip of the abyss, looking down into its unnaturally dark depths. Shadows bend within it, moving like a river of midnight. I pull

Leah away from the chaotic frenzy I can feel building within it. Within me. The pressure in my head spears down into my chest and out into my arms. Drips over the lead in my stomach and trickles into my legs. The trees behind the suffocating darkness begin to whisper and I slide my hand from Leah's, wrapping an arm around her shoulders as we face the barrier between us and Keela's horde, watching it crack. Dark fingers form, claws chipping away at our magic until there's nothing left. The barrier falls. Leaving only the pitch of night in its wake.

Keela strolls from the center of the life-swallowing darkness she's created, the gleam of red at her throat the only color left as we look out into the night that thickens with every stride she takes. "Come to me, Caroline." Keela's voice drips with venom, lines of Vampir forming behind her as she closes in on us. "Let me make all your dreams come true. While your lover watches."

Collin growls. The sound pathetic. One I'm making myself. "Allow me to introduce our resident demon." I look to the vampires behind her. "Do you guys know a demon made you kill your own family? That the *Dearg Dua* is your queen?"

A ricochet of gasps and gulps sound all around me but the Vampir are silent and Keela only smiles. "They know, and they are happy their maker has come. Relieved to have finally found nourishment at long last. They drink of my veins, and hunger for my sisters who will come to help me feed them."

"Keela," Rohan says her name softly. "This isn't you. Come home with me, so I can help you."

Talons grow thick and dark from her fingertips. "I am home."

Rohan shakes his head in argument but Jofir grips his arm, silencing him. I pull Leah to my chest and hold onto her, a part of my heart aching for Keela. Who she was in her human life and even who she was under Bishop's care. The redeemable vampire Rohan still believes in. The one who disappeared once Abhartack brought her to this evil place. What she is now holds no trace of who she used to be. No hope of mercy. I press a kiss to the top of Leah's head and the dark queen calls out to her. "Do you smell him on my breath, little wolf?" Leah's already stiff posture goes rigidly cold. Keela's laugh tickles at the boundaries of my faelight, Sóleyva and Riktr adding what they have to the glow that's trying to keep the shadows at bay. "Harlan made a nice meal, but his death was nowhere as satisfying as Sean Winkle's will be. The snack he gave me earlier makes me ravenous for the whole meal."

Leah shouts and screams, the sound muffled against my chest. I hold her tighter to me than she deserves but Keela doesn't get to see the pain she's inflicting reflected in Leah's eyes. That's what the demon wants. To hurt Leah. To strip her bare before she kills her. "Let them go, Keela."

"I will." Her words swirl like a tempest around us, a buzz building in the void behind us. "I will let them go to their deaths quickly."

"I have a better idea." I spin Leah and me toward Riktr, yanking Aether's stone from my pocket and slamming it against Riktr's chest. Runes ignite in flames along my arms and Sóleyva screams. I meet Riktr's stare. "It's time you had a voice. If you make it out of here, unite the Fae, and protect the Ulfr."

Riktr's eyes widen but he nods, Aether's power seeping into him, the stone turning to ash under my palm. A bone-chilling wind rises from the void with a howling screech, the buzzing turning into voices. I let go of Leah, handing her off to Riktr. He's my best shot at saving her. Collin is wrecked and already has Caroline to defend. With Aether's magic, the king is Leah's best chance and now, because of Aether's magic, Sóleyva can't make him stop.

I turn and face Keela. Wings of shadow spread out behind her, phantoms of her ancient demon. One like the others she lured us here to feed. That's what claws up from the pit behind us. The Lilitu are rising. Their whispers turn into shouts and the snap of their wings prepare them to fly. Keela opens her arms, her shadows lifting her into the air to meet those she calls sisters. "Vampir are guardians upon the threshold. Behold that which we have brought forth by blood and rite."

Rohan sucks in a gasp of air. "The Primordial Void. We stand upon the threshold of creation's gate."

Words spill from Monique's lips, fast and frantic. "Eclipse of light. A heart prepared. Harken loud ye woeful cries. The Eye aligns the blade of rite—"

"And the wolf stands at the gate where it all began," Leah screams.

The temperature drops and Keela laughs, shadows coiling all around our faelight as the beat of wings rises up behind us.

"Yggdrasil fights for its life," Monique screams, clamping her hands over her ears. "Yggdrasil fights against the destruction the void now hastens. Creator versus creation! To undo, redo, and forge anew."

"I'm the wolf at the gate!" Leah screams, clawing at Riktr's arms. He binds her to him with a pulse of glowing vines, eyes tracking between me and the edge of the ravine Leah's trying to get to. To jump into. I watch the blood drip from his arms as he commits to the charge I gave him. *Memory's blood.* A gate opened by memory's blood. I'm nothing but a vault of memories. Good and bad. My own and others.

I lift a hand, watching the faelight mingle with blue vines of Álfar magic, Beatrice's words mixing with Natalie's. The Eye was transformed by the all-knowing waters of Mimir's well. All-knowing because the cosmos runs through it. And the cosmos was created by Chaos. The pressure inside me hums, heat and light burning through my veins. "It's okay, Leah." I move to the lip of the void and face her, offering her one last smile and wishing I could see more than pain and heartache in her eyes. "You're not the wolf. I am. It's my fate that waits at the bottom of this pit, not yours." She screams and I fall backward into the swirling abyss, not needing to say anything more to her than I already have. My life sacrificed for hers is an easy choice to make. Not the one Odin created me for, but the one the Norns gave me. With the Eye, I can undo, redo, and forge anew. For Leah. Collin. Their future mates. And all of their family.

The Void roars up to meet me, wind screaming and darkness yawning. Slowly, I hear them. One voice separating from another. Things in the Void. Their sounds mixing with the screech of the Lilitu. Blood coats my tongue. My throat. I let go, releasing the pressure that's aching to be set free. Fire and faelight blaze out of me, one bright explosion of light, tendrils lashing out, dragging Keela's demons back down into the dark with me.

## ~22~

# Leah

The Void screams. An endless howl of rage storming up from the pit where Sean's body disappeared. Keela's shadows tear past our heads, surging down into the blanket of darkness, the hiss of her own rage adding to the sureness of death that already waits for Sean. For us.

I sink to my knees, Sean's name an echo of grief in my throat. Riktr's vines slough away, the Fae putting all his efforts into this one last futile attempt to fight off the Vampir surging forward behind us. Pushing us all toward the lip of the chasm where Sean gave us the gift of having to live these last minutes with the pain of knowing he's already gone. Collin's snarl wraps around my sorrow and pulls me from the ground. My brother is hurt worse than I am, and he can't afford to have his attention split between Caroline and me. He deserved Sean fighting at his side but now all he has is me.

I shift, moving to the far side of Caroline where I know Collin will most appreciate the dregs of my efforts to fight alongside him and the others. Even Monique is standing with us, what little magic she has on her own combining with Jofir's, Rohan lashing out between the two of them to make their strikes against the horde count. The horde that's too swollen with the demonic power of their queen to be stopped. One of them clamps onto my shoulder and I drop to the ground, pinning it underneath my body while Caroline screams at the bloody beast, calling it by name and getting no response from the glassy-eyed monster. I clamp my jaws around its throat and pull, beheading the only real way for Collin and me to kill them.

The next two vampires latch onto my neck and chest, ripping out my thick fur to get at my skin so they can feed. Collin gets swarmed by three, his front paw reaching out to pull Caroline underneath him. He lies down on top of her, relentless in his grim determination to shield her for as long as he can. My wolf cries out and behind us, a boom of thunder rattles the Void—terrible, awful cries of agony erupting from deep inside. The Vampir attached to my body pause in their frenzied efforts to rip me apart, a building sound rippling over us from the battlefield beyond our crumbling line. The vampires all open their bloody mouths, mimicking the spine-wrecking sound ripping from the throat of their queen.

I use the confusion to throw them off of me, the others doing the same. Vampir drop all around us and a hollow spot opens in my chest. I spin in the darkness, the air curdling, thickening with the sourness of death. It plumes up from the chasm and yet all I can concentrate on is *him*. My mate. He's here. I feel his presence in the hollowness—the wolf I've never met but whose terrifying presence I recognize all the same. He came to save *me*, but our bond has only brought him to his death.

I double over, a pinprick of wild, desperate need searing through me with nauseating force. Flames erupt from the Void, the thunder growing louder and the shrieking sharper. A great sizzling ball of faelight detonates in the blanket of darkness covering the Void. Shadows rise swift and wet with blood, shooting high into the sky as the ground underneath us quakes. Claws raking over stone echo up from the pit, something massive climbing up from the depths. A dozen winged beasts take flight ahead of it, their beautiful female forms firing like darts into the night sky, that terrible, awful screeching come from their mouths. Pain lances through me, white-hot and curling beneath my skin. Not mine...*his*. I shift back to my human form and scream his name. "Sean!"

Fire erupts skyward in violent arcs, blue sparks detonating against the smothering blackness. The winged beasts dive for me. All of them. I scream again, leashes of faelight whipping from the void, laced with Álfar magic to shatter against the bodies of the demons, cutting through wings and bones. Collin drags me into the huddle of our allies, away from the chaos rising out of the abyss. Flames tear across the sky, heavy with the glow of faelight and sizzling with blue vines. Vampir drop like flies around us as Sean's magic combines to eviscerate our enemies. Sean—my *mate*. The boy my wolf and I have always known to love. The boy who had the instincts to love us back, even when I didn't give him any reason to. *His choice was always us*. My wolf repeats the words Sean told us. *Always us*.

Massive white paws slam against the lip of the ravine, black claws crackling with blue sparks as they tear into stone. My knees buckle as the great wolf from my vision hauls himself out of the pit. He's twice the size of Collin and wreathed in flame, the tips of his fur burning and his eyes bright with faelight. A colossal beast of unimaginable fury. "The supreme alpha," I whisper, Collin yipping his agreement because he feels what I feel. Supremacy. Only Fenrir himself can hope to stand against Sean.

The white wolf paces away from the Void, shoulders rolling with power. His head swings in my direction and I freeze. "Watch out!" Rohan shouts, a streak of his sizzling blue magic cracking against a spear of dark shadow dropping down on us from high above. Thousands of them fill the sky. The great wolf throws his head back, unleashing a roar that rips across the battlefield with shattering force. The shadows fold in on themselves, snapping out of existence under the pressure of the rising canopy of fiery magic spraying up from every inch of Sean's magnificent coat. The ground moves under our feet and another enraged screech rips from Keela's throat as her shadowy darkness makes a violent retreat, pulling back away from us and rolling toward the tree line—heading back to where her wall of darkness came from. Light pours down onto my face, the sky above us now as clear and bright as a summer day in Midgard.

Threads of magic snap and hiss, exploding across the buckling ground in another wave of destruction. We all turn toward an angry boom of red magic. It shreds the space around it like tissue paper, a portal opening in its midst. From the center walks a witch taller than even Rohan, her arms lined with silver bracelets and her hair adorned with bones and feathers. Her dark eyes land on Keela—the queen still wrapped in shadows and her dark crown high upon her head. "Sisters!" the witch shouts. More women filter through the portal, fanning out behind her and linking their arms together. "Our mother was stolen from us, her life taken by the vampire queen. Now we destroy the queen."

Monique races to join them, her red hair and pale skin contrasting theirs as she offers her arm, lending her magic to the already blazing fury of the coven. They begin to chant and Jofir tugs at Collin's head. "Bishop...he's going to kill your pack."

### Sean

I leave a trail of blazing fire and smoldering ash behind me, Dökkbraek's ground thawing underneath my trail of terror. The sky splits, another portal opening. This one bringing the Fae army to this land whose magic is now broken by the force of my own. By Yggdrasil's might. The cosmos prompting fate to fight against the very thing that created it because the cosmos always knew the real battle wouldn't be between those things that live inside of it, but between itself and its creator. A right to the life granted by that which holds the power to burn it all down and start anew.

Leah and Collin race into the swarm alongside me, Sóleyva's magic spiraling skyward, twisting into living blades of light, signaling the ranks of her arriving warriors to spread out and save their queen. Their magic is as precise as it is devastating—to Álfar and Vampir alike.

Rohan portals himself to his father's side. Sleipner is on the ground and Bishop stands beside his sleigh, twisted by too many years of conquest to stop the slaughter of those defenseless Ulfr wrapped tightly in one another's arms. Rohan throws up a sizzling shield between the sleigh and his father but Bishop raises his staff over his head, streaks of red lightning crackling out of it to shatter his son's magic. Jofir appears next to Bishop, swinging her sword at the high elf. Bishop bats her away, sending her flying back across the battlefield. Rohan portals to her side, confused and afraid. I can smell his emotions. Smell the fear on my pack. On *Leah*. Odin didn't worry about the dragon he placed inside of me because female dragons are so rare, and true mate bonds between Fae are almost as rare. It was worth the gamble to let all of the souls be free inside of me, to rise to dominance when each was needed, a collective that would work together for the greater good of the power I could give them. Odin only needed to tame the wolf, locking him away in a cage that allowed me to access his senses but denied my wolf the opportunity of imprinting on his mate. But the gate to that cage was doused in the blood of my fighting wolf. He was awake the whole time, caged and forgotten, and clinging to the memories of the girl I was fighting to forget.

An ear-splitting roar booms out of me. Bishop hits the sleigh with an explosion of magic but it's too late. My wolves are already gone, my call breaking through the barriers around them. Faster than his magic can pick them off, the wolves shift and disappear into the woods behind them. Collin goes airborne, his jaws clamping around Bishop's staff-wielding arm. The ancient being hits him with a blast of thick red magic and I strike out with my own, hitting Bishop dead in the chest. He drops to his knees, but not because of my strike. He lifts his hands, yanking on the dagger lodged deep in his throat. "Don't bother." Caroline's trembling voice cuts through din. "It's tipped in bloodthorn, so you're already dead."

Bishop's magic fades away, leaving an old Santa Claus on the ground in front of us. I call to the wolves and they charge from the forest, circling around their dying captor. Bishop's skin blackens and curls, peeling away. Rohan moves forward, the wolves parting to make way for him.

He kneels by Bishop's side, eyes dripping with tears as his father flakes away, the stench of rot filling the air until there's nothing left of the High Álfar but his clothes and staff.

A steely calm falls over the battlefield, the shock of Bishop's death freezing the Álfar and Fae, the Vampir too defeated to make a difference now. Sihoma walks beside Jofir, the two women coming to stand at Rohan's side. "We yield." Sihoma's voice breaks. "The Álfar yield."

Tears drip from Jofir's eyes. "Please, we did not condone Bishop's actions. Nor Gelby's. Rohan tried to plead with them both but they would not hear him. So please." She sinks to her knees beside her mate. "Spare him. If you must take another life, take mine. Do not kill him for those things he could not control."

I look to Collin. His eyes are wide, face pale. He looks from Rohan to Caroline to me. "You are the supreme alpha. Our pack follows you."

I shift back into my human skin, not a stitch of clothing left on my body. "I'm guessing the magical eraser of Santa duties is pretty important to supernaturals, so Rohan can live if he agrees to continue doing that. Humans are better off thinking you're fairy tales instead of the monsters you really are."

Jofir's head shakes. "Yes, yes, Rohan will continue his family's duty to Midgard."

"And," I continue, "the Álfar will agree to relinquish control of Midgard to the Ulfr."

"What? No!" Sóleyva belts. "The Fae are the rightful—"

My growl cuts her off, my magic rippling out of me now without me even trying. Riktr walks forward, dipping his head to me. "The Fae yield to your demands. I will unite both Seelie and Unseelie, and we will *all* recognize the Ulfr as authority in Midgard."

"Good," I spit. "Because Collin is still the strongest alpha in all of Midgard. You answer to him, and if you don't, he'll send me after you." I bare my teeth at all of them. "Don't tick off my alpha."

I turn away from them and Collin's head shakes. I glare at him. "You lead and I'll stand beside you like I always have, but I'm not interested in your job so don't even try." I shoulder past him. "All I want is your sister." I cup Leah's face between my hands. "I told you your mate was going to be crazy about you."

Tears drip from her lashes, grief and relief bubbling through her. A nervous laugh forces its way across her lips and I rest my forehead on hers, pulling her body against my naked one. "You're going to have to stop doing that in front of people or I'm not going to be able to keep my wolf from doing what he's been dying to do since we hit puberty." I tremble with the need I have to mark her. To claim her. "Everything I am begins and ends with you. Always you, Leah."

A blade of shadow slams into my side, a second one hitting Leah. She yelps and I spin toward Keela. The witches have her pinned inside a magical cube but that isn't stopping her from pulling on whatever darkness will listen to her. Fire ripples from my palms and I shift back into my wolf form, feeling Leah's strong body thriving despite her injuries. I race toward Keela, a living cataclysm, taking out what remains of her horde. It was bad enough when they were normal bloodsuckers. Now they're even worse than the Jötnar, willing to kill their own family for one small taste of their queen. A taste I'll never be forced to have again.

I launch myself into the witches' magical box, registering Monique's shout as I detonate a sweeping bomb of sizzling faelight inside the protective barrier. Keela's crown snaps out of existence, the queen still fury incarnate even without the added benefit of the darkness the Void wanted her to command. Her taloned fingers lash out, dragging over my burning fur in blow after blow. I sink my teeth into her arm and slam her backward into the shrinking box. The air is growing thin. The witches are suffocating her. Wanting to watch her die slowly. A cruel punishment she might deserve, but not a satisfaction I'm willing to give them.

Keela's head comes forward, fangs sinking into my snout. Leah's wolf roars, her frantic presence outside the box the reason I'm not breaking the witches' magic. I slam Keela to the ground. Her taloned fingers dig into my legs and I clamp my jaws around her neck, teeth cracking through the bloody choker holding the power of the Void at her throat. The primordial pit of creation Natalie told me about. Natalie—another woman whose life I ruined. But like Leah, it was unintentional. The two of them wholly different from what I'm doing to Keela now. For the greater good of us all.

I sling my head side to side, a storm barely held in check as Keela's bones break and her skin splits, her neck ripping away from the rest of her. Her hands curl against my furry face, devoid of talons. They wipe against me, the motion soft and caressing as her head snaps free and her body drops to the ground beneath me, those hands falling down limp beside her. I place her head above her neck, the gem broken and colorless. The queen broken and free of darkness. I stare at the smile on her lips. Keela looks like a girl who is happy to have died.

I dip my head, running my nose along her cheek. I imagine the way she looks right now is why both Abhartack and Eric loved her. They both knew this girl. The one too innocent to have been Death.

I leave her body for the witches to burn, turning to meet Rohan's devastated stare from across the field. After so many centuries together, he lost his brother and father today, and now he's lost the person he thought he loved most in this world. But Rohan still has Jofir and like the rest of us, he's going to have to be happy with what he has left.

I shift back to my human form and catch Leah in my arms, her shift faster than mine. She wraps her arms and legs around me and I hold her tight, both us crying for different reasons. And for the same ones. "It's over," I tell her, nudging her off my shoulder. She lifts her head and looks down at me. I lift my mouth to hers, kissing her deep and hard, desperate to make up for lost time and ravenous to complete our mate bond. To claim her while she claims me so nothing can ever come between us again. *I love you.*

She shudders, our bond flaring bright and beautiful inside us. There's no more doubt inside of her. No more pain of uncertainty. Her voice is clear and steady inside my head. *You owe me a manicure. My nails are ruined.*

### Haldir

Wind howls over the southern cliffs like a wounded beast, soaring down to the valley floor below me. I stride along the rocky edge, looking down at the river cutting through the forest. My hands are numb. Senses dull. I can hear the ground crunching under my boots but I can't feel the loose rock or sharp edges. Still, I follow the edge of the cliff to a trail that turns to earth as I make my way from the mountaintop to the tree line, body moving with fevered compulsion to enter the ancient forgotten valley where all the Dreki kings were crowned. I know this is where I am, unable to shift and soar on the wind, because I've been here before. Long ago. When I first sought answers from the Norns.

The sisters brought me first to this valley where the Dreki temple stretches out in ruin, shrouded in a thick mist that hides all remaining traces of what was once a great and mighty kingdom. Then they took me to the end. They showed me how the transference of our tremendous power tipped the scales of destiny against the Dreki. How wars broke out and division grew among the remaining Dreki until they were weak and so scarce that only one royal line remained. A line that stood to inherit the strength, courage, and might of every Dreki heritage before it. One that, after a few centuries, died out, the last royal dragon gone—taking the threads of all Dreki with him. Our history and power lost. A dynasty ending. From that time, I and every other Dreki have been on our own, left to wander Yggdrasil without any family or culture of our own. Even our spirits have no one to claim them in the end.

I move toward the moss-covered stone and collapsed pillars of the decaying temple, stepping over crumbling remnants of a time when dragons ruled the skies. The floor is half-swallowed by twisted vines that grow up into the mist, covering the greatness of the open ceiling that once allowed the kings to land here on this very floor.

I keep going, heading for the altar where my spirit yearns to go. There's a snap of the twisted vines behind me. I turn, wishing I was flesh and blood instead of this...spirit that I am. Zara approaches, silent and unseeing as she passes by me, Firebrand, the sword of the kings, strapped against her back. It pulses and thrums. She draws the sword and kneels before the broken altar. Anger boils within me. I lunge at her, hands passing clean through her solid form.

Zara leans forward, using the tip of the sword to draw a rune in the air above the altar. Magic flares and a ripple tears through the open air, leaving an old woman's face looking out in its place. She smiles down at Zara. "You did well, my daughter. The Dreki heir has long been lost to fire and betrayal, but you have followed my training and brought home the blood of the kings. Now, finish what you must."

"Finish what I must," Zara repeats, gripping the sword, her hands making tight fists around the hilt. She raises it above her head and slams it down into the center of the crack in the altar. The sword ignites in flame and the floor of the temple trembles, marble columns crashing down around us and chunks of stone breaking from the cliffs above us. The old woman's eyes meet mine, as if she can see me. A flicker of orange light sparks to life in her stare, capturing my soul until I'm trapped within it. A burst of heat shoots through me and the world goes dark.

"Time to wake up," a melody of voices calls to me in the darkness.

I answer them with a low, echoing moan, my spirit back in my body and the stench of the decaying body next to me a paste coating my senses. A spark flickers in the darkness above me and the Norns step out from the space between worlds. "Wake up!" they shout, their screams forcing me to cover my ears. "Your journey awaits."

I lower my hands, staring up at them. Urd smiles, her soft voice a mother's caress as the trio fades, leaving me in darkness once again. "Find the sword. Save your kingdom."

# Acknowledgements

*"When the root is bitterness, imagine what the fruit might be." - Woodrow Kroll*

This book was a wild ride. It left a bitter taste in my mouth and a tear in my eye. But those are the perils we face when we try new things, work with uncooperative characters, and let our stories come to an end. One day, many of these characters will return with their own stories and I look forward to seeing those in print. Something that wouldn't be possible to dream of if not for the unwavering support of my husband. Joe – thank you for letting me talk about things that bore you to tears. You don't have to "get it", you only need to get me, and you do that each and every day.

Without the superior editing of Proof Positive's dear, nicer-than-my-dream-editor, Anita, there would be so many commas in my work you'd be able to nominate me for a world record award.

Marianne Nowicki—thank you for being attached to the very fibers of the universe, capable of knowing exactly what I want from a cover well before I know myself. Your cover designs are pure perfection!

I also owe a debt of gratitude to my friends and extended family for allowing me to ignore all of you while I fight with characters, sob for no reason, eat terrible things, and sleep such strange hours that I can't speak to you even when I want to do nothing else. Thank you for the texts, the photo dumps, and for calling Joe to have him make me answer my phone.

And you, my wonderful, patient reader—thank you! It's my honor to make your reading list and I'm grateful that so many of you flip through the pages of my ever-changing genres. An agent once told me that readers who like my style will make genre irrelevant and each day, you prove her right. Thank you for sticking with me, and thank you for making 2026 my best year yet.

# Also By Lee Dawna

Hinton Thriller Series – A serial-killer thriller trilogy.
Descend
Smother
Rise

Sierra: A Modern Psychological Thriller

Beller Ties – A four-book stand-alone romantic suspense collection
Something So Beautiful
Now And Always
Dawn Of Devotion
Marked By Forever

Eyes of Midgard – Norse fantasy trilogy
Day of the Raven
Night of the Dragon

# ECLIPSE OF THE NORNS

Join the mailing list for early release news!

# About Lee Dawna

Lee Dawna is a thriller, suspense, and fantasy author, and host of the Immortal Sunshine podcast. An avid traveler and outdoorswoman, you may bump into her along a remote trail where a meandering stream whispers her next story.
Visit **LeeDawnaBooks.com** for more on what the author is up to lately, and to **join her mailing list** for special announcements.
Member of the Alliance of Independent Authors. Find Lee on YouTube, Spotify, Rumble, X, Instagram, or Facebook.

www.ingramcontent.com/pod-product-compliance
Lightning Source LLC
LaVergne TN
LVHW040044080526
838202LV00045B/3475